A SIMPLE PLAN

"Perhaps we shouldn't have embarked on this adventure. Perhaps I should take you back," he said.

"No", she answered quickly. "Don't take me back. I haven't yet had a chance to . . . "

"Chance to what?"

Her plan. Dear Heaven, she'd come here with a plan, and he'd chased it clear out of her head. Just because she'd touched his sleeve and walked a few steps alone with him. Was this confusion what a chaperone protected one from?

She looked up at him and gave him what she hoped was her most pleasing smile. "I wanted a chance to ask you a favor."

"Anything," he answered, still gazing down at her.

"It's rather out of the ordinary."

"That doesn't surprise me."

"It's rather far out of the ordinary, I'm afraid."

His smile grew even warmer. "Now you have me intrigued, Miss Hamilton."

She took a breath. "I want you to help me dispose of some jewelry."

Other *Leisure* books by Alice Chambers
writing as Alice Gaines:
WAITANGI NIGHTS

Taming Angelica

Alice Chambers

LEISURE BOOKS   NEW YORK CITY

For my sisters of the pen.

A LEISURE BOOK®

February 2000

Published by

Dorchester Publishing Co., Inc.
276 Fifth Avenue
New York, NY 10001

If you purchased this book without a cover you should be aware that this book is stolen property. It was reported as "unsold and destroyed" to the publisher and neither the author nor the publisher has received any payment for this "stripped book."

Copyright © 2000 by Alice Brilmayer

All rights reserved. No part of this book may be reproduced or transmitted in any form or by any electronic or mechanical means, including photocopying, recording or by any information storage and retrieval system, without the written permission of the Publisher, except where permitted by law.

ISBN 0-8439-4682-2

The name "Leisure Books" and the stylized "L" with design are trademarks of Dorchester Publishing Co., Inc.

Printed in the United States of America.

Taming Angelica

Chapter One

London, 1865

Elizabeth Gates made quite a pretty picture as Will Claridge gazed down at her, even with her emerald eyes brimming with tears, as they were now. As thoroughly as she'd charmed him the moment he'd met her, as many delightful hours as he'd spent in her bed, as much as he savored the feel of her soft breasts pressed against his chest right now, he had to get her out of this room. And quickly.

"How *can* you cast me aside like this?" she said, sobbing. "How can your heart have hardened so toward me?"

"It hasn't," he answered truthfully, more or less. "That is, I'll always be fond of you, Elizabeth."

"Fond?" she repeated. "Only fond?"

What a colossal mess. He'd have to choose his words more carefully. "I'll always hold you in my heart," he said.

Good God, when had he started spouting rubbish like that? And speaking of the Almighty, why in His name had Elizabeth taken it into her head to declare her undying love at a party attended by half of London society? The woman normally had much better sense than that. He'd better help her come to her senses before they were discovered—as they surely would be—by some other couple looking for what laughingly passed as privacy at these affairs.

"Why can't we reclaim what we had?" she said, twisting her fingers into the linen of his shirt. "Don't you remember Paris?"

"Of course I remember." How could he forget? Beastly hot, overcrowded, and quite beyond his means to pay.

"We could be happy again, Will," she said. "If only you wouldn't turn from me."

"But my darling, you ended our affair, not I."

She shook her head, and a fat tear slid over her cheek to the corner of the heart-shaped mouth he'd kissed so many times. "I was wrong. I see that now."

He cupped her chin in his palm and turned her face up toward his. "You were noble and brave, Elizabeth. I've never been prouder of anyone. I swear it."

"No," she said in a moan. "No."

"Yes. We'd been hideously unfair to Horace, the two of us."

She pushed away from him. "Don't talk to me about Horace. I detest him."

"He's your husband," Will said. "He's the father of your children." At least he thought Horace was the father of her children—both of the boys looked like him, the poor devils. "He's a decent chap, and you two will be happy together again, I know it."

"He's flat as a failed soufflé," she declared. "He's as appealing as yesterday's fish. At the banquet of love, Horace Gates is a blancmange."

Taming Angelica

Perhaps, but culinary sensibilities aside, the man was also a great, strapping fellow and a decent shot, and bloody well sure to call Will out, even if they did have to cross the channel to take the field of honor. And of course, if anyone—anyone—found Elizabeth and Will together, word would get back to Horace before the end of the evening.

What in God's name had turned such a reasonable woman into a watering pot? How was he to escape this hellish situation with his skin in one piece?

"I can't face a life full of nothing but Horace," she said, gazing up into his face. "It's too bleak, too horrible."

"You seemed content enough when we met."

"That was before I'd known true love."

He put his hands on her naked shoulders, above the crimson satin of her gown. "But don't you see, my darling, that breaks our rule."

Her brows knitted together in an expression of pure astonishment. "Rule? What rule?"

"You made me swear to it yourself, Elizabeth. 'No matter what, we must not fall in love.' "

"I can't have said anything as ridiculous as that."

"But you did. You made me promise that we'd always be friends and nothing more. Amorous friends, but friends, nevertheless."

She twisted her hands together, wringing them. If he'd ever in his life seen anyone wring her hands, Elizabeth Gates was doing it right now. "That's preposterous. I've loved you from the moment I saw you."

"Quite the opposite," he answered. "You insisted it would all be a lark. You said that if one of us started making love noises, the other should run for the hills."

"And you believed me?" she demanded. She stared at him as though he were the world's prize idiot. "Even if I said that, you had to know I didn't mean it."

Dear God, such logic. Of course he'd believed her.

Any reasonable person would, and just look where it had gotten him. "You're upset," he said. "When you've calmed down, you'll see things much more clearly."

"I see only one thing clearly. I love you, Will Claridge."

Enough. The conversation had grown ridiculous. If he couldn't get her out of this damned sitting room, he'd get himself out before they were discovered and Horace demanded satisfaction. "Sit down, Elizabeth, and I'll go find you a nice cup of tea. Or some sherry or something."

"I don't want tea," she wailed. "I want you."

"But that's quite impossible. If sherry won't do, I'll find you something stronger."

She pressed the back of her hand to her forehead and swayed toward him, as limp as a boiled noodle. He bent and caught her before she fell, lifted her up in his arms, and carried her to one of the overstuffed settees. After settling her there, he knelt beside her and took her hand between his so that he could chafe her wrist. "Elizabeth, please. Whatever this is, you must come out of it. Someone's sure to come in and find you in this state."

Her eyes fluttered open, and she fixed an unfocused gaze on him. Her skin had taken on the color of ashes. Elizabeth had never swooned before. If he'd known her capable of it, he'd never have become involved with her in the first place. He couldn't abide swooning women. What on earth had happened to her?

Oh, no. Oh, dear God, no. "Elizabeth," he murmured. "You haven't . . . that is to say, you aren't . . ."

"What, Will?" she answered weakly.

"I couldn't have . . . we couldn't have . . ."

She didn't answer but just stared at him. He placed a hand over her belly. "That last night in Paris, you didn't . . . um, become . . ."

The color returned to her skin, and she batted his

Taming Angelica

hand away. "You think I'm *enceinte?*"

"You must admit you haven't been acting yourself tonight."

Her eyes flew open wide in an expression of perfect outrage. "You think I've conceived a child in order to trap you."

Put that way it sounded rather dreadful, but such things did happen. "I ask only because I'd want to do the right thing by you." Whatever *that* might be. "By any child of mine."

"How could you even think such a thing?" she cried. "How you must despise me."

"I don't despise you. After all we've had, I could never despise you."

"I'm not with child," she shouted—loudly enough for anyone on the other side of the closed door to hear. "And if I were carrying your child, I'd certainly never let you know, you beast."

"Whatever you say, Elizabeth. Only would you please say it a little more quietly?"

"How hateful of you to think so little of me," she cried. "How perfectly despicable."

"I'm sure I'm all those things. I'm certainly not worth getting into a state over," he said, still rubbing her hand between his.

She snatched her hand away. "Horace will defend my honor. Go find him."

Good God, anything but that. He might as well shoot himself and have done with it. "Do you really think that wise, Elizabeth? Let me fetch a woman friend for you, shall I?"

She wiped her eyes. "I don't want anyone. Dear heaven, I must look a sight."

"Not at all. You look lovely." He rose to his feet. "Let me go find Lady Smithson. She's always such a comfort to you."

"No," she cried. "Don't leave me. I'll never see you again if you leave now."

"But dearest, you'll see me all the time. We know all the same people, go to all the same parties."

"No!" She jumped from her seat and grabbed at his lapels, hanging on and sobbing uncontrollably. She'd gone quite hysterical. He put his arms around her and held her close while she poured her heart out onto his shoulder.

Poor thing. Somehow this had to be all his fault, even though he couldn't for the life of him make out how. For now, he had no choice but to hold her and comfort her and pray that no one came through that door.

"I'm afraid you have no idea what you're talking about, Lord Quimby," Angelica Hamilton said as she eased her way into a knot of wholly male, pigheaded British aristocrats. "Suffragists don't want to be men; we want only to enjoy the same rights as men."

"We?" One of Lord Quimby's bushy gray eyebrows shot up. "Am I to understand that you're one of those unnatural females, Miss . . ."

"Hamilton," Angelica supplied. "And there's nothing unnatural about a woman standing up for herself. I would think you English would understand that, given that your own Queen Victoria is a woman."

"You know nothing about Her Majesty or her subjects, Miss Hamilton," Lord Quimby said, looking down the length of his bulbous nose at her. "You're obviously not British."

"I come from Boston," she answered.

"Ah, American," he intoned, much to the amusement of the lords and lordlings around him, if their nasty snickering qualified as laughter. "A land full of red Indians and black slaves."

Taming Angelica

"We no longer have slaves, sir. And soon our women will be emancipated, too."

"Where did you learn such rubbish?" Lord Quimby asked. "Were you with that collection of harpies at Seneca Falls?"

"Of course not," she answered. "I was only a child in 1848."

"As you are now. If I were your father, I'd take you over my knee and teach you some respect for your betters."

What a lovely picture. No doubt his whole lap disappeared underneath his massive belly when he sat down.

"You're not my father, sir," she answered. Not that Papa was much better. But at least he didn't sneer like this overblown British potentate. Papa only scowled.

She took a breath. "You've misunderstood what Mrs. Stanton and the others hope for American women," she said. "Indeed, for all women."

One of the other dandies smiled—an oily, condescending expression. "Then perhaps you'll explain it to us, Miss Hamilton."

"We want fair treatment under the law, recognition for our labor, an equal partnership in our marriages. Is that so much to ask?"

"It's unnatural," Lord Quimby answered.

"I'll bet you know even less about the natural world than you do about suffragists," Angelica said.

"Here you are," Aunt Minnie said from right behind her. "Oh, dear, oh, dear, Angelica. What have you gotten yourself into now?"

"Your daughter was explaining why she wants to be just like a man," Lord Quimby said.

"Now you're deliberately misunderstanding me, sir."

"But this isn't my daughter," Aunt Minnie said.

Alice Chambers

"For that you have my heartiest congratulations, madam," Lord Quimby replied, to general laughter from the rest of the men.

"She's my niece, and I'll be in a fine pickle if my brother hears she's upset your lordships."

"Really, Aunt Minnie," Angelica said. "I hardly think I've upset anyone."

Aunt Minnie put a plump hand on Angelica's arm. "Come away, child. Let's go find the ladies."

Oh, yes, the ladies. Fine conversation they'd have with them—millinery, balls, and parties, each just as boring as this one. She'd escaped Boston, only to end up here. Now she had to escape London, too, or go mad with all this enforced femininity.

"A fine pickle," Aunt Minnie said. "Lawrence will be so angry with me if he hears of this."

"Father needn't hear a word unless you tell him."

"The ague," Aunt Minnie cried, her eyelids fluttering. "I'm going to have one of my spells."

"There now, young lady, you've upset your aunt," Lord Quimby declared.

"She'll be fine," Angelica said. "Won't you, dear heart?"

"It's the ague, I tell you," Aunt Minnie said, clutching at her ample breast. "I'll faint dead away if I don't get some air."

"Allow me to help," one of the younger men offered, extending his arm.

"No, no. Angelica can take me somewhere, but thank your lordship so very much."

"Of course." Angelica put her arm around her aunt's waist and guided her out of the circle of men. "Really, Auntie, am I not allowed to have a conversation of any substance?"

"I should hope not. You and your conversations will be the death of me." Aunt Minnie glanced around, her

Taming Angelica

eyes wild with one of her fits. "Now please get me out of this crush. It's all closing in on me; I swear it is."

It wasn't doing anything of the kind, as Angelica knew very well. Minerva Hamilton had the constitution of a draft horse—and the appetite—but once she got it into her head to act like a helpless female, there was nothing to do but humor her. Angelica supported her aunt as best she could while glancing around for an unoccupied love seat, a quiet corner, any place to set Aunt Minnie down.

"Do hurry, child," Aunt Minnie said with a gasp. "I'm all atremble."

Finally, Angelica spotted a closed door across a narrow corridor off a corner of the salon. It might be a sitting room or a cloakroom, for all she knew. *Only, please, let it be quiet and empty and have a stout chair in it.* "Over here, dear heart," she said, guiding her aunt. "Can you make it?"

"I suppose I'll have to," Aunt Minnie answered.

"All right. Off we go."

It took some work to get through the throngs of London's crème de la crème. All those crinolines took up a tremendous amount of room as couples swirled around the dance floor to the rhythm of a waltz.

All the glitter had impressed Angelica mightily at the first one of these parties she'd attended. Honest-to-goodness earls and dukes and their ladies—people who could trace their families back to kings and queens. All quite dazzling until she had realized that underneath the trappings of nobility they were merely men and women like those at home. Sillier, maybe, because they all took themselves so blasted seriously.

But none of that mattered because she'd be gone from here as quickly as she could book passage for an adventure to someplace exotic. This trip away from home was her only hope. If she didn't get away now, what would she do—live under her father's roof forever? Or worse, marry someone her parents found suitable? She shuddered at the thought.

"My dear, you're trembling, too," Aunt Minnie exclaimed. "You've caught the ague from me."

"Not at all, Auntie," Angelica answered.

"Lawrence will be so angry with me. You've been conversing again, and I did promise him you wouldn't."

"Talking to people is no crime."

"It is the way you do it. Or it ought to be," Aunt Minnie declared. "Oh, why did I let you talk me into making this trip without your father?"

"Because Papa would never have found the time to leave his factory, and I'd be a sour old maid by the time I got to England." As if she ever would marry. But Aunt Minnie still held out hope, poor deluded dear, and husband hunting had made a fine excuse for this trip, even though escape had been the real reason for it.

Aunt Minnie stopped in her tracks. "You'll end up alone anyway, if you keep offending people. Especially the gentlemen."

"Men like Quimby were meant to be offended. They were bred for it—the pompous old goat."

"Oh, child, what *will* I do with you?" Aunt Minnie's hands fluttered over her bosom. "I declare, I don't know."

"Let's get you to a quiet spot, shall we?"

"Please."

"Look, we're almost there." Just a few more steps and they were standing at the closed door. The crush and the noise of the party were behind them now, and a refreshing breeze floated down the corridor. With any luck, they'd find a comfortable seat for Aunt Minnie and she'd be back to herself in a moment. Angelica turned the knob and pushed the door open.

The sitting room on the other side was quiet and

dim, but unfortunately not empty. At the sound of the door swinging open, a couple stepped apart from each other. Indeed, the woman—a redheaded beauty with pale skin and enormous green eyes—took one look at Angelica and Aunt Minnie and jumped back as though she'd been stung. The tall blond man she'd been clinging to cleared his throat and smiled a guilty little smile.

"I'm so sorry," Angelica said. "Please excuse us."

The woman pressed the back of her hand over her mouth and gave a choking sob. Then she wiped at some tears in her eyes and rushed from the room, nearly knocking over Aunt Minnie in the process. Dear heaven, they'd come in on some sort of tryst—the type of affair everyone of "good" breeding winked at, all the while denying it ever happened. The type of affair that almost always sorted itself out at the expense of the woman involved.

Angelica steadied Aunt Minnie as best she could, glaring at the man the entire time. "I'm afraid we've interrupted something."

"Ended it, rather," he answered smoothly, "for which I can only thank you."

"Yes, I'm sure you do," she grumbled in response. "We'll go somewhere else."

"Oh, no," Aunt Minnie protested. "You'll only get into another one of your conversations, Angelica, and I couldn't bear it."

"Here, let me help." The man crossed the room in two strides and slid his arm around Aunt Minnie, letting her rest against the broad expanse of his chest. Aunt Minnie gazed up at him adoringly, as she always did with handsome men.

This one was certainly that, with his sparkling blue eyes, strong chin, and sloping nose that was just long enough to elevate his face from merely attractive to downright interesting. No doubt that poor soul who'd just run from the room had found it captivating.

"What seems to be wrong?" the man asked as he guided Aunt Minnie gently to a seat.

"I'm afraid she's having one of her fits," Angelica answered.

"We've had rather an epidemic of that lately," he said as he settled Aunt Minnie onto one side of the settee and stood nearby, holding her trembling hand.

Angelica sat down next to her aunt and stared up at the man. "Is that what was wrong with that lady just now?"

He smiled that same sickly smile again—one that just shouted of guilt. "In a manner of speaking."

"She seemed quite upset with you."

"For heaven's sake, don't question this young man, Angelica," Aunt Minnie said. "Introduce us."

"I'm afraid we haven't met," Angelica said.

The man bowed, still holding Aunt Minnie's hand in his. "Will Claridge, at your service, ladies."

Aunt Minnie gazed up at him and batted her eyelashes. "Our pleasure, your lordship."

"Really, dear. He may not be a 'lordship.' "

"I'm afraid I am," Claridge said, his smile broadening in earnest and taking on a positively wicked tilt. "Although it's my brother who's the duke."

"A duke," Aunt Minnie declared. "Did you hear that, Angelica? A duke."

"His brother's the duke," Angelica corrected. "Your older brother, I presume, Lord Claridge?"

"That's how these things usually fall out," he answered.

A younger son of a noble and no doubt very wealthy family. His type were the worst—rakes and scoundrels. The sort of man who raised a young girl's hopes in order to lure her into heaven-knew-what and then cast her aside as not worthy of his bloodline. "Are you in the military, Lord Claridge?"

"I haven't the inclination, I'm afraid."

"The clergy?"

"Good God, I should hope not," he answered.

"You disapprove of the clergy, do you?"

"Quite the opposite." He leaned toward Aunt Minnie and gave her a wink. "They disapprove of me."

Aunt Minnie giggled like a schoolgirl. How could a grown woman fall so completely under the spell of a man simply because he was nice to look at? All right—he was very nice to look at. Recklessly, indecently nice to look at. And polished and confident of himself to the point of arrogance—all the characteristics Angelica most detested in men.

"So what do you do to keep yourself busy, Lord Claridge?" she asked.

"Angelica," Aunt Minnie chided. "You shouldn't be rude to his lordship after he's been so kind."

Lord Claridge laughed, a deep and very pleasing rumble. "Have no fear, Mrs...."

"Miss," Aunt Minnie corrected. "Miss Minerva Hamilton, and this is my niece, Miss Angelica Hamilton."

Lord Claridge squeezed Aunt Minnie's hand—it seemed he'd grown quite attached to it. "You needn't fear your niece's offending me, Miss Hamilton. My brother interrogates me in very much the same manner every time I see him."

"So how do you pass your days, Lord Claridge? Breaking women's hearts?"

"Angelica!" Aunt Minnie said.

"What do you think he was doing when we came in, Auntie?"

Lord Claridge cleared his throat and managed to look quite ashamed of himself. As well he should be, if the display was at all sincere. "I say, I'd be most grateful if you wouldn't mind keeping quiet about what you saw here just now."

"I'm not a gossip, sir."

"Good, because the lady's husband isn't the understanding sort."

"Her husband?" Angelica rose from the settee and stared in utter amazement at the man. "Do you mean to say that woman is married?"

"Well, yes. I rather think so."

"You consort with married women?" Angelica demanded.

"Sit down, child," Aunt Minnie said. "His lordship's affairs are none of our business."

"But Auntie, the woman is married."

Lord Claridge dropped Aunt Minnie's hand finally and straightened to an impressive height. "That's between the lady, her husband, and me, wouldn't you say?"

"You are despicable, sir."

"Opinion appears unanimous on that score tonight," he said.

"At least you ought to have the decency to be ashamed of yourself."

"Now see here," he said. "You and your aunt intruded into my privacy, Miss Hamilton, not the other way around."

"That's quite true, child," Aunt Minnie interjected. "There's no reason to be so disagreeable."

"How can you say that, Auntie? If we were at home, Papa would give this man a thrashing."

"Oh, do hush, Angelica."

Claridge snorted. "I'd damned well thrash him back if he tried."

Angelica raised her chin and stared the man right in the eye. "Adding profanity to your charms, sir?"

"Stop it," Aunt Minnie shouted. "Stop it, both of you. You're giving me a headache."

Lord Claridge bowed toward Aunt Minnie. "My apologies, madam. I don't know what came over me."

Aunt Minnie let out a loud sigh. "You'd know better if you'd spent more time conversing with my niece, I'm afraid."

He stared at Angelica, his eyes taking on an appraising gleam. "You ought to keep her on a leash."

"Believe me, I've considered it." Aunt Minnie reached out a hand and touched his. "Now, if you'd be so kind as to leave us alone."

"Of course." He bowed to Aunt Minnie again and then to Angelica, as stiffly and as formally as if he had a plank down his back. Angelica didn't acknowledge him, but merely folded her arms over her chest and glared at the wall as his footsteps crossed the carpet and the door closed behind them.

"Child, child, child." Aunt Minnie sighed. "Why on earth did you have to make his lordship so angry?"

"Oh, blast the man," she said. "He's no better than the rest of them."

Chapter Two

Will leaned against the wall and ran his hand over his face. Good God, he felt as though he'd been in a fistfight. Who *was* that young woman?

A long, luscious thing, certainly, with hair the color and luster of sable and eyes that shot hazel sparks in her anger. She'd very naturally misjudged the situation she'd happened on. Anyone seeing him with Elizabeth under those circumstances would have assumed the worst, so he couldn't blame her for doing the same. At least only she and her aunt had seen them, not one of the gossipmongers.

"I say, dear boy," said a voice from nearby. "Elizabeth was harder on you than I'd imagined."

Will jumped and turned to look behind him. *Oh, no, Bertie Underwood.* "Elizabeth?"

Bertie appeared out of a shadow and smiled knowingly at Will. "La Gates," he said. "She returned to the party a few minutes ago. Looked like she'd been crying."

Taming Angelica

How like Bertie to notice, with his sharp eye for all social nuance and his uncanny ability to position himself exactly at the center of things. His habit of skulking in dark nooks and hiding places—just like this hallway—stood him in good stead, too.

"You know I don't discuss my friends, Bertie," he said.

The man's narrow eyebrow went up. "Or their wives?"

"Lady Elizabeth is my friend."

"I daresay." Bertie chuckled. "How do you do it, dear boy?"

" 'It?' "

"You know." Bertie gave him a conspiratorial wink.

Will just stared at the man. They both knew what Bertie was talking about, of course. Will had earned quite a rake's reputation for himself over the years—not without justification. But he wasn't about to go into the details of his romances with London's biggest gossip. So he stood there and watched Bertie's smile turn sickly as he floundered for something to say. Apt comparison that, as the fellow did rather resemble a fish.

Finally Bertie cleared his throat. "I just wondered how you managed to make so many female friends."

"Ah, there's a secret to that."

Bertie's eyes widened, and he leaned toward Will. "Do tell. I'm all ears."

Will looked up one end of the corridor and then down the other, as if checking to see if they could be overheard. Then he looked earnestly down into Bertie's face. "I talk to them."

"Hmm?" Bertie looked completely baffled, just as did every other man with whom Will had ever shared his secret for seduction. "I say. You talk to them?"

"Exactly, dear boy." Will reached up and clasped

Bertie's bony shoulder. "Couldn't have put it better myself."

"But what does it mean?"

"What it says—talk to them. Then once you've mastered that, listen to what they have to say in return. Ask their opinions and then listen to their answers."

Bertie stepped back and looked at Will as though he'd grown a second head. "I've never heard of such a thing."

"Most men haven't," Will answered. "That's why it works so well. Women expect all sorts of displays from men, but they don't expect a man to take any interest in their opinions. It throws them completely off balance."

Bertie chuckled. "Now I know you're joking, dear boy. Who's interested in their minds?"

"I know, I know," Will said. "But you must convince them that you are."

"I see," Bertie declared. "Yes. Pretend to care about their opinions in order to distract them from what you're really after."

"I wouldn't put it quite that way."

"Brilliant, dear boy." Bertie laughed outright. "And did you try that on Miss Hamilton just now?"

Dear God, what else had Bertie seen? "Miss Hamilton?"

"The Boston Blunderbuss. At least that's what the others are calling her."

"Boston," Will said. "That was the accent."

"Standard American husband hunter, or so they say." Bertie placed his hand over his heart in a woefully inadequate display of sincerity. "I prefer more tender terms."

"So she's rich."

"Oh, yes," Bertie replied, emphatically and with startling honesty. He must have startled himself with it, because he blinked his fish eyes once or twice and then settled a smile back onto his face. "But who takes any notice of such things? A woman's beauty resides in her soul, not her dowry."

Like hell it does. Most men didn't give a fig for a woman's soul—especially a man like Bertie, who could hardly see beyond his own pocketbook. Bertie'd lost money at the gaming tables that he oughtn't have wagered. If the stories were true, he'd also borrowed funds from people he oughtn't have borrowed from. Bertie needed money even more desperately than Will did, and a hefty American dowry could go a long way toward filling those needs. It was all so transparent.

So another rich American had landed in London looking to marry a title. Why would she be at one of these stifling parties except to make the sort of bargain that had become more and more common lately? Fine new money in exchange for a fine old name. Will could see nothing wrong with that.

This rich American was different from most of them, though. She had more than money and looks. She had backbone and spirit. She was rather more headstrong than his usual mates, but if all that passion could be put to better use, what a lover she'd make. And if she brought a healthy dowry with her, what a wife she'd make.

"I say, old boy, why are you looking like that?" Bertie asked.

"Like what?"

"As if you're contemplating something," Bertie said. "What could a fellow like you be contemplating?"

Will smiled at Bertie. "That's none of your concern, is it, *old boy?*"

"You can't be planning to pursue Miss Hamilton," Bertie declared.

"I don't see why not."

"She never shuts her mouth for more than a minute,"

Bertie said. He hesitated again and gave Will another insincere smile. "I find it endearing, of course."

"Never fear. I know how to shut a woman's mouth, for our mutual enjoyment."

Bertie's own mouth worked silently for a moment, completing the image of a grounded halibut. "But you'd never get anywhere with the likes of her. She's one of those suffragists—hates men."

"We'll see about that."

"Then I can't dissuade you from wooing such an obviously unsuitable woman?" Bertie asked.

"If she's suitable for you, I'm sure she'll suit me just as well."

"I can't prevail on our friendship?" Bertie said.

He really ought to ask Bertie what friendship that might be, but instead he just smiled at him pleasantly.

"Well then, we'll both pursue her," Bertie said after a moment, "and may the best man win." Bertie extended his hand.

"Indeed." The fellow didn't mean that, but Will took his hand and shook it anyway. "Good luck to you."

"Right," Bertie answered.

Of course, luck had nothing to do with winning a woman, but why waste his breath trying to explain that to someone like Bertie? Intelligent conversation, constant attention, unstinting affection—those things won a woman's heart. So did persistence, and he had plenty of that.

"I think I'll just pop off back to the dancing," Bertie said.

Bertie wouldn't, though. He'd take right off to try to find Miss Hamilton and win the advantage. And Will would be right behind him both to press his own claim and to ensure that Bertie didn't let any gossip about the encounter with Elizabeth Gates slip. Such self-serving "accidents" were an unfortunate part of Bertie's nature—especially if they won him something. In this case, the prize might be the woman Will now intended to marry.

Well, well, marriage. Will had to chuckle at himself. For the first time in his thirty-five years on Earth he was seriously contemplating marriage—with Miss Hamilton of Boston, she of the long limbs, fiery eyes, and all that money.

Why not? The time had come long ago, as his brother pointed out at every opportunity. The chase after married women had grown tiresome, and now, with Elizabeth and Horace Gates, outright dangerous. He couldn't bring himself to ruin virgins, and young, comely widows were in short supply.

Why not give the pleasures of the marriage bed a try? If that didn't work, he could always leave her ensconced at the ancestral estate at Brathshire. She could pursue whatever interests married women pursued while he continued on with his thoroughbreds, his wallet fat with American money. Perhaps his brother would even loosen the family purse strings if he thought Will had taken it into his head to act like an adult.

Why the devil not?

Will glanced around and discovered that Bertie had disappeared as quietly as he'd come. *Well enough.* Will would go after him. And later at home, he'd have a stiff drink and plan his strategy for getting into Miss Hamilton's good graces. And from there into her thoughts and dreams.

Minerva Hamilton was a finely plumed old bird, given to fluttering hand gestures and excessive expressions of delight, but she didn't fool Will. He knew when he was being sized up as marriage material, and the elder Miss Hamilton had embarked on a thorough, if not overly subtle, investigation of his husbandly qualities. No matter—he'd grown accustomed to these interrogations over the years, and in truth this lady had a great deal more charm than most of his inquisitors.

She smiled at him sweetly as she poured a cup of tea and held it out toward him. "So you're the youngest of your family, your lordship?"

Translation: How far are you in line from the dukedom?

"There were only two of us," he answered, taking the cup from her. "My older brother and I."

She poured herself a cup of tea, put an ample spoonful of sugar into it, and stirred. "Your brother's a family man, I imagine."

Translation: Does the duke have heirs?

He really ought to find that last one offensive, but she had no access to that sort of information without asking. Female heads of other households had only to hear the name Will Claridge to know who, and what, they were dealing with. Miss Hamilton didn't know his situation, and with any luck he could keep it that way for a while.

"My brother's childless so far," he said.

She clucked her tongue in sympathy. "What a pity."

"We have high hopes that will change soon."

Translation: Don't count on my making your niece into a duchess.

She blushed, not the lovely flush of anger that had colored her niece's cheeks last night when they'd met, but a flattering pink, nevertheless. "I hope you don't think I'm prying, your lordship."

Translation: How much can I ask without making you angry?

He didn't answer immediately but took a long sip of tea. Letting her worry for a moment would help him to keep the upper hand. "Not at all, Miss Hamilton. I do admire you Americans and your directness."

She took a sip of her own tea, gazing at him out of

sparkling blue eyes as she did. She seemed rather an accomplished flirt for a spinster, and with her looks she must have broken quite a few hearts when she was younger. Her niece must have inherited the upturned nose and long, graceful fingers from Minerva's side of the family. And while the younger woman's figure was nowhere near as plush as the older's, she still had soft curves that promised to blossom into full womanhood with the loving attentions of a man.

Yes, Minerva must have been almost as appealing in her youth as Angelica was now. Why had she never married?

"Oh, your lordship," Minerva said, lowering her gaze. "If I were a younger woman, I'd swear you were staring."

"I was. Please forgive me."

She covered her mouth with her fingers and giggled into them. A pleasing sound, actually—musical and full of honest delight, unlike the practiced laughter of the women of his set. Angelica would laugh like that— or would her voice come out deeper and richer? With any luck he'd soon hear her laughter for himself.

Minerva recovered herself sufficiently to pick up a plateful of tiny sandwiches and extend it toward him. "I haven't been much of a hostess, have I?" she said. "Do have one of these. They're delicious."

"Thank you." He took one and popped it into his mouth—cucumber. It was, indeed, very tasty, and the china it was served on so fine as to be translucent.

The Hamilton ladies had done themselves up right in this grand town house just off the park. Whoever had furnished it for them had chosen everything to shout out good taste and hang the expense. If he had any eye for such things, and he most assuredly did, he could read money and lots of it in each detail—from the warm mahogany of the furniture to the muted tones of the Oriental carpets to the long string of perfectly matched, tiny pearls that graced Minerva's bosom.

Those pearls alone would not only buy a racehorse with good lineage but would keep it in oats for a year. With any luck some of her family's funds would be doing exactly that, and soon. Bless the Americans and all their money.

"Thank you for being at home to me," he said.

"Not at all, your lordship," she answered. "After Angelica's behavior last night, I was pleasantly surprised to receive your card."

"She's a high-spirited girl."

"I don't know how she manages to have any spirit. It's certainly nothing her mother or father ever taught her."

"I admire spirit in a woman," he said, although he didn't add that in the main he most admired spirit in a bed partner.

"You do, sir?"

"Certainly."

"I'm so happy to hear you say that, your lordship." She leaned toward him like a conspirator or a confidante. "May I be frank?"

"Of course, Miss Hamilton."

She sat back and gazed into her teacup, twisting it around and around in its saucer. "You see, Angelica is quite a remarkable girl."

She set the cup down and looked at it some more. "Quite admirable in her own way," she continued, "if a gentleman is prepared to grant her some . . . well . . . some latitude."

"Latitude," he repeated. What did that mean? That he was to give Miss Hamilton a wide berth?

She looked up at him and smiled. "I'm so glad you see my point," she said. "Most young girls are too malleable, don't you agree?"

First *latitude,* now *malleable.* The conversation had

started out probable enough, but somewhere it had shifted course.

"Yes, I suppose so," he answered, for lack of anything better to say.

"Oh, your lordship." She reached over and laid her hand against his arm. "I'm so glad you understand."

He smiled and sat in silence, allowing her to think he understood. In fact, he hadn't the faintest idea what she was talking about.

"Mind you, I wasn't easily shaped at Angelica's age," she said after a moment, "but shape me they did. My father was a master at that, and then there was Lawrence."

"Lawrence."

"Oh, my, yes," she answered.

He had no idea who Lawrence was, of course, but it seemed he could maintain his end of the conversation by repeating key words from time to time.

"And then, of course, he found Katherine," she said.

Katherine. Lawrence and Katherine. Who or what in hell were they talking about now? Perhaps he could guide her back to inquiring into his background. At least he'd understood that.

"She never had a thought that some man didn't put there first, that one," Minerva said. About Katherine, no doubt. Whoever she was. "I imagine she's happy enough, but it's been quite a trial for Angelica."

"A trial?"

She nodded vigorously enough to make the pearls bobble against her ample chest. Obviously he'd repeated the correct word again. "A young girl needs to be governed, of course, but she doesn't need to be told how and when to breathe."

"Certainly not," he tossed in to please her.

It must have worked, for her smile broadened to beatific. "Angelica has such dreams. I can understand that because I had dreams myself. Not like Angelica's, mind you, with those giant turtles and the finches. You'd think we have enough finches in Massachusetts, wouldn't you?"

"You'll find we have splendid finches in England," he said. "More than enough of them for the most devoted finch lover." Giant turtles were another matter, but he wasn't planning to worry about that until he had some idea what he was talking about.

"Well, there you are then," she declared. "Given a splendid collection of finches and the right man to devote herself to, Angelica is sure to forget about all that other nonsense."

"The turtles," he offered.

"Exactly."

"And that would please Lawrence and Katherine, would it?"

"Oh, you'll please them mightily in any case; have no doubt about that. Just wait until they meet you," she said. Abruptly she covered her mouth with her fingers again and giggled into them. "But I'm getting ahead of myself, aren't I?"

"You've gotten quite ahead of me," he admitted.

"Oh, your lordship," she declared and laughed some more. "I had no idea you and I would be such kindred spirits. In fact, I had no idea we'd even meet again. If I'd known you planned to visit today, I wouldn't have let Angelica step out with that other one."

"That other one?" Now here was something he really did need to understand. If Miss Hamilton was stepping out with another man, he'd have to race his way into her affections before the other chap got there.

"Oh, what was his name?" Minerva said. "We met him last night shortly after we met you."

Oh, no, not Bertie Underwood. "An agreeable sort of fellow?" he prompted.

"Yes, I'd say so," she replied. "In fact, I thought to

Taming Angelica

myself that even though he wasn't overly impressive, he was very pleasant."

"Almost too pleasant?" he asked. "As though he weren't being thoroughly honest?"

"Why, yes," she said. "I knew there was something about him that didn't ring quite true."

"Did he look rather like a fish?"

She tilted her head back and laughed outright. "Bless you, your lordship," she said after a moment. "That's exactly what he looked like. What a fine judge of human nature you are."

"Then you'll take a bit of advice from me about him?"

"Of course."

"Don't trust him. Especially with any information you wish to remain confidential." *For example, the position you found me in with Elizabeth Gates last night.*

Her eyes widened. "Oh, my, you don't suppose he'd do anything to disgrace Angelica, do you?"

"No. I wouldn't worry on that account." Angelica Hamilton could take care of herself around Bertie Underwood, and she'd most likely have enough sense to keep her mouth shut when with him. At least he hoped she would. "Just don't trust his pleasantness too far."

"Thank you, I won't. Oh, here they are now."

Will glanced over at the door and found that it had already been opened, and Angelica Hamilton and Bertie Underwood stood on the threshold. She made a perfect vision in a walking costume of lemon yellow lawn and with a healthy glow to her cheeks. Will rose immediately.

"You won't what, dear heart?" Angelica asked as she approached her aunt, bent, and planted a kiss on the older woman's forehead.

"I'm afraid it's a secret between Lord Claridge and me," Minerva answered. "You remember his lordship from last night, don't you?"

"Of course." Angelica straightened and studied him. Her gaze held none of the previous night's hostility in it, but neither was it an open and friendly greeting. She appeared rather to be making some mental calculation, as though she couldn't easily decide whether she wanted him present or not.

Finally she smiled at him and nodded, but even that gesture held a tiny threat or dare—he couldn't tell which. She looked for all the world like a woman who was up to something, something that involved him. And to think only moments ago he'd been telling her aunt not to trust Bertie. He'd better watch his step with her instead.

He had no trouble reading Bertie's expression, as full as it was of displeasure at his finding Will there. Bertie crossed the room and took up a position near Angelica as though marking out his territory. They'd see about that.

"Did you have a pleasant walk?" Minerva asked.

"Very pleasant," Angelica answered.

"Did you see any finches? Lord Claridge tells me England is just full of finches."

Bertie's expression brightened. "You're fond of finches, Miss Hamilton? I'll make certain we spot some on our next stroll."

"Thank you," she answered. "But that's not exactly the point."

"I'm wild about birds myself—grouse, whippoorwills, doves," Bertie said.

What an ass. The man obviously didn't give a fig for birds. He wanted only to ingratiate himself with Angelica Hamilton. Surely she could see that.

"Are you fond of birds, too, Lord Claridge?" Angelica asked.

Taming Angelica

"Don't know the first thing about them."

She smiled in earnest, and the expression filled the room with sunlight. Somehow he'd gotten the right answer. He'd happily deny knowing anything about giant turtles, too, if he got the opportunity.

"Would you care for me to point out a few of your local species?" she asked.

"Certainly," he answered. "Whenever you like."

"How about right now?"

"Angelica, you've just come in," Minerva said.

"Yes," Bertie added. "We had a lovely walk."

"So lovely that I'd like another," she said. "Why don't you stay here and have some tea with my aunt, Lord Underwood? I have something I'd like to discuss with Lord Claridge."

"I'm at your complete disposal, Miss Hamilton," Will said.

"But . . ." Bertie tried.

"Do keep me company, Lord Underwood," Minerva said. "And have some tea."

"Now see here," Bertie sputtered.

"There's a dear," Angelica said. She turned toward Will. "Now that that's settled, let's have our walk."

"Certainly." He escorted her to the doorway.

"Take the maid," Minerva called from behind them.

"But Auntie," Angelica answered. "She'll only slow me down again."

"Take the maid," Minerva repeated, some authority in her voice this time.

"Oh, very well," Angelica answered.

Chapter Three

Angelica had already found that the park on a sunny afternoon at teatime made a marvelous place for a discreet meeting with a gentleman. Unconcerned with protocol and social niceties, the birds stayed at their posts, searching for seeds and insects along the lawns. The flowers, in all their botanical wisdom, stood in place to serve as diversions to the conversation.

The natural world remained—if such a perfectly tended place could be called natural—while humanity had for the most part disappeared. All Angelica had to do was get rid of her maid, and she'd have Lord Claridge to herself.

"Nice of you to come out with me," he said.

She glanced at where he walked, not more than an arm's length away, an impressive figure at several inches taller than her own not unimpressive height. "It was nice of you to ask me."

"That's odd," he said. "I thought you'd asked me."

"My heavens, no," she lied. "I don't go around asking strange men to take me for walks."

"You'd only just come in from a stroll with Bertie Underwood."

"I didn't ask him either." At least that was true. Only, why did he seem determined to make her out to be so eager for masculine company?

"Are you sure?" he insisted. "Bertie's not usually the walking sort."

"Of course I'm sure. And why is this so important to you?"

He smiled, just the tiniest curl to his lips, and shrugged. "I don't know. I don't suppose it is important in any real sense."

"All that's important is that we're here," she said.

"Quite."

"And that it's a lovely day, and that we can share some intelligent conversation."

Intelligent conversation would be a relief after her futile attempts at discourse with the simpering Lord Underwood. The man's entire vocabulary consisted of compliments and invitations. *"I must say you look fetching, Miss Hamilton. What a lovely dress." "Might I invite you to visit my box at Vauxhall tonight?" "Would you care to ride in the park tomorrow morning?"*

He'd completely missed her hints at her plan to acquire some cash, even when she thought she'd made it clear that he would profit, too. He was either unbelievably thickheaded or didn't need money. Whichever, he was of no use to her.

But now she had Lord Claridge. She hadn't expected him to appear at the house after she'd acted so rudely toward him last night, but here he was, and he'd suit her plans wonderfully. If he objected to them, she'd threaten—subtly, of course—to reveal the details of the scene she and Aunt Minnie had witnessed in the drawing room.

She had no real desire to cause that poor woman any embarrassment, but she was desperate. And if he were any kind of gentleman at all, he'd agree to help her rather than harm his paramour any more than he already had. Yes indeed, Lord Claridge would suit her purposes well.

"Then we'd best have at it, don't you suppose?" he asked.

"I beg your pardon?"

He stopped and turned to her, looking down at her with amusement clear in the blue depths of his eyes. "We'd best have some intelligent conversation. What did you think I meant?"

"I'm certain I have no idea what you meant."

"You claim you invited me here for intelligent conversation, but instead you've been quite lost in thought. Is something amiss?"

Concern from him, with an offer of assistance sure to follow. Here was the perfect opportunity to ask for his help. If only she could get him truly alone. She glanced over his shoulder and found her maid approaching. She'd already run the poor girl all over the park on their walk with Lord Underwood, and Mary had tried to slow her down on this trip. It shouldn't take much to get her to sit down and let them wander off a bit on their own.

"There you are, Mary," she called. "Are you feeling quite well?"

The girl curtsied. "Bless you, miss, I am a bit tired. Would you care to go back now?"

"Not at all. I haven't shown Lord Claridge those magnificent dahlias yet."

"I don't remember any dahlias, miss," Mary said.

"They're here somewhere," Angelica answered. She glanced around for something, anything, that might look like a dahlia. Preferably something at a good distance. "Maybe just down that wooded path."

Mary's face fell as she peered down the path in question. "We've already been down there, and I don't remember dahlias."

"I'm certain that's where they were. Come along."

"Please, miss, haven't we had enough exercise already?"

"Nonsense." Angelica took a deep breath and let it out loudly. "You can never have too much healthy exertion and fresh air."

Never mind that the air wasn't at all fresh but full of the smells of too many horses and too many people all living on top of each other—city air and barely breathable, but adequate to her point. She put her hands on her hips and looked at Mary, who appeared to be breathing heavily at the mere idea of more exertion.

"Lord Claridge is ready for a walk," she said, turning toward her escort. "Aren't you, sir?"

"I'm sure I'm ready for whatever you're ready for, Miss Hamilton," he answered.

"His lordship hasn't already been around the park," Mary muttered.

"Oh, very well," Angelica said. "I suppose you'll have to sit down instead. Go and find yourself a bench somewhere. We'll be back in a few minutes."

"But I'm not to leave you and his lordship alone. Mr. Davidson would have my hide, he would."

Lord Claridge's brow went up. "Mr. Davidson?"

"The butler," Angelica explained. She looked back at Mary. "Mr. Davidson will know only if you tell him. I have no intention of doing so; do you, Lord Claridge?"

"Not at all."

"There you are, then. Go find a place to sit before you drop."

Mary bit her lower lip. "But it isn't respectable, miss."

"Oh, blast respectability," Angelica declared. Really, she'd had more than enough of the girl and her constant presence for one afternoon. "I'm a grown woman, and I'll do as I want. Lord Claridge is hardly likely to ravish me while we're alone, in any case."

Claridge made the correct huffy noises in his throat. "I should hope not."

"There, you see?" Angelica said. "Now off with you."

Mary didn't move but worried her lip some more with her teeth. Finally Angelica shooshed the maid off with a wave of her hands and then turned to her escort. "Shall we?"

He offered his arm. "Certainly."

She looked at his arm, at the smooth wool of his sleeve and the elegance of his hand with its long fingers. She hadn't counted on actually touching him. That seemed too intimate somehow.

Now that she thought about it, he was standing close enough that she could smell his shaving soap. For the first time since realizing that he might be at her disposal to carry out her plan, she had to wonder at the wisdom of using him. She'd spent over an hour with Lord Underwood, and the entirety of that man had left her unmoved. This man could shake her by simply extending his arm.

She stood there perfectly still, lost in indecision, until she'd made herself ridiculous. Until he looked down at her with open amusement in his eyes. Worse than amusement—a definite challenge in his eyes and in his smile. Well, she certainly wasn't going to back down from any challenges. She lifted her arm and twined it through his, resting her hand lightly on his sleeve.

"There you are. I won't bite, you know," he said. He

Taming Angelica

bent toward her until she could feel his breath on her cheek. "Unless you ask me to, of course."

"Really, Lord Claridge."

"Really, Miss Hamilton."

"Then let's have at it."

His eyes widened, and a laugh of surprise escaped his chest.

"Our walk, sir," she said. "And intelligent conversation. Let's have at it."

"What a delicious prospect," he answered.

She led him to the wooded path and then down it, half expecting to find dahlias and not really caring whether they did or not. The trees met overhead, casting them into dappled shade. Here, away from the sounds of carriages and out of sight of the rest of humanity, Angelica could almost imagine herself in the wilderness.

Not that she had any true idea of what wilderness would be like—never having been away from civilization before. But she'd read about Darwin's voyages on the *Beagle,* and she'd listened to Miss James's descriptions of the Sandwich Islands—Hawaii, as the natives called them—and she'd imagined herself there among dense, green forests and the majestic volcanoes.

And at sea. She always imagined herself at sea. She'd found the Atlantic crossing glorious, but eventually they'd ended up here in a place more suffocating than Boston—though she'd hardly imagined that possible. To take off for tropical waters, ah, that would be heaven. To wear trousers rolled up to her knees as the sailors did. To feel the wind in her hair by day and to gaze at unfamiliar constellations by night.

She was young and intelligent and rich, and the only thing that held her back was her gender. But she'd outsmart all her masters and get away. To that end, Lord Claridge would prove invaluable.

She glanced at him and found him looking back at

her. A light of something she couldn't read shone from his eyes, as though he'd seen something inside her. As though he'd dreamed her dreams with her and approved. What would it be like to have a partner in adventure instead of countless persistent adversaries intent on holding her back?

"That's very appealing," he said.

"I beg your pardon?" She seemed to be saying that sort of thing to him all the time. How did he manage to constantly surprise her?

"You're blushing," he answered. "It's very appealing."

Indeed, her throat was warm. The realization made her flush even more until the heat crept up and over her cheeks.

"You have no idea what that does to a man of . . ." He cleared his throat. "Um, a man of some experience."

"I don't know what you mean, sir." In fact, she didn't, but some part of her knew. Her chest tightened, and the oddest sensation started in her belly—a sort of fluttering, uncertain but not entirely unpleasant. No, not unpleasant at all.

"Perhaps we shouldn't have embarked on this adventure. Perhaps I should take you back," he said.

"No," she answered quickly. Being here with him, isolated and alone, was an adventure. Not the kind she hoped for ultimately, but an adventure nevertheless. The odd feelings he created in her certainly bore exploration. Systematic and scientific exploration to broaden her education and nothing more. If she was to understand the world, she needed to understand her own nature, didn't she?

"Don't take me back," she said. "I haven't yet had a chance to . . ."

"Chance to what?"

Her plan. Dear heaven, she'd come here with a plan,

and he'd chased it clear out of her head. Just because she'd touched his sleeve and walked a few steps alone with him. Was this confusion what a chaperon protected one from? It didn't seem dangerous, only perplexing and definitely enjoyable, nothing she needed protection from. She'd explore it further, but right now she had other matters to attend to.

She looked up at him and gave him what she hoped was her most pleasing smile. "I wanted a chance to ask you a favor."

"Anything," he answered, still gazing down at her.

"It's rather out of the ordinary."

"That doesn't surprise me."

"It's rather far out of the ordinary, I'm afraid."

His smile grew even warmer. "Now you have me intrigued, Miss Hamilton."

She took a breath. "I want you to help me dispose of some jewelry."

"Dispose of some jewelry?" Will heard himself echo her but made little sense of the words. "In what sense *dispose?*"

"In the sense of sell it," she answered, as though she were talking to a child. "What other sense could there be—throw it into the Thames?"

"But why?"

"To get money, of course," she said. "I suppose you're far too rich ever to need money, being the brother of a duke and all. Maybe that's why you seem so surprised."

Now there she had things completely, one hundred and eighty degrees wrong. He needed money all the time, but he'd never thought she did. What on earth for? She had an elegant town house in the most elegant part of town. She had elegant furnishings, elegant clothes, elegant food. What else did she need? Giant turtles and finches?

Unless . . . good God, Bertie couldn't have been wrong about her family's wealth, could he? "If you and your aunt are temporarily short of funds . . ."

She cocked her head in a curious way, studying him. "Why, Lord Claridge, how kind. But we could never take a loan from you. Why, we don't even know you."

Just as well. If they did, they'd know he didn't have two shillings of his own to rub together. Of course, he could always appeal to his brother on their behalf. As long as the duke knew that not a penny was to go to Will, he might even help.

"Besides," she said, "we have plenty of money. Boatloads of it, in fact."

Well, thank heaven for that. Marriage, even for money for his thoroughbreds, hadn't interested him before last night. But now that he'd settled on Miss Hamilton and her smiles and odd ways, he'd grown rather used to the idea. He didn't really care to be changing his goals again so abruptly.

"But I don't understand," he said. "Why would you want to exchange some jewels for money if you already have boatloads of it?"

"*We* have the money, not I. And *I* need it."

"Then why don't you simply ask your aunt for some?"

"I can see you've never been a woman, Lord Claridge."

Very well. The niece was as daft as her aunt. Younger, more beautifully packaged, and more attractive when she blushed, but certainly as daft. "What does my gender have to do with anything?"

"A woman may ask for anything she wants as long as it's appropriate to her station. I could ask for acres of satin, a mountain of lace, buckets full of diamonds, and no one would flinch."

"I suppose that's true."

Taming Angelica

"But let me ask for funds to spend at my own discretion—no matter how little—and just listen for the howls of outrage."

"People only want what's best for you."

She started to pace across one side of the walkway and back again. "Best for me? *Best* for me?"

Clearly he'd said the wrong thing this time, because her skin flushed again, with anger this time.

"Can't anyone believe that *I* know what's best for me?" she cried, still pacing. "Is everyone so convinced that I haven't a brain in my head, just because I'm female?"

"Certainly not." That *had* to be the right answer.

"Then why am I treated that way? Why am I given no freedom to make my own decisions? Why am I kept dependent for everything? First on my father and now on my aunt, who is no more than his substitute no matter how sweet she is."

"Surely they only care about you."

"A fine way to care, to keep a woman from her heart's desire. To kill her dreams."

"And you want my help to dispose of some jewels so that you may pursue your dreams."

She stopped her pacing and walked straight up to him, placing her hands over his. "You do understand."

Not a bit. Not for an instant. Ever since Minerva Hamilton had stopped checking into his background, nothing about either woman had made any sense. And yet he seemed to do so well with them when they thought he understood. So well, in fact, that at this very moment she stood only inches from him, gazing up into his face with an expression of such earnestness he ought to laugh.

But he didn't feel like laughing. Quite the contrary. He wanted to lift his hand and ease the tension in her brow. He wanted to unpucker her mouth, softening her

Alice Chambers

lips with kisses until they parted on a sigh. He'd almost done it a moment ago, until her talk of selling jewelry had quieted the stirrings in his loins. The stirrings were back now, and if she wasn't careful, he'd pull her off into the bushes and kiss her senseless.

"Are you quite well, Lord Claridge?" she asked softly.

He straightened and gave her hands a squeeze. "Quite."

"You looked rather odd for a bit there."

Odd. Didn't the woman know what a man looked like when he wanted to kiss her? Could she really have had so little experience? No doubt there were many ways to find out the answer to that question, but only one came into his head at this particular moment—to try to kiss her and see what happened. He lowered his face toward hers, parting his lips to let his breath dance over her cheek.

She studied him warily as his mouth neared hers, but she stood her ground, even leaned into him ever so slightly. But then, maybe he imagined that because he wanted it so desperately. Suddenly nothing in the world seemed as important as kissing this woman—this silly creature of finches and giant turtles and fictitious dahlias. This impossible innocent with skin like flower petals and eyes like amber flecked with gold.

She closed her eyes, her dark lashes fluttering lightly against her cheeks. An invitation if ever he'd seen one. He bent lower and touched his lips to hers.

She was awkward at first, holding herself stiff while he tasted her tightly closed lips. But he didn't give up. He moved softly, slowly, now over the top lip, now brushing against the corner of her mouth. After a moment, she yielded to the kiss with a sigh that parted her lips enough for him to press the advantage.

He tilted his head and took her mouth with more

authority, using his own lips to part hers further. She made a tiny noise in the back of her throat, halfway between a gasp and a squeak, as though astonished at what was happening to her. But she didn't retreat from him. Rather, she rested her hand against his chest and tipped her head back, bringing her face closer to his.

No practiced response could have inflamed him more. No coy cat-and-mouse game could have heated his blood any hotter than her tentative explorations. When her tongue came out, just the tip grazing his lower lip, it sent a jolt of need through him. Pure, undiluted lust in a current that shot right to the center of him and below. *Damn.*

He made his hands come up to her arms and push her away. God only knew where he found the strength. He took a few breaths and made himself look over her shoulder at a point in the distance. If he saw the flush that must be coloring her skin, he would come quite undone.

"I'm so sorry," he said with a gasp, short of air. "That was unforgivable of me."

"No," she answered. "That is, yes, I suppose it was. That is, I don't know."

He looked down at her and discovered that her cheeks were, indeed, an appealing rose. "You don't know?"

She took a few shallow breaths. "I know I should be shocked, even angry. But that was really quite remarkable, wasn't it?"

"Remarkable?"

She brought her fingertips to her mouth, as if feeling for a reminder of his own lips there. "I've heard that kisses could be pleasant, but I never dreamed of this."

"No one's ever kissed you before?"

"No. Except for my family, of course. I'd remember if someone had kissed me like *that*."

Alice Chambers

Her first kiss—he'd been right about her innocence. Her very first kiss, and he'd had it. *How infinitely precious.* The thought filled him with a sort of fierce tenderness—a very strange feeling, a desire to protect her and own her at the same time—contradictory and impossible and irresistible, unlike anything he'd ever felt about a woman before.

"Maybe we'd better go back," she said. "I think I really have had enough exercise for one afternoon. Yes, and I have quite a bit to think about."

About what a perfect cad he was, no doubt. Not that he could blame her. "Not until you've allowed me to apologize."

"That really isn't necessary."

"But it is," he insisted.

"I could slap your face if that would make you feel better."

"I deserve no less," he answered. "Please just let me explain."

She stood in silence, looking up at him as though he'd gone quite mad. Perhaps he had. What the devil was he to explain to her when he didn't understand himself?

She laughed, a pleasing enough sound but with a hint of worry behind it. "Nothing to explain, Lord Claridge. Nothing at all."

"Allow me to escort you home," he said hastily, like an overeager schoolboy. What had gotten into him?

"No need. I'll just find Mary, and we'll be on our way."

"I may see you again, mayn't I?" Damn, now he was begging. "You'll still need my help with your jewelry. To pursue your dreams."

None of that made any sense to him, of course, but it stopped her. She fidgeted for a moment, clearly torn between staying to discuss it with him and running from him. "Yes, I will. Only not right now. I need some time alone. To think."

"Then I may depend on your company in the future?" he asked. "The near future, I hope?"

"Yes." She set her shoulders and looked at him squarely. "The near future."

Chapter Four

If only it were anatomically possible to kick herself where she should, Angelica would gladly do it now. The hall clock chimed again, two in the morning this time, and she set aside the book she'd been trying to read for the last hour. What in heaven's name had made her run from Lord Will Claridge when she'd nearly won his cooperation?

That kiss, of course. One didn't experience something like *that* and just go on about one's business. That kiss required some thought, some analysis. All afternoon, all evening, and now into the small hours of the morning, the memory of that kiss had played itself over and over in her mind. Even now, all she had to do was close her eyes to re-create the feel of his lips against hers.

She'd always imagined men to be little more than bullies. Certainly her father ordered all the women of his household around—from his sister to his wife to

Taming Angelica

both his daughters. Then her sister Penny had found her own husband, become Penelope, and moved away to follow her own master's orders, leaving Angelica as the last female to be browbeaten into submission at the home of Lawrence Hamilton. Now she'd gotten free of all that—almost—only to discover that a man's gentleness could prove even more powerful than his temper.

That kiss.

She closed the book and set it on the table at her elbow. The candle's light barely reached beyond the chair she sat on, and she could imagine any number of surprises in the dark corners of the library.

All of them were tall and blond with laughing eyes and an attractively sloped nose. Lord Claridge in his evening dress as she'd first seen him in the study at the ball. In the suit he'd worn this afternoon, with the pleasantly scratchy wool of his coat that she'd rested her hand against as he kissed her. In her father's robe de chambre—the only man's dressing gown she'd ever seen. The image came through so clearly she almost expected him to step from the shadows and tell her, *It's late, Angelica. Come to bed.*

A shiver of something ran through her, as though he really did stand there. As though she really had heard his voice in the stillness. An order—*Come to bed.* And yet it held more entreaty than command. She'd heard that uncertainty this afternoon when he'd apologized for kissing her. She'd liked it then, but not nearly as much as she liked the invitation she'd thought she'd heard just now.

Oh, dear heaven. She'd completely lost her mind. She hadn't heard him just now. She'd only imagined him, and in her father's robe, too. What a silly goose she'd become, just because a man had kissed her. No matter how nice, it had been only a kiss.

What followed kisses hardly held any appeal, if

she'd read her mother and her sister's reactions correctly. Her mother shut up tighter than a miser's pocketbook at the mention of "wifely duties," as she called them. *Wifely duties*—what an ugly pair of words.

Penny hadn't told her much more, no matter how hard she'd pushed her questions. She made the act sound like little more than an invasion of privacy while one's husband made strange noises, eventually satisfied himself, and then slipped off to his own bedroom. It hurt like the very blazes the first time, and it made you bleed. Penny had made sure to tell her that much. All in all, the whole business sounded nothing more than unpleasant.

And yet—that kiss.

Yes, that kiss. At least she could turn it to her advantage. He'd seemed honestly sorry he'd behaved so forwardly, and maybe she could use his regret to get him to help her. She couldn't tell anyone else that he'd kissed her. That would reflect back onto her much more than it would onto him. But if he had a conscience, maybe she could make use of it for her own purposes. That and the little difficulty she'd found him in at the ball.

She'd been close to winning his cooperation this afternoon before that kiss had shaken her. If only she kept her head at their next encounter, she'd prevail. Let him kiss her again if he wanted. That would put him even more in her debt, and the next time she wouldn't lose the upper hand by letting her own feelings confuse her.

He'd asked to see her again. In the near future, he'd said. Very well, he'd see her again. In just a few hours, if she could only manage to get some sleep. She rose from the chair and picked up the candle.

It's late, Angelica, a deep voice whispered in her head. *Come to bed.*

Taming Angelica

* * *

"Claridge, you bastard, I ought to call you out."

Good God. Just the voice that Will had been dreading. He held firmly to the gray's bridle and turned to look over the stall toward the stable door. Horace Gates's silhouette filled most of the space, built as he was like a draft animal. A very large draft animal.

"I say, old fellow," Will said. "Great day for a race. If you want a tip, wager a bit on my gelding here in the third. He's going to give them all a surprise."

"I didn't come here to watch the races," Gates replied.

"Odd. That's why most people come to the track."

Gates took a few steps into the stable, his size appearing to increase with each one—until he resembled a coach more than an animal. A very large coach. Finally he stood, his hands clenched into fists by his side. "I came here to see you, Claridge."

"Very nice of you, Gates, but totally unnecessary. We see each other all the time at parties."

"I came to see you alone," the man rumbled. "And you know why."

Will looked at his horse, feigning nonchalance. "I have no idea what you're talking about."

"Damn you, Claridge," Gates thundered.

Will jumped. So much for nonchalance. He turned to face his adversary head-on. "Very well, get on with it. I have a race to run."

"What have you been doing with my wife?"

"Nothing." That was true enough, at least since she'd broken off their affair months ago. He hadn't even been alone with her since then, except for that unfortunate scene in Lady Kimball's sitting room.

"Then why is she constantly mooning over you?" Gates demanded, his pale cheeks turning a decidedly ugly red.

"How do you know she's mooning over *me?*" Will said. "Women moon over any number of things. It can vary with the . . . well, the moon."

"I should think I know why my own wife moons."

Will studied him. With his broad shoulders and overmuscled arms, he might make a good draft horse, after all, but he hardly appeared the type to be sensitive to a woman's nature. And the stubborn set to the jaw and light of dim intelligence in his watery blue eyes didn't promise much talent in reading people. He was probably a bully at the dinner table and a buffoon in bed. No wonder Elizabeth had taken lovers.

"Has Lady Gates told you that I've done something to offend her?" Will asked.

Gates's eyes narrowed to resentful slits. "No."

Thank God for that, anyway. Elizabeth might have lost her reason enough to fall in love with a cad like Will, but it appeared she'd maintained enough reason not to confess herself to her boor of a husband. "Have you seen me behave in any way untoward with your wife?"

Gate's fists clenched so hard, Will would have sworn he could hear the knuckles cracking. "No."

"Then what on earth makes you think that I have?"

"There's a rumor floating about of you and an unidentified lady at an unidentified ball. The rumor has it that the lady was crying her eyes out, that you'd broken her heart."

"Don't go around believing rumors, old fellow. You know how people like to talk. Besides, what on earth makes you think Lady Gates would behave so stupidly?"

"Because she's turned into a bloody watering pot all of a sudden," Gates answered. "All I have to do is look at her to set the river Jordan to gushing."

Will tried stiffening his own shoulders and staring at the man in mock indignation. It was rather hard to summon up the real thing when he was so thoroughly guilty as charged. "With all due respect, dear chap, that sounds like it has more to do with you than me."

"Don't try any of that, me buck. Not if you know what's good for you."

"I don't know what you mean, Gates."

"You and your clever ways," the man said in reply. "You may be good enough to take in women—lots of them, if I've heard right—but you can't fool me."

Next to Will, the gray stamped and snorted softly, his breath fogging in the unseasonably cool morning air. Will patted his neck and crooned to the horse, glad to turn his attention from the snorting, stamping human male on the other side of the stall.

"Everyone knows what you are," Gates continued. "A bed monkey. A mongrel cur with the morals of a serpent."

"A one-man menagerie, eh?"

"Don't laugh at me, Claridge." Gates stepped closer, until he towered over Will. "I won't have it."

"Then you oughtn't to make yourself laughable."

He'd gone rather too far with that last. Gates's nostrils flared, and he fairly snarled at Will, making him far more bestial than Will could hope to be on his most primitive days. Even the horse sensed the threat from the man, and he tossed his head and danced in place until it was all Will could do to keep him under control.

"You've been toying with my wife," Gates said between clenched teeth. "I haven't seen it myself, and I haven't been able to get Elizabeth to admit it. Yet."

Dear God, if Elizabeth had withstood this sort of inquisition and kept quiet, she had more backbone than he'd ever given her credit for. Somehow he'd have to find a way to thank her—when she'd done with hating him, too, of course.

"But one way or another I'll get the straight story,"

Gates continued. "Elizabeth will confess, or I'll find someone else who's seen the two of you together. Either way, I'll have the truth."

Will stared back at him as calmly as his shaking knees and restless horse would allow. "There isn't any truth to have."

"You're a damned liar."

"Now see here—"

"I'll have the truth, Claridge, and when I have it, I'll beat your face in with my bare hands until no woman in England would want you. Then I'll drag your sorry hide onto a boat and across the channel and fill you so full of holes you won't be able to hold a glass of water."

Will didn't have any answer for that. He knew damned well that Gates was perfectly capable and willing to carry out the threat if given proof of his affair with Elizabeth. He could only hope that the rumor remained that and nothing more.

"Make no mistake," Gates said, punching a thick finger into Will's chest. "When I have particulars and can prove what I already know, I'll have justice. You won't be doing to any more men what you've done to me."

"To you?" *Unbelievable.* Elizabeth and her feelings mattered not a whit—only what he'd done to Horace. Husbands could be such asses.

"To me. Mark my words, Claridge. One word of support for what I've heard about you, and you'll find yourself facing me in a duel."

Will pushed away Gates's finger with his free hand and straightened the fabric of his coat. "I've heard you, Gates. Will that be all?"

"There you are, Lord Claridge." A feminine voice from the doorway. Gates took a step back, and Will could see the source. ***Dear God, Angelica Hamilton.***

Taming Angelica

Of all the people in the world, only Bertie Underwood could be more of a disaster.

Gates took another step back, crossing his arms over his chest. He glared at Will for a moment and then looked toward Miss Hamilton.

"You're here to see *him?*" Gates asked with a contemptuous nod of his head in Will's direction.

"Why, yes," she answered.

"I'd watch my step with this one, miss," Gates said. "He has a reputation, if you know what I mean."

"For the love of God, Gates," Will said.

"I'm very aware of the rumors," she said. "I've experienced them at first hand."

Gates dropped his hands by his sides and stared at her in amazement. "You have?"

"Just the other evening," she said.

Well, that does it. Now the whole story would come out, and Gates would have his hide. Will glanced around—assessing his chances of getting out the door and losing himself in the crowd before Gates could grab him. He'd have to run to the Continent, of course, but even France wouldn't be far enough away to escape this particular irate husband. Perhaps Italy.

"I'd appreciate it very much if you'd repeat the details," Gates said.

"I'm afraid I'd become very upset over an argument I'd been having with Lord Quimby, and Lord Claridge happened on me as I was crying my foolish eyes out."

"You?" Gates asked.

"Lord Claridge only did what he could to comfort me. It looked rather intimate, but it was wholly innocent."

What the devil? What in the hell was she talking about?

Gates eyed her as if he couldn't believe the story. But the man had no reason to doubt Angelica Hamil-

57

ton, who appeared the very picture of sincerity with her wide amber eyes and the youthful glow to her skin.

"You were the woman in the sitting room at Lady Kimball's?" Gates demanded.

She looked down at her feet and managed a tiny blush. "Yes, I'm afraid I was in quite a state. And all this time Lord Claridge has been protecting my identity to keep me from disgrace."

"Has he now?" Gates asked.

"Of course I have," Will volunteered. If Miss Hamilton would willingly lie to cover his sins, the very least he could do was help her. "It was only the decent thing to do."

Gates snorted and glowered at him.

"And it's cost him," Miss Hamilton continued. "I've heard ugly rumors that he was found in a compromising position with a married lady. It's so unfair."

"Say nothing of it, Miss Hamilton," Will said.

Gates snorted even more loudly.

"In fact, I've come here to thank Lord Claridge for his chivalry," she said. "I'd hoped to be discreet, but it appears I've been found out again. Silly me."

Dear God, the woman was good. She could simper with the best of them if it proved to be in her interest. Will could learn a few tricks from her, or so it appeared.

"I do hope I can rely on your silence regarding this visit," she continued. "Lord . . ."

"Never mind." Gates grunted. "I wasn't here. I never met you. None of this happened."

"Thank you, sir." She dropped a curtsy, overdoing it just a trifle.

Gates waved his hand in disgust at both of them and walked toward the door. When he got there, he turned for one more glower. "Just keep your wits about you with Claridge. He isn't to be trusted."

She smiled sweetly at Gates, and he crossed the

Taming Angelica

threshold and disappeared. She turned back toward Will, her expression triumphant. "You'd better close your mouth, Lord Claridge. You're beginning to look like your friend Lord Underwood."

"Why did you do that?"

She didn't answer but continued to smile at him, gloating for all she was worth. "Was that man the husband of one of your flirtations?"

Will cleared his throat. "A gentleman doesn't tell."

"But you aren't a gentleman, are you, sir?"

"You've found me out, Miss Hamilton."

"My aunt has." She approached the stall, intent on the horse, but still smiling smugly and glancing at him out of the corner of her eye. "Not that I was surprised after the position I found you in the other evening with . . . was she that man's wife?"

Now that was a question he wasn't going to answer, so he just stood enjoying her nearness and the faint scent of flowers that surrounded her. She reached up and stroked the horse's nose, bringing herself so close to him that he could sense the heat of her body.

The feeling was entirely too pleasant, too seductive. It reminded him of the kiss they'd shared the day before. Thank God there was a wall between them.

"What has your aunt found out?" he asked, more to distract himself with conversation than to gather information.

"You don't have any money, for one thing," she said.

"My family is quite wealthy."

"Your brother is, and he doesn't approve of how you spend what little he gives you. On racing and horses."

"Everyone in London society knows of my situation."

She stared up at him, a look of steely determination behind her dark lashes. "You have quite a way with the wives of your friends."

"Their wives *are* my friends," he corrected.

"You're a rake, sir. Even worse than I'd thought at first. A perfect scoundrel."

"Ugly words." He took a breath. "So does all this disqualify me from keeping company with you?"

"Not at all. You're a man, and you come from a good family. That's all my aunt cares about, and that's all she plans to tell my father."

"She still wants me to court you?"

"Yes." She rested her hand against his arm. "And I want you to court me, too."

Good God. Could it really be that simple? A few months of the proper attentions, and Miss Angelica Hamilton with her soft mouth and hot sighs could be his?

"As a diversion only," she added. "I don't plan to marry you or any man. Ever."

"Why not?"

"That's my business. But I need a man's help, and a fiancé would be perfect."

"What would I have to do?" he asked.

"First, help me to sell some of my jewels."

"Excuse me for asking, Miss Hamilton, but are they truly yours to sell?"

She waved her hand. "A legality."

"I'm afraid I don't know anything about selling stolen jewelry."

"Use one of those racers," she answered.

"A horse?"

"Of course not. One of those people from Bow Street."

"Runners," he said. "Bow Street runners. They aren't in the business of selling stolen jewelry either."

"You'll manage somehow." She crossed her arms over her chest and gave her head a determined nod. "Then I want you to help me book passage to South America."

"South America? Why in God's name would you want to go to South America?"

"As I said, that's my business."

He dropped the horse's bridle and crossed his own arms over his chest, staring at her with equal determination. "And why should I do all this for you?"

"You'll get part of the money from my jewels. You can use it on your horses, and your brother will know nothing about it. We'll both get what we want."

"So you think you can buy me for some money?"

She ran a fingertip across the top of the stall, glancing at him coquettishly from under her lashes as she did. "That, and my continued cooperation in fooling the gentleman who just left here."

He smiled despite himself. "You have it all figured out, do you?"

"I think so." She extended her hand. "Do we have an agreement?"

He took her hand in his and shook it. "Indeed, we do."

She grinned at him, thoroughly satisfied with herself by all appearances. *Clever little thing.* She just hadn't reckoned on one fact—if he married her, he wouldn't get part of her money. He'd get it all.

A week after saving Lord Will Claridge's hide in that dim stable, Angelica spotted the man himself among the flowering orchids in the Crystal Palace. He didn't see her, standing as he was at some distance and conversing with a woman who appeared somewhat older than he but strikingly beautiful nevertheless. As she watched, the two of them smiled at each other in a very familiar manner, and he inclined his head ever so slightly toward hers.

Angelica turned away and concentrated on the nearest plant, a particularly spectacular specimen of the genus *Cattleya*. It was the beauty of the flower that made her insides shudder—the magnificent spread of the petals and the frilliness of the lip—not the fact that Lord Claridge had decided to woo another woman in broad daylight. What he did with his own baser instincts was his own affair and none of hers.

But wait. It *was* her affair. They'd struck a bargain that he would pretend to court her in order to help her escape London. How could he be courting her if he was seen in the company of another woman at a busy flower show? *Blast the man.*

"Oh, my, aren't all these flowers lovely?" Aunt Minnie exclaimed as she approached on the arm of Lord Bertie Underwood. "Do they grow in England, Lord Underwood?"

"Oh, I say . . . they must do," he answered, all British joviality.

Angelica would get a real headache if she had to endure much more of the man's good spirits. "The cattleyas and their relatives are all native to Central and South America."

Aunt Minnie assumed her stern look—the one that was supposed to scold but only managed to make her look oddly perplexed. "You're not going to start talking about South America again, I hope."

"Of course not," she snapped. "Why would I want to talk about South America or the Galápagos or any place interesting? Why would I want to talk about anything but hats and parties and tea cakes?"

"You needn't get testy about it," Aunt Minnie chided. "Testiness is so unattractive in a young girl."

"I'm sorry." Aunt Minnie was right. She needn't get angry with her aunt or even Lord Underwood because Lord Claridge was making a spectacle of himself with another woman. She cast a quick glance at where he stood, still deep in conversation with the other woman. Now he even held something behind him where Angelica couldn't see it. No doubt the other woman

Taming Angelica

found his coyness appealing. She only found it annoying.

She looked back at her companions. "You're right, Auntie," she said. "I apologize, Lord Underwood."

He smiled at her—the same unctuous expression he'd been using on her all afternoon. "No need, Miss Hamilton."

"What I meant to say was that the cattleyas are New World orchids. Any reference to South America was purely unintentional."

"I'm sure you know your orchids, Miss Hamilton," he said. "But I can assure you that these are English orchids because they're owned by the Royal Horticultural Society and grown right here."

He laughed heartily at his own joke for a minute. Angelica tried sharing his amusement but could only manage a titter. Aunt Minnie just stood on, staring at him, perplexed.

"You see, Miss Hamilton," he said to Aunt Minnie when he could manage a breath, "what I meant was that these orchids have to be English . . . because they live here . . . in this very conservatory . . . in England. You see?"

"Yes." Aunt Minnie looked at him as though he wasn't quite right in his head. "Of course, Lord Underwood. Whatever you say."

"Ah, yes. Well." He cleared his throat. "A bit of a joke, that."

Aunt Minnie continued staring at him. "Very funny, I'm sure."

"Amusing the Misses Hamilton again, Underwood?"

The voice, deep and masculine, came from directly behind Angelica. She turned and looked up at the source, but the light coming through the panes of glass blinded her, making Lord Claridge into a hazy figure. She could smell his shaving soap again, though, and the fragrance brought back memories of another afternoon in the park. An afternoon when he'd kissed her.

"You again, Claridge," Lord Underwood said behind her, disapproval ringing clearly in his voice. "You do keep popping up."

"No more than you do, Underwood."

Angelica reached up and shaded her eyes. She found the man whose image crowded her imagination more and more now, even invading her dreams. It wasn't just his good looks that made him so intrusive—although he had plenty of that. It was more the way being near him made her heart beat uncertainly. And she just couldn't get that kiss out of her mind. Too bad she couldn't use someone safer to carry out her escape. But fate had given her Will Claridge, and she'd use the man she'd been given.

"Good afternoon, Miss Hamilton," he said evenly. An innocent-enough greeting, but then nothing he did seemed entirely innocent. He glanced toward Aunt Minnie. "And good afternoon to you, Miss Hamilton."

Aunt Minnie didn't answer but just giggled behind Angelica. Lord Claridge looked back down at her and produced something from behind his back. An orchid flower—a cattleya flower, pure white with a splash of yellow in the throat. "For you, Miss Hamilton."

She took the blossom from him. "Thank you. It's very beautiful."

"No more beautiful than the lady who receives it."

Lord Underwood made a strangled sound. Lord Claridge glanced toward him. "You don't mind if I spirit Miss Hamilton away for a moment, do you?"

"Now, see here . . ." Lord Underwood replied.

"Not too far away," Aunt Minnie said. "You mustn't be careless with your reputation, Angelica. It's the only one you'll ever have."

"I'll take care not to bruise her reputation, Miss

Hamilton," Lord Claridge answered. "You may depend on me."

"Really," Angelica muttered as she stepped around him and walked down the path between towering palm and rubber trees. On either side, orchids of every color and shape created a chaos of beauty.

Lord Claridge fell into step beside her. "Really, Miss Hamilton?"

"Really, Lord Claridge. You shouldn't act so solicitous of my reputation when you don't give a fig for any other woman's."

"I beg your pardon?"

She stopped and glanced over her shoulder to make sure Aunt Minnie and Lord Underwood wouldn't hear them. "That lady I saw you talking to," she said quietly. "You were openly flirting with her."

He laughed heartily. And loudly, blast him.

"Keep your voice down," she said.

He leaned toward her. "Jealous, Miss Hamilton?"

"Certainly not." *The very idea!* "I only wish you'd be a bit more careful in public."

"The lady's a cousin of mine and an old friend."

"Oh."

"Her husband, Lord Brabant, is president of the Royal Horticultural Society. She gave me leave to pick that flower for you."

"And that's what you were discussing?" she asked, holding up the cattleya. "Whether you should pick this?"

"Without Lady Brabant's permission, my wrist would be soundly slapped for picking that. I might even be tossed out of here bodily."

"Oh," she said again. Not very intelligent commentary, but the best she could think of under the circumstances. "Thank you."

"My pleasure," he answered. "In the process I

learned some fascinating things about orchids." He moved closer to her, and a mischievous gleam entered his eyes. "Would you like to hear them?"

Her heart fluttered at his nearness, but she stood her ground. "Of course. I'm interested in all the natural sciences."

"Well, then." He reached over and ran a fingertip across the lip of the flower. "It seems that the orchid flower is characterized by two things. One is this very elaborate and beautiful lip, which is actually the flower's third petal."

She watched his finger move over the flower, and her throat threatened to close. She managed to get a breath. "And the other?"

"This complex structure," he said as his finger moved to a column that stood erect between the petals. "It has the sexual parts of the flower—male and female—hidden just behind this little nubbin at the tip."

"Oh," she said yet again. Why would nothing else come to her?

"The fact that it's both male and female means that it's a perfect flower," he said. His gaze moved from the flower to where her heart raced under the silk of her blouse. Could he hear it beating? "In the same way that a man and a woman perfect each other."

If she said "oh" one more time, she'd wither with embarrassment, but the only other thing she could think of was "My, isn't it warm in here?" So she just kept her mouth shut.

"This flower is considered quite desirable," he continued, taking the orchid from her and raising it to her cheek, "because of its firmness and the fine texture. And how the petals have opened so completely."

"Well, thank you, Lord Claridge," she said, taking the flower from him. Another moment of that sort of talk and she would have melted into his arms. "It's a very wonderful flower, and as soon as I get home I'll put it into water or under glass or press it in a book or whatever."

He put his hands behind his back and smiled down at her pleasantly, the scoundrel. How could he remain so cool when her own pulse was racing? "I'm glad I found you here," he said after a moment. "I have some news."

"News?"

"About your plan. To sell some of your jewelry."

She glanced over her shoulder quickly. Aunt Minnie and Lord Underwood were engrossed in conversation and far enough away that they wouldn't overhear. "What news?"

"I've found a buyer for them. A rather shady fellow. Are you ready for an adventure?"

"Yes," she answered. "When?"

"Tomorrow afternoon. I'll collect you just before teatime."

Chapter Five

"Ah, yes." Mr. Thaddeus Rush, if that was his real name, peered at Angelica's diamond necklace as though he planned to eat the stones, not appraise them. For heaven's sake, if he held them any closer to his face they'd leave marks on his skin. "Ah, yes," he repeated. "Well, well, well."

"Mr. Rush," she began.

Lord Claridge reached over from where he sat in the adjoining chair and squeezed her hand. She glanced at him, and he gave his head an almost imperceptible shake. He'd warned her that this meeting would resemble a tiny drama, with each of them playing their respective parts. But he hadn't told her it would drag along so.

She pulled her hand from his and interwove her fingers together in her lap. Across the desk, Rush opened a drawer and fumbled inside for a moment, finally pulling out a jeweler's loupe. "Ah, here you are," he proclaimed.

Taming Angelica

Oh for heaven's sake, did he have to talk to the thing? At least maybe now they might make some progress. "Yes, indeed," she volunteered. "Right here."

He smiled at her—a quick parting of his lips that exposed teeth that were far from perfect. "Quite so," he said.

"Quite."

Lord Claridge cleared his throat softly, a soft but definite command for her to keep quiet. He was right, no doubt, but if she didn't return to the house soon, she'd miss tea with Aunt Minnie, and she really didn't care to raise any suspicions on the day her diamond necklace turned up missing. And it might turn up missing, despite all her precautions.

She'd taken great care getting the necklace out of the house. First she'd had to find out without asking where Davidson kept her and Aunt Minnie's jewels. Then she'd had to find his keys. All in the space of one day. If she hadn't discovered quite by accident sometime before that their butler had a penchant for sneaking off to the wine cellar for a nap in the middle of the day, she'd never have managed any of it. And now this weasel-faced fool was going to make her late returning to the house. *Really.* Even a swindler had to live by a schedule, didn't he?

"Ah, yes," Rush said, as he stared into the center of the largest diamond. "A nice stone. A very nice stone."

"Nice?" Angelica snapped. "My fa . . . husband paid an unbelievable price for that necklace."

The man looked up at her, not even removing that *thing* from his eye. "As I said, nice."

"Forgive my sister," Lord Claridge said, covering her hand again and giving it a rather unpleasant squeeze this time. "She's distraught after the sudden loss of her husband, I'm afraid."

Rush eyed her clothing—a stylish walking costume

of pink sateen—with a scrutiny tantamount to a challenge. "Very sudden his death was, then?"

"Very," she answered. She took a breath and prepared to launch into the story she and Lord Claridge had discussed on the way to Rush's shop. "I'm from the United States, as you may have gathered, and my poor Charles was killed in a riding accident. I need funds for the burial and can't wait for money to arrive from home."

"Ah, yes," Rush said.

"As you can see, I haven't even had the time to have mourning clothes made."

"Interesting family you have there," Rush said.

"I beg your pardon?" she said.

"Seeing as how you're from the United States and your brother here sounds English. Very interesting."

"We were separated when we were small," she answered.

"My sister hasn't always lived abroad," Lord Claridge said simultaneously.

"Ah, yes."

Curse the man. They all three knew what kind of business they were conducting. Why didn't he just quote them a price and get the whole sordid thing over with?

Lord Claridge straightened in his chair and gave Rush a pleasant but very insincere smile. "My sister needs your help, Mr. Rush. We know you won't disappoint us."

Rush set down the necklace, took the loupe out of his eye, and rested back in his chair, smiling at them just as insincerely as Lord Claridge had at him. "As I said, it's a nice piece. I'll give you five hundred pounds for it."

Angelica did some quick calculation, changing the amount into dollars. "Why, it's worth four times that amount!"

Taming Angelica

"Now, Angelica," Lord Claridge said, sounding for all the world like Aunt Minnie.

"But my fa—"

"Charles," Lord Claridge interjected.

"Charles." Curse all this deception. "Charles, my husband. Charles paid a great deal of money for that necklace."

"I'm sure Charles would understand the necessity of selling it," Lord Claridge said. "Even at this price."

She looked from him to where Rush sat smiling at her as though he'd won some sort of bet. He had won, in truth. He'd make a small fortune off this transaction. But what choice did she have?

"Very well," she said. "Five hundred pounds."

Rush opened another drawer and pulled out a cash box. Still smiling, he opened the box and counted out several bills, finally handing them to Lord Claridge.

Lord Claridge didn't even count the money but merely slid it into the pocket on the inside of his coat. He rose and picked up his hat and gloves from where they lay at the edge of Rush's desk and then reached down a hand to help Angelica up. "We'll be on our way. Thank you for your time."

Rush rose as well, walked to the door, and held it open for them, still grinning like an overfed predator. How galling it was to have to leave that beautiful necklace in this dingy office with a nasty little man who made his living taking advantage of people who were desperate for money. If only *she* weren't desperate for money, she'd tell the man exactly what she thought of him and snatch her necklace back. *Odious man. Detestable creature.*

When she and Lord Claridge reached the door, Rush made a tiny bow and then looked up at them, his smile insufferably broad. "Do come again. I've enjoyed doing business with you."

Now, that was too much. Angelica's back stiffened.

She did her best to ignore the pressure of Lord Claridge's hand at her elbow and straightened to her full height. "You, sir, are no gentleman."

"Ah, yes."

Lord Claridge pulled her, not gently, into the hallway.

Out on the street, Lord Claridge finally released Angelica's elbow from his death grip and stopped to put on his hat. Angelica crossed her arms over her chest and glowered at him. "You had no reason to pull me along like that," she said.

"I wanted to get you away from Rush before you'd soured the deal completely," he answered.

"And what a wonderful deal it was. Out-and-out robbery, I'd say."

"I'm sure you have a great deal to say," he said as he hailed an approaching hansom cab with the hand still holding his gloves. "But I think I'll get you out of this place before you say it."

Angelica glanced around. The area was, indeed, an unpleasant part of town, full of run-down buildings and dark corners that could hide any number of people conducting unsavory business. The cab pulled up to them, and Lord Claridge opened the door. Angelica climbed in while her escort gave instructions to the driver. Maybe they still had time to get home for tea without arousing Aunt Minnie's suspicions of where she'd gone to be away so long.

Lord Claridge joined her just as she had finished straightening her skirts and settling her reticule on top of them. He crowded the little enclosure with his long legs and broad shoulders—just as he had on the trip over. Then Angelica had pressed herself against the opposite side of the cab to give him room. This time she stood, or rather sat, her ground, not moving an inch to accommodate his larger frame. Why should she? He'd dragged her along the corridor outside of Rush's office and then down a set of stairs and onto the street. He'd handled her like a naughty child, and she didn't tolerate that sort of treatment. Not even from Aunt Minnie.

He removed his hat, put his gloves into it, and settled the whole into his lap. That done, he crossed his arms over his chest and settled back against the wall of the cab, stretching out his legs until they rubbed up against hers quite indecently.

The pose spoke volumes about him, about studied carelessness and a tendency to rule those around him with his mere physical presence. The expression on his face betrayed a mix of emotions—impatience, amusement, and confidence that bordered on arrogance.

Angelica stared back at him. He really was a handsome man. Quite a feast for the eyes with his shining, golden hair and blue eyes. With his strong jaw and elegant nose. Some women might find him irresistible. Thank heaven she had more sense than that.

"Well," he said finally.

"Well," she repeated.

"I don't suppose five hundred pounds is near enough for you to pursue your dreams."

"Four hundred and fifty," she corrected. "Fifty is your share."

"Oh, yes," he replied. "We might have both done a bit better if you hadn't been in such a damned hurry."

"I?" *Of all the unmitigated gall.* "You're going to blame this fiasco on me?"

"Who else was fidgeting in her chair and tapping her foot and harrumphing every other moment?"

"I do not harrumph."

He narrowed his eyes and looked at her as if she were a child he'd just caught in a lie. If only he knew

Alice Chambers

how it made him look like a pompous jackass. A very handsome pompous jackass.

"I do not harrumph," she repeated.

"I've never seen anyone who looked quite as guilty as you did. Or quite as desperate. No wonder he offered next to nothing for the necklace. The man's not stupid."

"I wish you'd thought of that before you made up such a silly story about why we wanted to sell those diamonds."

"Silly story?" His eyes widened, and he sat up straight. "What was so silly about it, I'd like to know?"

"For one, that I was a widow," she answered. "Imagine, a widow in pink sateen."

"That wouldn't have presented a problem if you'd worn black."

"I don't own anything black. And the ridiculous idea that we were brother and sister. Who would believe that?"

He opened his mouth to say something and then shut it again. Finally a sheepish little smile curled his lips. "I didn't expect he'd believe that part of it. We had to have some sort of story to tell him, and it was the best I could think of."

"Thank you." He looked so agreeable when contrite that she couldn't help but return his smile. "I don't suppose I helped matters very much either."

"Thank you."

"We'll just have to plan better next time."

He shot up so straight his head hit the trapdoor in the top of the cab. "Next time?"

The door opened and the cabbie peered in. "Anything wrong, guv'nor?"

"No, just continue," Lord Claridge said to the man. The door closed, and Lord Claridge fixed her with his irritated glare again. "Next time?" he asked more quietly.

Taming Angelica

"Of course. You just said yourself that five hundred pounds isn't enough."

"Lord give me strength," he muttered.

"Four hundred and fifty pounds," she corrected herself. "There must be more Thaddeus Rushes in London."

"I don't know any. I had a devil of a time finding this one."

"How did you find him?"

He leaned against the side of the cab, looking fatigued and put-upon. "I have a friend who runs up gaming debts. From time to time he, um, enlists a bit of the family jewelry to get him out of a spot."

"A friend?" she repeated. "You're not referring to yourself, are you?"

He sat straight up again and glowered at her, the very picture of outrage. "Certainly not."

Oh, for heaven's sake. The man was starting to act perfectly stuffy and proper, when they both knew he was the worst kind of scoundrel. "There's no need to act offended, Lord Claridge."

"You've just called me a thief," he answered.

"Only of what belongs to your family. We both know you're capable of worse."

"Worse?" Now he looked downright wounded. "What have I done that's worse than stealing from my own family?"

She shrugged. "That lady we saw you with . . . that married lady . . . she can't have been the only such affair you've had."

"You don't know what you're talking about, Miss Hamilton."

"I don't?"

"No."

She squared her shoulders and studied him evenly. "Then why don't you explain it to me?"

"Very well, but it's not easily done." He sighed,

weary of the world again, to all appearances. He glanced out of the cab for a moment, watching the shops and buildings of a new neighborhood roll by—much nicer than the one they'd just left. "A man has needs. Women do, too, of course, but not usually until they've had some experience and are a bit older."

Needs? She had asked about scruples, and he answered with needs. "I'm afraid I don't understand."

He looked at her and blushed. "I'm trying to explain it to you."

He looked back out the window, and Angelica watched him again. He'd blushed, of all things. What could make such an admitted rakehell, a breaker of women's hearts, blush? Embarrassment? The knowledge was so intimate it took her breath away, leaving her with the same sort of dizzy feeling she'd had when he kissed her: sweet, warm, and intoxicating.

The space inside the cab grew even closer as she became more and more aware of the man sitting next to her—of his leg where it brushed her skirts, the long fingers that played across his cheek in his contemplation. She sat as quietly as she could, savoring the moment. Trying to memorize everything so that she could analyze it later when her head had cleared.

After a long moment he turned back to face her. "Men and women, they enjoy a certain sort of congress together."

"Congress?" she repeated.

"Please. You're not making this easy."

"I'm sorry."

"Lack of this, um, congress can be keenly felt. In fact, it can drive a body quite mad after a while. The marriage bed is one solution, of course, but if one isn't in a position to marry . . . well, one has to be creative."

As badly as he was confusing her, she didn't dare say anything for fear that he'd stop altogether. The marriage bed made some sense, but congress didn't. The

Taming Angelica

English had a parliament, didn't they? That couldn't be what he was talking about.

He stopped for a moment and cleared his throat. "I don't believe in taking advantage of innocent young women."

"I should hope not."

He glared at her, and she fell silent again.

"And paying for pleasure holds no appeal," he added.

Angelica didn't reply. After all, everything she said on the subject seemed wrong.

"So," he said and cleared his throat again. "That generally leaves married women of an, um, adventurous nature."

"Well, thank you for explaining it to me." *I think.*

"There's no need to adopt that tone, Miss Hamilton," he said.

Now what had she said? "What tone?"

"That tone. That Boston, if-we-were-at-home-Papa-would-thrash-him tone."

She felt her own cheeks redden. "I am sorry about that."

"As you should be. A jewel thief has little reason to feel superior to anyone else."

"I'm not a thief."

He leaned toward her, his smile growing downright smug. "How is what you've done any different from what my gaming friend does?"

"Why . . ." She caught herself sputtering and stopped. "There's a world of difference."

"How?"

"Well, it's my necklace, and I need the money for a good reason, not to cover a gambling debt."

"And what reason is that?" he demanded.

"I've told you."

"To fulfill your dreams."

Before either of them could say more, the cab pulled

77

to the side of the street and stopped. "Why are we stopping here?" she asked. "We aren't anywhere near home."

Lord Claridge pulled his gloves out of his hat and put his hat on his head. "Because I'm taking you to tea."

She glanced outside the cab. "Here?"

"Treadwell's," he answered. "Famous for its ices. You'll love the food."

"But I have to get home before Aunt Minnie wonders where I've been."

"We won't be long."

"But you don't understand," she said. "I don't want to be missed at all. If Davidson notices my necklace is gone, I don't want him to do it on a day when I've been out on a mysterious errand."

"You're being rather melodramatic, don't you think?"

"No, I don't." Really, the man could be so pigheaded.

"What if we see someone we know? What will we do then?"

He leaned toward her until his nose almost poked into her face. "Simple. We won't volunteer that we've been out selling stolen jewelry."

"It isn't stolen."

"Very well," he said, straightening. "You can try to convince me of that *inside*."

"I don't understand why you're being so stubborn about this."

"Because," he said, "if I'm going to be stealing your family's jewelry, I'm damned well going to know about these dreams of yours that I'm helping to fulfill."

"But—" she began.

"Or perhaps you'd prefer to discuss that over tea with your aunt?"

Taming Angelica

She crossed her arms over her chest. "Don't be ridiculous."

He yanked the cab door open. "Come along, Angelica."

For heaven's sake, now he sounded like her father. She gritted her teeth and glared at him. *All right.* She'd come along, but only long enough to get him to stop doing *that*.

Once inside, Will keenly felt the collective—albeit subtle—attention of the patrons of Treadwell's on him and Miss Hamilton. No doubt part of that attention came from the fact that she looked rather like a confection herself in that pink fabric. And no doubt part of it came from the fact that she hadn't quite finished sputtering over the gentle but firm pressure he'd used to get her into the shop. But no small measure of the attention came from the mere fact that they were an unmarried couple—alone and unchaperoned. Exactly what he'd hoped for.

She felt the reaction, too, he could tell—a ripple of tension over the muted sounds of heavy silver contacting china. A hush of the nearest conversation. A glance cast quickly at them and away. She lowered her eyelashes and glimpsed around her.

He leaned toward her. "Afraid to be seen in public with such a notorious bounder and cad?" he murmured.

"Of course not," she answered. "What a ridiculous idea."

Good. He'd known she'd never admit to any trepidation. At least not to him. Foolhardiness was the very best trait an opponent could have, as far as Will was concerned. And while Miss Angelica Hamilton of Boston, Massachusetts, United States of America, was no enemy, she certainly was an opponent. "Very well, then. Let's have something to eat," he said. "Larceny always gives me an appetite."

"We did not—" She shut her mouth abruptly and glanced around. "We did not steal anything," she whispered.

A waiter appeared and bowed to Miss Hamilton and then to Will. He led them to a table, pulled out Miss Hamilton's chair, and then waited for their order.

"I'm positively ravenous," Will declared. "I'll have the turtle soup. And the lady would no doubt like one of your famous ices."

"Pineapple, if you have it," Miss Hamilton said. "And a cup of tea."

The waiter left, and Miss Hamilton looked around the room. *How delightful.* Instead of hunching her shoulders and trying to pretend she wasn't in a public place with the Duke of Brathshire's scandalous younger brother, she was ensuring that everyone present knew she was here. In truth it pleased him mightily to have her seated across the table from him. It gave him an almost possessive pride that this vision in pink belonged to him and no one else for the entire afternoon.

She turned back and found him staring at her. She picked up her napkin and put it in her lap, then lowered her eyes.

"It's time you told me, don't you think?" he said.

She looked back up at him, raising an eyebrow. "Told you?"

"About your dreams," he answered. "It appears I have quite a bit more to do toward fulfilling them. I ought to know what they are."

"Oh, that."

"That."

She laughed lightly, and color flushed her cheeks. "You'll think I'm silly. Everyone does."

Taming Angelica

"I don't think you're silly," he said.

She studied him, a light of cautious surprise in her eyes. "You don't, do you?"

"Of course not." He meant that. Really. Any number of words could describe Angelica Hamilton—impulsive, innocent, more honest than was usually found flattering in a young lady. Exasperating, fascinating, admirable—but certainly not silly. "Now tell me. To what purpose did we endure Mr. Rush's company just now?"

She bit her lip for a moment, clearly not sure whether to say anything. Finally she took a breath. "I want to see the world."

"Yes?"

"I don't mean by that I want to see Europe, or even Asia, I suppose. I want to see the world the way God made it. I want to study nature."

"And your family thinks that's silly?"

"Most of them." She sighed. "Papa gets apoplectic if I even bring up the subject."

"I see."

"You don't think that women are helpless little flowers, likely to perish outside our little hothouses, do you, Lord Claridge?"

"I certainly wouldn't describe you that way, Miss Hamilton."

She leaned toward him, her expression intent. No doubt she didn't even realize that her hand rested against the table, only inches from his own. "Women have souls, just like men. We have minds—minds that need to be stretched and challenged. Just like men."

He leaned forward, too, closing those few inches between their hands. To anyone observing, they'd appear more than casual acquaintances by holding hands in public. He supposed he ought to warn her about that, but she must be as aware of society's niceties as he. Besides, he wanted to do the right thing by her, and if a little pressure from some raised eyebrows helped, so much the better.

The waiter chose that moment to arrive with their food, and Miss Hamilton snatched her hand back. He immediately missed the warmth against his own palm and the feel of her gloves under his fingertips. But he'd be touching her again, and soon. Kissing her, too, if he got half a chance.

He leaned back and watched as the waiter served her and then put a steaming bowl of turtle soup in front of him. The picture of efficiency, the fellow disappeared as soon as his job was done, and Will picked up his spoon and tasted his soup. Delicious, of course, just like the woman opposite him.

"And so, Miss Hamilton," he said. "You want to study nature."

She swallowed the bit of ice in her mouth and set down her spoon. "I have it all planned," she said. "As soon as I have enough money, I'll book passage on a ship to South America."

"South America? All the way across the Atlantic and around Cape Horn? Couldn't you study nature a little closer to home?"

"Oh, no. I want to follow Darwin's route—visit the natives of Tierra del Fuego. See the giant tortoises of the Galápagos."

"Tortoises." He dropped his spoon into his soup. "That's what your aunt was talking about."

"Aunt Minnie was talking about tortoises?"

"She called them giant turtles."

Angelica smiled. "The dear. She does confuse things."

"Things and people. She had me thoroughly baffled," he replied. "Does this explain the finches, too?"

"Oh, my, yes," she answered. "You see, the tortoises

Taming Angelica

and finches of the Galápagos were instrumental in Darwin's observations about the development of species. It's all so wonderful, really."

"I know something of Darwin, but I can't say I remember the finches."

Her eyes widened as her expression took on an enthusiastic glow. "You see, the finches on the Galápagos occupy the same places in nature's grand scheme that many different birds do in other lands. It seems that just a few birds managed to get there, and their descendants were somehow modified to play all the different roles birds play in, say, England or the United States."

He understood that, more or less. Perhaps he ought to try reading more. "And the tortoises?"

"Oh, the tortoises," she declared. "Each island has its own species. As if all the tortoises had a common progenitor but changed over time until each species was unique unto itself."

"And this change is . . ."

"Natural selection," she said, raising her hands in a gesture of victory. "Horse breeders select for the best qualities in racers. Why shouldn't nature select for the strongest traits, too?"

He sat and drank in the sight of a young woman with a purpose. Something beyond capturing the adoration of every man at a ball. Beyond capturing the most prestigious title available that season. He couldn't claim to understand everything she was saying—maybe not even the bulk of it—but he could admire her devotion to the subject as much as he could enjoy the glow it brought to her skin and the fire of intelligence in her eyes.

"When I read Darwin," she continued, "I felt as if the sun had come out and made all sorts of mysteries clear."

"So all this selling of jewelry is simply meant to get you to the Galápagos?" he asked.

"Everything is meant to get me to the Galápagos," she answered. "I only came to England to escape my parents. I told them I'd stand a better chance of finding a husband here."

"Perhaps a husband could help you to get to South America."

"I suppose a husband could, but how many *would?*"

"A great many," he replied. For example, he could easily imagine himself with her on an isolated island, splashing naked in the surf by day and making love under a tropical moon by night. In fact, he could picture the image all too easily. He could get quite lost in it in the middle of Treadwell's.

"No, Lord Claridge," she said. "I've seen how husbands act, even the nice ones. They keep their wives like shadows—attached to them constantly, but always behind them and always silent. I don't intend to live my life as some man's shadow."

"But surely not all marriages are like that."

"Too many are." She squared her shoulders and looked him directly in the eye. "I won't take the risk. I'll simply never marry."

They'd see about that. She might have her heart set on permanent spinsterhood, but Will had other plans for her, and unless he very much missed his guess, he was about to get some help in that direction. Headed right toward them was none other than Bertie Underwood. Will reached quickly across the table and caught her hand in his again. "I understand, Miss Hamilton."

She gazed at him with just the right hint of admiration in her eyes. "You do?"

"Certainly."

"Well, well," Bertie said from right behind Miss

Taming Angelica

Hamilton's shoulder, his face in a pucker of displeasure. "Claridge and Miss Angelica Hamilton. In public. In a restaurant. Alone."

Miss Hamilton looked up at Bertie, and her mouth dropped open in horror.

Chapter Six

Aunt Minnie wasn't alone when Angelica and Lord Claridge arrived there. An older gentleman—tall and vigorous of frame but with only a fringe of white hair surrounding a shiny bald head—sat on a chair almost near enough to Aunt Minnie for their legs to entangle. At the sight of Angelica, he shot out of his chair, still holding a teacup, cleared his throat, and smiled guiltily.

Aunt Minnie jumped without leaving her own seat. "Well," she said and then laughed nervously. "Yes. Well, well. There you are, aren't you?"

"Perhaps we've interrupted some business or other," Lord Claridge said softly. "We can leave again easily enough."

"Yes," Aunt Minnie answered. "That is, no. That is, yes. Mr. Foxworthy is our solicitor, Angelica, and he's here to discuss business."

"How do you do, Mr. Foxworthy? I'm Miss Hamilton's niece, Angelica."

Taming Angelica

Mr. Foxworthy nodded. "My pleasure, miss."

"Odd, though," Angelica said. "I don't see any papers. Lawyers in the United States always bring lots and lots of papers."

Lord Claridge squeezed her elbow. Just the gentlest pressure, but then, he needn't have done anything. He had to know she was only teasing Aunt Minnie. She could tease her own aunt, couldn't she? She looked at him out of the corner of her eye, trying to scold with just a glance. He didn't respond but just continued to smile pleasantly at Aunt Minnie and her Mr. Foxworthy.

"Oh, yes, the papers," Aunt Minnie said. "We finished with the papers some time ago and decided to have some tea. You might have joined us, you and his lordship, only you weren't here, were you?"

"We're here now, and we've already had our tea at a place called . . ."

"Treadwell's," Lord Claridge supplied.

"So why don't you sit back down and finish your own tea, Mr. Foxworthy?" Angelica said.

"Eh?" he answered. The question appeared to have pulled him out of a reverie of embarrassment. "Oh, no, I really must be going."

"Yes, we're quite through with our business," Aunt Minnie said.

Mr. Foxworthy set down his teacup and bowed crisply, first to Angelica and then to Aunt Minnie. "It's been a pleasure, Miss Hamilton. I'll just see to the details we discussed and bring the papers back for your signature."

Aunt Minnie smiled at him, more broadly than she'd ever smiled at their lawyer in Boston. "Please do. We appreciate all your efforts on our behalf."

Angelica appreciated him well enough, despite the fact that until a moment ago she never realized he existed. He seemed to put a glow in Aunt Minnie's cheeks and a sparkle in her eye. And if he kept her aunt occupied, Angelica might find it a bit easier to get about on her own. Besides, after years of spinsterhood in the house of a tyrannical brother, Aunt Minnie deserved a little happiness.

Aunt Minnie's eyes followed Mr. Foxworthy from the room, and she gave a little sigh as the door closed behind him. Angelica walked to her chair, bent, and planted a kiss on her aunt's forehead. She caught the scent of rose water as she did—for Mr. Foxworthy's benefit, no doubt.

"And where have you been, I'd like to know?" Aunt Minnie said.

"Here and there," Angelica answered. She straightened, resting her hands on Aunt Minnie's shoulders. "As I told you, we had our tea at a restaurant."

"A restaurant?" Aunt Minnie repeated, looking from Angelica to Lord Claridge. "Unchaperoned? You disappoint me, your lordship. I know my niece has no sense in these matters, but I expected better from you."

He managed to look embarrassed, the scoundrel. "Your niece looked faint and needed refreshment," he lied smoothly. "But if I could have your permission, I'd like an opportunity to make amends for my forwardness."

Aunt Minnie's face melted into a delighted smile. "What sort of amends?"

"The Duke and Duchess of Kent are having a ball tonight. I'd be most happy if you and your niece would accompany me."

"Oh, my," Aunt Minnie declared. "A duke and duchess. Oh, my."

"Not another ball, dear heart," Angelica said. "Please."

"Of course we'll accept, your lordship. Thank you so much for thinking of us."

"Stuffy, boring balls," Angelica said. "I've already

been to more than enough of them for an entire lifetime."

Aunt Minnie ignored her pleas, instead beaming a smile at Lord Claridge. "Do tell, your lordship. What does one call a duke? 'Your worship?' 'Your dukeship?'"

"'Your grace,' usually," he answered.

"This is so exciting," Aunt Minnie said. "I must consult my *Burke's*. Where did I put that book?"

Angelica squeezed her aunt's shoulders. "Don't overtax yourself, Auntie. You wouldn't want to have one of your fits."

"But I don't know what one says to a duke. I wouldn't want to give the wrong impression."

"Kent and his wife are wonderful people," Lord Claridge said. "I practically grew up with their son. He loves hunting, and she potters about in her garden. She's quite dotty about her marrows."

"Marrows?" Aunt Minnie repeated.

"We call them squashes," Angelica said.

"Squashes. There, you see, Angelica, you'll have something in common—you with your finches and she with her squashes."

"The two have nothing to do with each other."

"Of course they do. They're all"—Aunt Minnie waved her hands in the air—"outdoors."

Lord Claridge smiled. "Then I'll send my carriage around for you this evening."

"We'll be ready," Aunt Minnie said.

He glanced at Angelica, his eyes full of warmth and his smile full of victory. "Until then, Miss Hamilton?"

She hesitated. She knew very well that she'd attend the ball. If she tried to refuse, Aunt Minnie would give her no peace until she relented. But having to agree openly went against her nature somehow. She hated surrender, even this small. Still, she didn't seem to have much choice in the matter.

"Until then, Lord Claridge."

Alice Chambers

* * *

With the afternoon all but done, little time remained to prepare for the evening. Especially not an evening that held so portentous an event as a duke and duchess' ball. Angelica had no time even to collect her thoughts about the events in Mr. Rush's office or the restaurant before she found herself seated in her small clothes at the vanity in her room.

She especially hadn't had the time to ascertain whether anyone had missed her diamond necklace. So far there'd been no outcry, although she'd jumped at every noise that sounded louder than normal. But with each passing hour she'd felt more secure. If the "theft" wasn't discovered for days or weeks, it wasn't likely to be connected with her excursion this afternoon.

She sat in front of the bank of mirrors, her hairbrush clenched in her hands. On a tray at her elbow sat a light meal of vegetable soup and a meat pie. Normally the delicious aromas would have tempted her, but tonight she hardly noticed them.

"Let me take that, miss," Mary said from behind her.

"Hmm?" she answered. "Take what?"

"The brush. Before you strangle the life out of it."

"Oh." She handed the brush to Mary and stared blankly at her own reflection. "Do you think women really like balls? Or do you think they just pretend to like them?"

"Lord, I wouldn't know. I've never been to one." Mary clucked her tongue and began running the brush through Angelica's hair.

She didn't know why she hated balls as much as she did. She loved to dance and always indulged herself in the elegant dinners afterward. The company was usually like any other gathering of human beings—some smart and some not, some nice and some not, some amusing and some not. But she really would prefer to be free to dance, unfettered by bone stays and crinolines. She really would prefer to eat heartily, not be restricted to ladylike bites and portions.

As to the company, she always felt that she didn't quite measure up. Unlike her more modest mother and sister, she was too loud, too earnest, and far too forthright in her opinions. But what was the point of having a mind if you didn't use it? Being a woman seemed a complicated and thankless job, the more she thought about it, and the sooner she got away from here the better. For tonight, she'd have to get through the ball for Aunt Minnie's sake.

"You should eat something," Mary said from behind her. "You won't have another chance before the wee hours."

Angelica looked at the perfectly good food, and her stomach did a flip-flop. "I don't have any appetite, I'm afraid."

"Men don't like an overly slender woman, or so I've heard."

"And of course, the world revolves around what men like," Angelica answered.

"They do rule the world. Won't do us poor women no good to pretend they don't."

"I know. I just wish . . ."

"Wish what?" Mary asked.

What, indeed? That a man could be a true mate, a partner, a helpmate, the way a woman was supposed to be. If someone like Lord Claridge could expend all that cleverness on helping her instead of expecting her to bend to his wishes, he'd earn her devotion and more. He could have all of her. He could have her heart. But she didn't dare surrender any of that until she knew he'd make an equal contribution.

What a silly female she'd become. Men didn't do

that. Certainly not men of Lord Claridge's type—blessed with wealth, a superior station in society, and an overabundance of good looks. She'd best take advantage of what he would give: his grudging help in her plan and maybe more of those kisses.

Yes, maybe he'd kiss her again. Maybe she'd make sure he kissed her again tonight. Maybe it would be her reward for attending the blasted ball. That might make the whole thing worthwhile.

"Why, miss, what a wicked smile. You look like the child who's just found the prize in the pudding," Mary said.

"She certainly does," came Aunt Minnie's voice from the doorway. "You look just like I did the afternoon I . . . Oh, no, I don't think I'll get into that."

"What, dear heart?" Angelica asked.

Aunt Minnie bustled into the room, the layers of lace on her dressing gown flouncing with every step. "Just girlish foolishness, and if you'd ever allow yourself to, you might just have some, too."

"Why would I want to be foolish?"

"Because it's expected of young girls. And it's fun, and you ought to try it while you have the chance."

"I'll remember that." Whatever it meant.

"You may leave us, Mary. I can take care of things here." Mary set the brush back down on the vanity, curtsied, and left.

"Now then, let's have a look at you." Aunt Minnie studied Angelica's reflection in the mirror. "Why, you're not even dressed."

"Neither are you."

"Oh." Aunt Minnie looked down at herself. "So I am. That is, I'm not. Oh, dear."

"We still have plenty of time." Angelica picked up the brush and tackled her own hair.

"Yes, and thank heaven for that," Aunt Minnie said.

Taming Angelica

"I only wish we'd had enough notice to have new gowns made."

"I have enough gowns. I haven't even worn this one before."

Aunt Minnie glanced over to where Angelica's dress of robin's-egg blue satin lay over the bed. "It will have to do, I suppose."

"Of course it will do. You loved it when the seamstress made it for me."

"But I didn't know you'd wear it for a duke and duchess," Aunt Minnie gushed. "I didn't know you'd wear it for a beau as handsome as Lord Claridge."

"He's not my beau," Angelica replied.

Aunt Minnie waved her hand. "Beau, admirer. It's all the same."

"He's not my beau."

"Whatever you want to call him, he has a discerning eye. We'll have to do something to make you really stand out tonight." Aunt Minnie paused. "What jewelry were you planning to wear?"

"Jewelry?" The very last thing she wanted to discuss. "I thought I'd wear Grandmama's pearls."

Aunt Minnie clucked her tongue. "Pearls are for old ladies like me. You need something more . . . I don't know . . . dazzling."

"Grandmama's pearls are the most beautiful necklace I own."

"I know—your diamonds. I'll send Davidson for them immediately."

Angelica put down the brush and grasped Aunt Minnie's hands before she could go for the butler. "Not the diamonds, Auntie. They're far too flashy."

"But they're beautiful. And so very impressive."

"Too impressive."

Aunt Minnie cocked her head and stared at Angelica. "What does that mean?"

93

"We don't want people to think I'm *trying* to impress them," she answered. "Especially Lord Claridge. He can't think I've set my cap for him, can he?"

"Ah." Aunt Minnie smiled like a cat who'd caught the goldfish. "You *are* planning to catch his eye, aren't you?"

"Not at all." She already had all she needed of him and more. "I just don't want to look like I'm desperate for his attentions."

"Very wise, child. It's about time you started thinking like a lady."

Heaven forbid. Anything but that. At least it seemed she'd gotten Aunt Minnie's attention away from her diamonds. "Tell me about that afternoon and your foolishness," she said.

Aunt Minnie looked puzzled again. "My foolishness?"

"You said when you came in that I reminded you of that afternoon when you'd been foolish. I'd like to hear that story."

"Oh, yes. My foolishness." Aunt Minnie eyes got a faraway look in them, and she sighed. "I was much younger then. Younger even than you are now; it was that long ago. The secret was so impatient inside me that it couldn't help but come out in my face, I imagine. Take care with your smiles, Angelica. They can be so traitorous."

"I don't understand."

Aunt Minnie looked down at her and smiled. "No, of course you don't. That's the goodness in you, isn't it?"

"Goodness?"

"Your honesty," Aunt Minnie answered. "I was as forthright as you, and where did it get me?"

Angelica squeezed Aunt Minnie's hands. "That's what I'm asking, dear heart. Where *did* it get you?

Taming Angelica

Please, just start at the beginning and tell me the story."

"It started with Sean O'Malley. Big, strapping, handsome Sean O'Malley—a man with a wicked laugh and a golden tenor singing voice. Sean O'Malley, the man who stole my heart."

"Auntie," Angelica declared. "You fell in love."

"Love hardly describes it. I came alive the day I met Sean."

"Tell me, how did it happen?"

Aunt Minnie giggled. "I'd slipped my tether one day and gone for a walk in the spring air. All alone."

Angelica stared at her aunt in surprise. "You?"

"I had my own independent streak once. Don't think you invented it."

"I don't," Angelica replied. "I'd just never thought you felt the same way."

"I think and feel a great deal more than you imagine. More than anyone would imagine."

"I don't doubt it, not for a minute," Angelica said. "Only, please go on with the story."

Aunt Minnie's eyes misted over again with her memories. "It was a wonderful day—the sort you think will never end when you're young—and I wasn't attending to where I was or where I was going and I stepped into the street in front of a beer wagon. A great, lumbering beer wagon."

"Was Sean O'Malley driving the wagon?"

"Of course not. He owned a dry-goods store. Why would he be driving a beer wagon?"

"I'm sorry," Angelica said. "Please go on."

"Mr. O'Malley—Sean—just happened by and saw the disaster about to happen. Without thinking of the risk to himself, he jumped into the street and pulled me to safety." Aunt Minnie wrapped her arms around her shoulders, hugging herself. "It was the first time I'd ever been in a man's arms. I don't think I'd ever been touched by any man. My father never played with me when I was small, and certainly Lawrence never did, either."

That wasn't hard to believe. If Angelica hadn't seen pictures of her father in his short pants, she would never have believed the man had been a child.

"Then when Sean was through lecturing me in his wonderful brogue, he told me I had pretty eyes," Aunt Minnie continued. "I fell in love on the spot."

"And did he love you?"

Aunt Minnie blushed and smiled shyly. "He said he did. Over and over."

"Then why didn't you marry him?" Angelica asked.

"Father and Lawrence wouldn't hear of it."

"Because he owned a dry-goods store?"

"That," Aunt Minnie answered. "And then, Sean was Irish."

"Damn them!"

"A lady doesn't resort to profanity, Angelica. It isn't attractive."

"I don't care." She dropped Aunt Minnie's hands and rose from her dressing table. What those two men had done to Aunt Minnie deserved worse language than *damn*, if only she knew some. She barely remembered her grandfather, but he was as big a bully as her own father. No young girl could possibly have withstood the two of them if they stood together. But look at what their pigheaded prejudices had done to poor Aunt Minnie—forced her into spinsterhood when she had so much love to give. If God were a woman, those two would have a great deal to answer for at the Pearly Gates.

"Papa and Grandpapa—what a pair they made." Angelica paced to the canopied bed and turned back to her aunt. "We'll just have to fix what they've done, won't we?"

Taming Angelica

"I don't know how," Aunt Minnie answered. "I'd never find Sean O'Malley again, and if I did, he'd probably be married with children and grandchildren by now."

"No, but you've found Mr. Foxworthy, and by heaven, you'll have him."

Aunt Minnie blushed and waved a hand. "Don't be silly."

"It's not silly. He admires you. I could see it in his eyes."

"But your father would never approve of my marrying, not at my age. Even to an Englishman."

"Blast Papa," Angelica said. "It's none of his affair whether you marry or not. It was none of his affair when you wanted to marry Sean O'Malley. Men! What makes them think they have the right to rule us?"

"It won't do to work yourself into a state, Angelica. It isn't good for the skin, and you do want to look your best for his lordship tonight."

"Blast him, too. We have more important things to worry about."

Aunt Minnie crossed the room and took Angelica's hands in hers. "There's nothing more important than your first love, my dear."

Angelica pulled her hands away. "I don't love Lord Claridge."

"Maybe you don't know it yet, but I can see it in your eyes."

"Don't be silly," Angelica answered. "I've seen him only a few times."

"It only took one glance for me to fall in love with Sean."

"That's different. You're you, and I'm . . . well, me. We're not at all alike."

"He cares for you, too, Angelica. It's written all over him."

Now, *that* was perfectly ridiculous. Lord Will Claridge preferred regal women like the one they'd surprised him with that first night they'd met. He tolerated Angelica's presence only because she could get him money for his horses. Although not homely by any means, she could never hold the attention of an aristocrat. If she tried, she'd only get her heart broken for her efforts.

Still, he had sought her out on his own, the very day after they'd met. And he'd been so engaging—charming, even—in the cab this afternoon. Explaining his "needs" like a shy little boy. Maybe he did harbor some feeling for her. Some tenderness, if nothing more.

No, she wouldn't get caught up in that trap. He didn't care for her, which was all for the best, because she wouldn't tolerate being ruled by any man, not father, brother, or husband.

"You know I'm right," Aunt Minnie said. "You're fighting it, just as you've fought everything since you were a tiny child."

"You're being silly, Auntie."

"*You're* being stubborn. I've seen that look on you since you were old enough to toddle around."

"What look?"

Aunt Minnie took Angelica's face between her palms and looked into her eyes. "That look, and you should stop because it isn't attractive in a young girl."

"Really." Angelica tried to turn away, but Aunt Minnie held her firmly.

"Now you listen to me, Angelica Roberta Hamilton," Aunt Minnie said. "When you find love, you take it. Grab on with both hands and don't let it go."

Angelica reached up and gently removed her aunt's hands from her face. "Love is for you, dear heart, not me. You lost your Sean, but now you have Mr. Foxworthy. Everything will work out for the best for both of us. You'll see."

Taming Angelica

A throat cleared at the doorway. Angelica looked over to find her maid standing there. "What is it, Mary?"

"There's a carriage outside, miss."

A look of pure horror flitted over Aunt Minnie's face. "Lord Claridge. He must be early. What will we do?"

"Begging your pardon, but it isn't Lord Claridge," Mary said. "It's Lord Underwood, and he'd like a word with you, Miss Hamilton."

Oh, no, not him. Not the man who'd caught her out and about this afternoon, in places where she shouldn't have been. Still, he could only threaten to reveal that she'd been in a restaurant. He couldn't know about the other things. Not even she could wear *I've just stolen my own diamond necklace* on her face. Could she?

"Tell him I'm not dressed," Angelica said. "Tell him to come back some other time when it's more convenient. Say, next week. Or next month."

"He doesn't want to talk with you, Miss Angelica, but with Miss Minerva."

That settled it. Lord Underwood had come to report something to Aunt Minnie. With any luck, his gossip would be about restaurants and nothing else.

"What a bother," Aunt Minnie said. "Tell him *I'm* not dressed."

"I did, miss. He said he'd wait."

Aunt Minnie put her hands on her hips. "What do you suppose the man wants?"

Angelica didn't answer. She didn't have an answer. She could only hope for the best.

Bertie Underwood. Twice in one day. Will wasn't quite sure he could stomach seeing the fellow again. He had little choice in the matter, though, given that Bertie's carriage was standing outside the Hamiltons' house and the man himself was just emerging from the sitting

Alice Chambers

room as Will entered the front hallway. He didn't look any happier than he'd looked when he had confronted them at Treadwell's.

Bertie caught a glimpse of Will and came up short. "Claridge," he said.

"Bertie," Will answered. "I thought you and I were close enough to use our first names."

Bertie made an unpleasant little sound in the back of his throat. "Will. You're here?"

"I'd rather say so."

"I mean again. I mean every time I see Miss Hamilton, you're with her."

Will smiled at him pleasantly. "Nice how that works out, eh?"

Bertie didn't answer that, but his eyes bugged and his jaw clenched. He was not a happy fellow, it appeared, and that suited Will just fine.

Another figure appeared in the doorway—Minerva Hamilton. "May I see you for a moment, Lord Claridge?"

"Certainly." He gave Bertie another nasty grin and stepped around him toward the sitting room. Miss Hamilton's aspect did nothing to reassure him, however. She was doing her best to scowl at him. The attempt fell somewhat short, given her round face and usually happy demeanor, but it conveyed her displeasure nevertheless. He switched his smile to the one that used to get around his governess when he was small and followed Miss Hamilton into the sitting room, closing the door behind them.

Her bearing would have done the queen proud as she gracefully sat in one of the upholstered chairs and indicated another one to him. "You told me this afternoon that you and my niece had taken tea at a restaurant," she said.

"Yes. That we did."

"Tea is one thing. Restaurants are quite another."

Taming Angelica

"Treadwell's is a respectable establishment," he said.

"And being observed taking tea in a restaurant is yet another thing altogether."

"Ah, Bertie's been carrying tales from school."

She straightened in her chair until her back was ramrod stiff. "I'm afraid we have a situation on our hands, Lord Claridge."

A situation fully of his own making. One he'd calculated to be just improper enough to start some tongues wagging, but not so dire as to cause Miss Hamilton to banish him from Angelica's company. "I can only apologize again," he said. "I was very hungry, and I thought your niece would enjoy one of Treadwell's ices."

"When it comes to Angelica, you'll have to do all the thinking, Lord Claridge. You can't depend on her to do any."

"Odd, she struck me as a young woman with a lot of ideas."

Minerva Hamilton's eyebrows lifted. "Exactly. All of them bad."

It was just that tendency toward unpredictable behavior that set Angelica Hamilton apart from a crowd of young women as lovely as or even lovelier than she. It made her fascinating, in fact. And it was just that tendency he hoped to use to win her for himself. Right now he needed to take care not to push the elder Miss Hamilton too far. "I'll do what I can to discourage your niece's rebellious nature."

"Thank you. You men can be so male, but occasionally your better natures win out, I suppose."

"My maleness and I will try to bear that in mind."

"Good." She let out a sigh of relief. "Now then, do you suppose Lord Underwood can be trusted to keep the fact that he saw you together to himself?"

"He might." Will cleared his throat. "But that isn't his normal way."

"Oh, dear."

"In fact, the man's quite a gossip."

"Oh, dear. Oh, dear." She rose and paced to where a small fire crackled in the grate. "Nothing like this must happen again."

"I am sorry."

"I won't have my niece compromised. I'd never forgive myself, and certainly her father would never forgive me."

"I'll be more careful in the future." He intended quite the opposite, of course, but Minerva would forgive him when he was her lawfully wedded nephew.

"Please do, Lord Claridge. Actions have consequences, sometimes unpleasant consequences."

"You wouldn't forbid me to keep company with your niece, I hope."

"No." She rested a hand on the mantelpiece and studied him evenly. "I believe you're a sobering influence on Angelica."

Sobering? Not exactly the word he'd use, but he let it pass.

"But actions have consequences," she repeated. "If you and Angelica misstep too broadly, you'll have to pay those consequences. I hope I'm making myself clear."

"Quite clear." And exactly what he'd wanted her to say. Obviously she meant marriage. If he and Angelica were caught in too compromising a position, they'd have to marry. Maybe a direct order from her aunt would thaw Angelica's stubborn objections to matrimony. Maybe the disapproval of all of society and his own most ardent declarations of devotion would do the trick. If not, he'd have to think of something else, because Angelica Hamilton *would* be his wife.

The door opened, and Angelica stood on the threshold. Will rose, and his maleness took total control over his mind as he looked at his future wife. Her skin pos-

Taming Angelica

itively glowed above the low bodice of her ball gown. A long string of pearls hung from her throat and trailed over her graceful collarbone to her bosom. And beneath the pearls—dear Lord—beneath them her breasts rose, small but full, pressing against the blue satin that held them captive. A tiny waist and yards and yards of skirts followed, ending where her hem just brushed the floor. He looked at her face and found her studying his obviously too-intent gaze with some uncertainty. She bit her full lower lip in a manner that would have made him groan if he hadn't caught himself.

Damn, but he wanted her—beyond any wanting he could remember. He'd have her eventually, but not tonight. Tonight he'd have to suffer the quadrille until he could take her in his arms in a waltz.

Chapter Seven

Will did suffer the quadrille—dancing with Kent's youngest daughter, a child barely out of the schoolroom, because Miss Hamilton didn't know the steps. After that, he settled Minerva Hamilton into an energetic conversation with the duchess about the sorry state of etiquette in today's young people. Then, and only then, could he finally take Angelica Hamilton onto the dance floor and slip an arm around her slender waist. He wasn't disappointed—she fit next to him perfectly, her nose just reaching his chin, and her soft breasts pressed against his ribs.

He gazed down into her upturned face and felt a silly grin spread across his face. "I must say you look . . ."

Words failed him at that. He could say the obvious—*lovely* or *beautiful*. He could try any number of adjectives—*fetching, ravishing, divine*. But he'd used all those before, and they just wouldn't do now.

Taming Angelica

She cocked her head and studied him with some amusement. "How do I look, Lord Claridge?"

"Extraordinary, Miss Hamilton. You look extraordinary."

She laughed lightly, never missing a step of the waltz. "I'll take that as a compliment."

"Please do." She had no idea how great a compliment it was. He seldom found himself at a loss for words, especially where women were concerned. But then, he'd never before met a woman with her combination of conventional female beauty, innocent charm, and iron determination. Somehow she made the combination plausible.

"What did Aunt Minnie have to say to you?" she asked.

"Hmm?" he said, quite lost in the amber depths of her eyes.

"In the sitting room. Before we came here. She didn't ask about my diamond necklace, did she?"

"Not at all." He pulled her an inch or two closer to his chest. "She had a few words with me about taking you to restaurants where we can be observed by Bertie Underwood and his ilk."

"Thank heaven it was that."

"We really must be more careful, or your reputation may suffer."

"Blast my reputation," she declared as she slid her hand along his shoulder, moving herself closer to him. "Once I'm gone from here, I won't need a reputation."

"Actions have consequences. That's what your aunt said, and she's quite right."

"Do they?" A positively wicked light shone in her eyes. "Actions such as your kissing me the other day?"

"Most especially. If we'd been caught . . ."

"That wasn't the kind of consequence I meant," she

said. "I meant something more like those needs of yours."

"Oh," he said, his throat suddenly dry, "that."

"I'd like to know about that," she said, moving so close that she rested fully against his chest.

He cleared his throat. "*That* that?"

"Most especially *that* that."

He slid his arm around her until it almost circled her waist completely. The action snuggled her against him, her body pressed against him in the most delicious manner imaginable. His member stiffened in response. Another moment of this and he'd be fully erect, and he didn't care.

"What would you like to know about *that?*" some devil made him ask.

She blushed and looked up at him from under her eyelashes. "What comes after kissing, I suppose."

"Ah, but I'm afraid you're not ready for that." He was ready for that and becoming more so by the moment. But if he told her that, he'd frighten her, and fear wasn't the emotion he wanted to engender in her. Not at all.

Anger flashed in those remarkable eyes. "What makes you think I'm not ready? I'm a very quick student. Any of my teachers would tell you so."

"These aren't lessons to be hurried through," he said. "Once we've thoroughly explored the subject of kissing, we can move on to what comes after."

She made a soft sound in her throat, halfway between a gasp and a sigh. "I'd like that."

Dear God, how had he managed it? In another moment she'd be begging him to kiss her. He'd oblige, of course, because he was the worst sort of scoundrel and because it would further his plan to get her to marry him. And because more than anything in the world, he wanted to taste her sweetness again.

Taming Angelica

The waltz chose that exact moment to end. She made a great show of fanning herself with her hand. "It's grown quite warm in here, Lord Claridge, don't you think?"

She had no idea how warm.

"Would you take me outside for some air?" she asked.

"We should get a chaperon," he offered, giving her a chance to save herself from what would undoubtedly happen if he got her in private.

"Blast a chaperon," she said.

Bless her and her stubborn nature. "I'd be honored, Miss Hamilton," he said, extending his arm.

She took it, smiling at him shyly as he led her toward the door that led toward a balcony and the gardens beyond. Once outside, he found the evening cool, but not overly so. A full moon shone over the extensive gardens, casting trellises and rose bushes in magical light and shadow.

"It's lovely," Miss Hamilton exclaimed. "Who would have dreamed of having such a garden in the city?"

"The duchess can't bear to be parted from her marrows, even for the London season."

"Do you mean she's growing vegetables in this glorious garden?"

"Unless I miss my guess, they'll be just behind that hedge," he said, pointing into the near darkness.

"I'd like to see that."

He studied her. She wore the smile of a bad whist player with all the trumps. She didn't have the faintest interest in marrows but rather lessons in kissing, with him as instructor. *Fine.* He felt up to the job. He bent his head toward hers, until his lips were mere inches from her ear. "Allow me to show you."

She laughed lightly, a delightful sound that floated

out over the silvery landscape as he led her across the balcony and down the steps toward where the duchess always used to plant her marrows. He might look foolish if she'd decided to skip her horticultural efforts this season, but no doubt he'd find something else to discuss.

Under a bower of fragrant roses, past a hedge, and off to one side, he found them. "Here you are," she said, gesturing. "Marrows."

She dropped her arm from his and turned to face him directly. "They're lovely."

She hadn't even glanced at the blessed things, of course, and he wasn't about to waste his time pointing that out, not while he could look at her in the moonlight. Her hair formed a perfect frame for pale skin, large eyes, a delicate nose, and full lips. Lips just waiting for his own. "Lovely," he repeated as he lowered his mouth to hers. "Just lovely."

She rested her hand against his chest and raised herself up to him, so close he could feel her breath mingle with his own.

"Lovely," she whispered, just before he closed the distance and took her mouth in a tender kiss. He explored her lips, gently moving along the upper and then to the fullness of the bottom one. She tasted like tea with honey, toast with marmalade—all citrus and innocence. Soft, so soft and giving and inviting. He moved along to kiss the tip of her nose, her eyelids, and back to her lips, and he felt rather than heard the sigh that escaped her.

She clenched her hand into a fist against him and leaned into the caress, her own lips taking up the steps of the dance his ached to teach her. She nibbled at him and tasted him, finally tentatively reaching out with her tongue to search for his. He didn't respond immediately but allowed her to grow bolder on her own.

The restraint cost him dearly, as the heat of the kiss spread through him. She whimpered and pressed herself against him, sliding her hands up and around his neck.

He lifted his face from hers and buried it in her hair, smelling the scent of roses and soap.

"Oh, my." She gasped.

"Do you like this?" he whispered.

"Oh, my, yes."

He nipped at her earlobe and then kissed the spot just behind it. "And this?"

"I had"—she took a ragged breath— "no idea, um . . ."

He bent to nuzzle the corner of her jaw and then nibbled along the length of her throat.

"No idea," she continued, "that horticulture . . . oh, my . . . could be so . . ."

He reached her collarbone and then proceeded up the other side of her neck.

". . . stimulating," she said in a little cry.

He straightened and took her face between his hands. "My dear Miss Hamilton," he said, his own breath coming ragged and shallow. "If you only knew."

"Teach me," she whispered. "Show me."

"Lord help me." He did as she asked. He took her mouth again in a ravenous kiss, lips, tongue, breath, heartbeat, every part of him given to possessing her. His sex grew thick and hard, throbbing and ready to plunder her. Damn, but he wanted her, now, in this garden in the moonlight, smelling the grass as it gave way beneath them. To hell with marrows and ball gowns and fancy parties. He wanted to love her the way women were meant to be loved—until she was naked and writhing beneath him in ecstasy.

Dear God, what was he thinking? He straightened and held her away from him. "We have to stop."

"Why?" She looked up at him, her eyes glazed over with unspent passion, her breasts rising and falling as she tried to get air. "I didn't tell you to stop."

"You should have. My dear Miss Hamilton, don't you realize what would have happened in another moment?"

"We would have progressed beyond kissing?"

"For the love of—" He stopped himself. He had to get some control over his frustration, sexual and otherwise, or he'd end up screaming at her. He took a few unsteady breaths. "We'd have progressed far beyond kissing, I'm afraid."

"Well, why not?" she asked.

"Because you deserve better than a fast tumble in someone's vegetable garden." She deserved a soft mattress and clean sheets and a husband skilled in the techniques of love, but he didn't dare tell her those were exactly his plans for her. "Besides, someone might have happened on us here."

She looked at him, her eyes wide with amazement. "You would have had your way with me?"

"Thank heaven I had more control than that, but only by the narrowest of margins."

"You want me?"

He groaned. How could he be angry with her innocent and perfectly honest questions? And yet how could she question the fire that had inflamed them both? It would take only the placement of one of her delicate hands against the front of his pants to show her just how much he wanted her, and God, how he'd love to have her do it. He groaned again. "Yes," he gritted from between his teeth. "I want you."

"Astonishing." She raised a hand to her mouth. "Truly astonishing."

"Astonishing, perhaps, but not surprising in the least."

"What's even more remarkable is that I want you,

too." She smiled and ran the tips of her fingers over her throat and down over her bosom. "That's what this feeling is, isn't it? This odd, fluttery, and very pleasant feeling?"

Mercy. If God had any mercy at all, He'd make her stop doing that—touching herself in that provocative manner and telling him she wanted him. It was too much for any man to endure, and the last of his willpower would crumble at any moment if he didn't get away from her.

"I have to take you back inside," he said. "To your aunt."

"And what about you?"

"I plan to find a bucket of very cold water and stick my head into it." He grasped her firmly by the elbow and started back to the ball.

After that miraculous encounter among the squashes, the rest of the ball proved quite a disappointment. Angelica didn't even see Lord Claridge for hours. Maybe he had found that bucket of water, but surely he couldn't still have his head in it. She couldn't endure waltzing with other men, after being in Lord Claridge's arms, and if she had to listen to one more complaint about the inadequacies of the current generation from Aunt Minnie, she'd scream. Finally she set out to find their escort. He was going to have to see them on the drive home anyway, and couldn't avoid her completely.

Leaving the dancing behind, she proceeded down a corridor until she detected the aroma of cigar smoke and the sound of male laughter. If she'd found the gentlemen, no doubt she'd found her quarry.

She ended up standing near the threshold of the billiard room. Partially hidden in the dim light of the corridor, she stopped and observed two men engaged in a game and another one looking on. None of them were

Alice Chambers

Lord Claridge, but she enjoyed watching them without the "civilizing" presence of any ladies. They moved so easily, unhampered as they were by corsets or skirts or any of the trappings females had to endure. What would it feel like to enjoy that sort of freedom?

"I say, old fellow," a strapping blond man said to another one who was leaning against his cue in a corner of the room. "A bit of bad luck you got caught."

A third man, shorter and stout, with a mop of red hair, picked up his own cue and bent over the table. "At least it was the upstairs maid, Reggie. Mere banishment wouldn't have been good enough if you'd boffed the daughter of a peer of the realm."

The leaner moved closer to the light, showing him to be of average height, average weight, and average appearance except for a pronounced thinning of his hair for such a young man. "Exactly why I chose the upstairs maid."

The blonde laughed. "God will punish you for that, or so the vicar keeps telling me."

"God hasn't caught me yet," Reggie replied.

"Perhaps you'll encounter Him on your journey," the redhead said. "Isn't that why young men get sent away—to discover their Creator by studying His creations?"

"More likely to keep them from despoiling nice English girls," the blond said. "Old Reggie here is likely to be plowing the females of Tierra del Fuego for some time."

"Tierra del Fuego!" Angelica blurted.

All three men straightened and stared at her in horror. The blond one recovered his powers of speech first. "I say. How long have you been standing there?"

"Only a moment," she answered. "I didn't mean to eavesdrop."

"You managed nicely, nevertheless," the blonde said.

Taming Angelica

"I'm very sorry. It's just that I . . ." *Oh, bother. Why apologize?* She had more important things to do. She entered the room and walked up to the average-looking man, Reggie. "Are you really going to Tierra del Fuego?"

He glanced at her pleasantly. "Afraid I am. But I'd rather the reason for my trip stay within this room."

"I wouldn't repeat anything I overheard," she said.

"Thank heaven for that," the blonde said.

She stared at him. "I said I was sorry."

"That she did, Ned," Reggie said. "I say, we ought to give her the benefit of the doubt."

Ned snorted and resumed his casual pose, this time leaning against the billiard table. "Suit yourself."

Angelica turned back to Reggie. "Will you be leaving soon? Do you think there's room for one more passenger on the expedition?"

"Looks like you might have a travel companion there, old man," the redhead said. He followed it with an evil-sounding laugh.

Reggie's smile widened as he looked down at her. "It's not the sort of trip a lady would enjoy."

"How do you know what I would enjoy?"

"See here, Miss . . ."

"Hamilton," Angelica supplied.

"Miss Hamilton," Reggie said. "You'd best go find your governess or chaperon or whoever brought you here and leave us to our game."

So he'd dismissed her. *Fine.* She didn't really want to hang around these grinning, laughing fools.

Now that she knew he was leaving for South America soon, she'd get the information she needed from him somehow. He knew of an expedition—when it was leaving, whether there was room for one more passenger, what she'd have to pay to join it. That was more than either she or Lord Claridge had been able to find out so far, and he could make things go faster if he'd cooperate. The fact that he didn't appear at all cooperative wouldn't stop her.

"Thank you for your concern," she said. "I'll be on my way."

She turned on her heel and left the room in a flurry of skirts. Behind her all three of them laughed. Well, let them. Reggie, or Reginald, or whoever he was hadn't seen the last of her.

The atmosphere in Lord Claridge's carriage seemed fairly charged with tension, especially after Aunt Minnie fell asleep, leaving everything silent except for her snoring. Angelica sat and tried to find a safe place to rest her gaze—on the walls, her skirts, the London streets as they passed by. Anywhere but on the man opposite her. For his part, he seemed equally ill at ease, glancing at her occasionally and giving her an insincere smile, only to look away again.

The silence—this not-talking—would make her crazy. How could she understand what had happened to them in the garden if he wouldn't discuss it with her? She couldn't ask Aunt Minnie for an explanation. Maybe she could have asked her sister, but Penny was in Boston, and she might not give an honest answer anyway. Lord Claridge had been forthright about his "needs" before and the fact that he wanted her. Why couldn't he talk to her now about what had just happened between them?

"Lord Claridge," she began.

He turned in his seat and looked at her as if she'd startled him. "I'm sorry. I'm afraid I'd lost myself in thought."

"About what we did in the duchess's vegetable garden?"

He didn't answer, but looked pointedly toward Aunt Minnie and then shook his head.

Taming Angelica

"Oh, don't worry about my aunt. She drops off like this all the time and never hears a thing."

The carriage jostled over a bump, and as if on cue, Aunt Minnie snorted. She settled back down immediately, her breath returning to its even rhythm.

"You see?" Angelica said.

"Still, I don't think we should talk about . . ." His voice trailed off.

"About what?" she demanded. "We shouldn't talk about what?"

"That," he said, and stared out the window again.

For heaven's sake, he'd gone back to "that" again. How would she ever learn anything if he persisted in speaking in code? "Well, I think we should."

"My behavior toward you was beastly tonight, and it embarrasses me to go over it."

"It was not beastly."

"Yes, it was."

"No, it wasn't."

"Miss Hamilton," he said, looking at her again. "I think I know beastly when I see it, and my behavior was beastly."

Dear heaven, the man had started to sound like a perfect prig. He hadn't done anything with her that he hadn't done with women before, maybe dozens of times. Maybe hundreds. What had made him develop scruples now? *Men.* If you couldn't depend on them to take advantage of every opportunity, what could you count on?

"I don't understand you," she said. "Neither of us dragged the other out there, and neither of us made any pretense of why we were going."

He glanced again at Aunt Minnie. "I don't want to talk about it."

Aunt Minnie snorted again, and Angelica crossed her arms over her chest and rested back against the seat. All right, he didn't want to talk about what happened in the vegetable garden. Maybe he could supply some other useful information. "Do you know a man named Reggie?"

"Who in London doesn't know a man named Reggie?" he replied.

"My, aren't we being testy all of a sudden?"

He sighed. "I'm sorry. To which Reggie were you referring?"

"I met a man in the billiard room tonight. A young man, unremarkable-looking, balding."

"Reginald Montrose," he answered. "Second son to Viscount Dansby. You met him?"

"I happened on him and a couple of others who were playing billiards."

"Is there anyplace you didn't get to tonight?"

"I don't understand what's putting you so on edge," she said.

He brought a hand to his face and rubbed his forehead. "No, I don't suppose you do."

And she wasn't likely to understand until he would talk to her frankly and openly about how he felt. If he didn't want to do that, so be it. But he'd have to take care of his own headaches. He wouldn't get any sympathy from her. "Do you know where this Reginald Montrose lives?"

He sighed again, thoroughly put-upon, and waved his hand. "In Mayfair, I believe. On Grosvenor Square." He looked at her then, and his eyes widened. "Why do you want to know?"

She shrugged. "Just curious."

"Oh, no." He leaned forward in his seat. "You will *not* pay a visit to Reggie Montrose."

She stared at him in amazement. "I don't believe you're in any position to tell me whom I may visit."

"The man's a notorious womanizer," he said, his volume rising. "He'd think nothing of taking every advantage of someone like you. Stay away from him."

Of all the nerve. What colossal audacity. "How dare you order me around?"

"I dare because I must." He raised his hand and stuck his finger almost right into her face. "Now you listen to me, young lady."

She pushed his hand away. "You're starting to sound like my father."

"Sweet God in heaven," he exclaimed.

The last woke Aunt Minnie finally. She snorted twice and then sat upright. "What—are we there yet? The ball?"

Angelica put her arm around her aunt. "Not quite, dear heart. We're on our way home."

"I must have dozed off," Aunt Minnie said. "You English keep such ungodly hours."

"You might have had some sleep," Angelica said, looking pointedly toward Lord Claridge, "if *someone* had kept his voice down."

Lord Claridge didn't answer that, but crossed his arms over his chest and huffed. For heaven's sake, he was sulking. First he issued orders, and now he sulked.

"I thought I heard something," Aunt Minnie said. "I hope you two weren't arguing."

"Argue with your niece?" Lord Claridge said. "There's a pointless undertaking."

Angelica scowled at him.

"Good," Aunt Minnie declared. "We have plenty of that in Boston. Oh, look, here we are."

The carriage pulled up in front of the house and stopped. After a moment the door opened, and the footman offered his hand to help Aunt Minnie out. With the two of them alone for just the briefest of moments, Lord Claridge waved his finger at Angelica again. "I'm warning you. Stay away from Reggie Montrose."

Angelica didn't dignify such arrogance with a response, but jumped from the carriage before the footman could help her. Tomorrow at her first opportunity she planned to do the exact opposite.

Chapter Eight

Even in the middle of the day, Reginald Montrose wasn't fully clothed when Angelica came to call. He wore no coat at all, and his tie and shirt both hung unfastened, revealing brown hairs curling over his chest. He seemed unconcerned with his appearance as he rose from behind the desk in his study. In fact, he seemed to enjoy her discomfort.

He walked around his desk and approached her, his hand extended. "What a pleasant surprise, Miss . . ."

"Hamilton," Angelica said.

His manservant chose that exact moment to close the study door behind her. The latch caught with an audible click that made her heart lurch. Leaving the door open would have been a much better idea.

"Do come in and have a seat," he said, his hand still extended. She pointedly kept her own hands curled around her reticule, walked to a wing-back armchair in the center of the room, and dropped into it, crossing her ankles primly under her skirts.

"Yes, well." He walked to his desk and lounged against a corner of it, extending his legs as far in her direction as they could go. "To what do I owe the honor?"

"I came to ask you about your trip to Tierra del Fuego."

"That's right. You're the one who wants to go to South America."

Angelica studied him. So far the conversation had gone normally enough, despite his state of dress. She must have imagined the gleam in his eye—average eyes, just like the rest of him. Or maybe just a tiny bit beady and close-set. No, she was imagining that, too. She cleared her throat. "I want to go to the Galápagos, actually. Do you suppose your expedition will be going there?"

He shrugged. "Who knows? I think the captain just follows his nose on these expeditions, taking you to any god-awful place he pleases."

"I don't know how you can talk like that, Mr. Montrose."

One unremarkable eyebrow rose. "You don't?"

"No. To some people a trip like that would be the opportunity of a lifetime."

He smiled a bit too broadly. "To someone like you, perhaps?"

"Yes." Good heavens, why did she feel as though she'd just made a confession? Why did she feel that her answer gave him some advantage over her? Why did she feel that the whole idea of coming here today was an enormous mistake?

"Do you want me to take you with me?"

"No," she said, maybe a bit too loudly. "That is, I'd like you to convince the captain to let me join the expedition."

"And that's the reason for this visit."

"Yes."

Taming Angelica

He rose from the desk and she jumped. He must have found that amusing, because he laughed. Not pleasantly. "Would you like a drink, Miss Hamilton?"

In the middle of the day? "No, thank you."

"I think I'll have one." He walked to a bookcase and opened the glass door, revealing a decanter and tumblers. He lifted the decanter in her direction. "Are you sure?"

She shook her head. He poured himself a stiff drink and swallowed it in one gulp, tipping his head back with a flourish. Finally he set the tumbler back down with a thud. "Now then, let's discuss why you really came here today."

"I've told you why."

"Don't be silly," he said. "No woman wants to go to a place like Tierra del Fuego."

"I do."

He crossed the room in three strides and perched on the arm of her chair, so close that she found herself staring into the hair on his chest. She leaned as far backward as she could, twisting herself into an impossible position. "Thank you, Mr. Montrose, but I think I'd better be on my way."

He leaned across her, grabbing the opposite wing of the chair and blocking any hope of a graceful exit with his body. He peered down into her face and smiled. "But you've only just arrived."

She put her hand against his chest and pushed—hard—but he wouldn't budge. "Really, sir, you're making a spectacle of yourself."

"Ha-ha, am I? Well, you may push as hard as you like, my little fox, but you aren't going anywhere until I'm quite through with the chase." He lowered his face toward hers until she could smell the liquor he'd just drunk. Dear Lord, he was going to kiss her. He had her trapped in this blasted chair and he was going to kiss her. Just the thought turned her stomach.

She pressed herself back against the cushions, still pushing against his chest, now with both hands. The chair rocked with her efforts, but his face loomed closer and closer, his eyes half-closed and his lips parted. *What a revolting sight.* She pressed her feet into the carpet and pushed with all her strength. The chair toppled backward with a loud crash, and Angelica managed to slither out from under him and scramble to her feet.

Unfortunately he got up only a heartbeat behind her, at a spot between her and the door. The two of them stood in the center of the room with only the upturned chair between them. Angelica made a move to her right, trying to get around him, but he made an agile countermove, sending her back to her original position.

"So you want a fight, do you?" he said, a triumphant gleam in his eyes. "Fine with me. The taste of blood can be such an aphrodisiac."

"Blood?" she repeated in horror. "You're sick."

"Whatever sickness my fox prefers," he said.

Angelica tried dodging again, this time to her left, but he kept right up with her, damn him. "Let me go, sir."

"Good then, shout. Scream. Whatever sort of play you want, I'm game."

"I don't want to play," she cried. "I want to leave."

He laughed and lunged for her, catching her sleeve. He started to pull her toward him, but she struggled for all she was worth. She broke free finally, and the fabric of her sleeve ripped as she ran to the closest haven she could find—behind his desk.

He came toward her, rested his hands against the desktop, and leered at her. "No one's put up a struggle like this for some time. It's very exciting."

She put her hands out toward him, half fending him off and half offering him peace. "Please understand. I don't want to excite you. I only wanted your help in getting to South America."

He laughed again. "What a delightful liar you are, my fox."

"Blast you, I'm not lying."

"And with a wicked mouth, too!" he declared.

"Oh, dear heavens." She made a desperate try for freedom, skirting the desk as quickly as she could and heading toward the door. But he caught her hair as she went by, pulling her hat off and the pins out of her coiffure so that her hair fell all around her shoulders, except for what he had in his fist. She twisted and kicked as hard as she could. Her foot made solid contact with his shin, and he dropped her hair, howling.

She headed toward the door again, only to see it fly open and crash against the wall. Will Claridge stood on the threshold, white-hot fury written on his face. She flew into his arms.

"Go downstairs, get into my carriage, and wait for me there," he ordered.

"I'm all right," she said. "Don't do anything rash. Please."

"Downstairs, Angelica," he ordered. "Now."

She obeyed, stepping into the corridor and heading toward the stairway. After she had taken a few steps, the door to the study slammed shut behind her. She paused for a moment. What in heaven's name was Lord Claridge going to do to that man? Whatever it was, he probably deserved it. She continued down the stairs.

When Will finished with Reggie Montrose, he found Miss Hamilton sitting, obedient and for once quiet, in his carriage. Aside from the tear in her sleeve and the disarray of her hair, she appeared unharmed. But what if he'd been a few moments later in getting to her? Dear God, that didn't bear thinking about. He ought to shake her silly. Instead he climbed into the carriage and pulled her into his arms. "What in hell were you thinking, coming here?"

"I don't know. I don't know." She began to tremble. He held her, stroking her back, but she only shook harder.

"Did he harm you?" Will demanded. "By God, I'll kill him if he hurt you."

"No," she said, still shaking violently.

"Then why are you trembling like this?"

"I'm not."

"You're not trembling?" he said.

"No." Her teeth had started to chatter, and she barely got the word out.

Lord, what an impossible woman. Next she'd deny that her sleeve was ripped and her hair had all come loose, falling in a cascade over his chest. "Stop trying to pretend you're fine when you're not," he said. "Put your head on my shoulder and have a good cry."

"I don't cry," she said, still quaking in his arms like an aspen in the wind.

"Fine then. But my shoulder's as good place as any to put your head while you don't cry. Don't you agree?"

She didn't answer with words but made a little noise that sounded remarkably like a sob and put her head down right where he'd told her. He couldn't help himself but nuzzled her hair and kissed the top of her head. That brought the tears in earnest as her shoulders shook and more sobs tore from her chest.

Disturbing her as little as possible, he slipped his hand into his jacket and found his handkerchief. He handed it to her. "You might want this if you're going to not-cry for a while."

She took the handkerchief from him without protest and dabbed at her eyes with it. "I'm sorry," she said, so faintly he almost didn't hear it. "I've been very stupid."

"I can't disagree with you there, I'm afraid."

"How could I know he'd behave like that?"

"You might have trusted my judgment," he answered. "I don't say things just to annoy you."

"I know." She sniffed once more and sat up straight. "It only seemed so lucky that I'd meet someone who was going to South America. I didn't want to miss the opportunity."

"And so you went around to a man's house all alone in the middle of the day."

She looked down into her lap, where her fingers had twisted his handkerchief into a knot. "I've admitted it was stupid."

"He might have hurt you. Badly." *In ways too horrible to think about.*

"He didn't," she said. "I was getting away from him when you came in."

"What if you didn't? Dear God, Angelica, what if you didn't?"

She didn't answer but just sat looking at him, her eyes wide as a frightened doe's. Her skin was so pale and her eyes puffy, and her lips were pressed in a delicious-looking pout. His heart melted at the sight of her—sweet and innocent and so unbearably precious.

"Oh, my d—" *Darling.* He'd almost called her his darling, and at that very moment she was, God help him. He reached out a hand and stroked her cheek, finding it as soft as flower petals and as warm as a spring breeze. *My darling.*

She looked at his fingers and gasped. "Your hand. What happened to your poor hand?"

He glanced down at his hand, at the purplish bruises along his knuckles. Until this moment he hadn't noticed the pain from where he'd pummeled Montrose. "My fist ran into dear Reggie's cheekbone, I'm afraid."

She looked perfectly aghast. "You hit him?"

"Well, yes."

"You *hit* him?"

"It seemed like a good idea at the time."

"And I kicked him in the shin," she cried. "Just look where my foolishness has brought us."

"He deserved it, Angelica. He was trying to force himself on you."

"You didn't deserve it. I'm sorry. I'm so sorry."

She started crying again. She brought his handkerchief to her face and sobbed into it as though her heart would break. Will put his arms around her and pulled her against his chest again. With the exception of Elizabeth Gates, no woman had ever cried for him, especially not because he'd punched someone who needed punching.

What sort of woman went to a man's house unescorted during the middle of the day and then was surprised when he tried to take advantage of the situation? What sort of woman managed to get the upper hand with the bastard and then dissolved into tears only moments later? What sort of woman then regretted kicking the fellow in the shin and sobbed because another man got bruised giving the cad a very satisfying beating?

Angelica Hamilton did all those things, it appeared. Fiercely independent, wonderfully strong, impossibly innocent Angelica Hamilton. If he wasn't careful, she'd steal his heart completely. If she hadn't already.

He kissed the top of her head again and pulled her closer. Why shouldn't he give her his heart? After all, he was going to marry her and give her his name. Caring for her only made things better. Loving her made things better.

Taming Angelica

Dear God, did he love her?

He slipped a finger under her chin and raised her face to his. She looked up at him, her warm eyes full of trust and gratitude. He kissed the tip of her nose and then guided her head back down onto his shoulder, his heart full of what he'd seen in her face. She sniffed a few more times as he cradled her against him.

If this wasn't love, it was as close as he expected to get in his lifetime. And if he loved her, he *would* win her for his wife—he had to. He'd better do something soon, before she got herself into trouble again. As set as she was against marriage, he'd have to find some way, and he would. No matter what it took.

For once, luck smiled on Angelica. There was no sign of Aunt Minnie as she crossed the foyer and headed toward the staircase. She really didn't want to explain how her hair and dress had gotten into such a mess or why she'd been crying. She just wanted to go to her room, take off her clothes and stuff them somewhere, and order a bath, even in the middle of the day.

She had her hand on the newel post and her foot on the first step when the sitting room door opened behind her.

"Where have you been?" Aunt Minnie asked from behind her.

Angelica didn't turn. Maybe she could mumble an excuse and escape before Aunt Minnie got a good look at her. "I took a walk. Now I'd like a nap."

"A nap? That doesn't sound like you."

"Really, dear heart," Angelica said, trying to keep her tone light. "I've developed a slight headache. I'd like to lie down." She took a few more steps up the stairs.

"Angelica Roberta Hamilton, you turn around and face me."

Angelica sighed. There was no point arguing when Aunt Minnie used her full name. She stopped her ascent and turned around.

Aunt Minnie's eyes widened in horror as she studied Angelica. "Child, what happened to you?"

Angelica did her best to smile. "Nothing. That is, nothing important."

"Your hair. What happened to your hair?" Aunt Minnie cried. "And your dress. Where's your hat?"

"It's nothing."

"And you've been crying."

Angelica took an unsteady breath. She just wanted to wash herself clean and snuggle into her bed. If Aunt Minnie forced her to talk about what had happened, she'd start crying all over again. *Silly, silly tears.* "I'll tell you later. Truly. Just let me go now."

Aunt Minnie walked across the floor, her footsteps echoing in the foyer despite the carpets. She climbed the steps and put her arms around Angelica. "You'll tell me, and you'll tell me right now."

"Oh, Auntie, I did something incredibly stupid."

"A man," Aunt Minnie replied.

"Could you tell?"

"Only men can make us stupid. It's their one great talent." Aunt Minnie sat down on the steps and pulled Angelica down with her. "Tell me. It wasn't Lord Claridge, was it?"

"No," Angelica declared. "Not him."

"I didn't think so."

Lord Claridge had been wonderful, far more comforting and understanding than she'd ever imagined a man could be. He hadn't blustered, hadn't yelled, hadn't lectured. He'd simply held her and stroked her and then honored her wishes to come inside alone. She'd never seen a man act that way, and she liked it. Maybe too much. She'd certainly enjoyed resting against his chest far too much for her own good. What

Taming Angelica

an enigma the man presented—first to arouse such hungers with his kiss and now to provide such a warm haven.

"So who was it?" Aunt Minnie asked as she smoothed a stray lock out of Angelica's face.

"A man I met at the ball. I went to his house to ask him something."

"Angelica," Aunt Minnie chided. "How could you have so little sense?"

"I'm sorry."

"Did he hurt you, child? What did he do? Oh, dear, oh, dear."

"No, he didn't hurt me. Please don't be upset. I got away from him, and then Lord Claridge brought me home."

"Thank heaven for his lordship. You owe him a great deal."

"He was very nice."

"I hope he understands your going to another man's house," Aunt Minnie said. "It isn't done. What were you thinking?"

Angelica shrugged. "I thought he was a gentleman. He seemed so, well, ordinary."

"You can't trust a man because he seems ordinary. Ordinariness protects you from nothing. Neither does dullness or anything else. You have to use common sense where men are concerned, and even that doesn't work half the time."

"I guess I found that out."

"Well, I don't like you finding things out," Aunt Minnie said. "In fact, I've been sent here specifically so that you won't find things out. If your father finds out what you've been finding out, he'll never let me hear the end of it."

"Father will never hear of this. I promise."

"I have my responsibilities, and I'll live up to them. You may think me a silly old fool—"

"No! Never."

"That's all well and good, but even if you *do* think me a silly old fool, I'm going to keep my word to your father. I'm going to protect you, whether you like it or not."

Angelica placed a hand on her aunt's arm. "Please don't exert yourself over this. I've learned my lesson."

"You'd better have, young lady." Aunt Minnie waved a finger into Angelica's face. "If anything else happens, you'll learn more lessons than you thought I knew."

Angelica put her arms around Aunt Minnie and hugged her. "Nothing will. I promise."

"See that it doesn't, Angelica. Actions have consequences."

Now what did *that* mean?

Will could have watched the stallion all day. It ran as though the devil were after it. Or inside it, rather, as though some demonic force drove it to impossible speeds—all the while imbuing its every movement with an almost preternatural grace.

"He's a good'un, Black Diamond is," Jonesy said. The trainer stood beside Will, watching the stallion complete yet another circuit of the practice track.

"Do you think he can do it?" Will asked. "Can he win the Derby?"

"He's the best horse I've ever trained. Great heart. Loves to run. Most of all, he won't let no one beat him."

"I know. And he's ready." Will clasped Jonesy's shoulder. "This year we're going to do it."

"Yes, sir." Jonesy rubbed the back of his neck. "Only . . ."

"Only what?"

"Beggin' your pardon, but you've been away in

society too long. We need more money if we're going to last till the Derby."

Will looked at Jonesy, really looked for the first time in . . . how long? Weeks? "You mean we don't have enough money to last until the Derby?"

"We don't have enough to last out the month."

"Good God, man. How much do we have?"

Jonesy's face colored, and he stared out over the track, avoiding Will's gaze. "Enough for board and feed for a week, I guess. The boys and me are already working without pay."

"That bad?" Will said.

"We won't be able to stable the horses here after the week's up," Jonesy answered.

"We'll promise the owner a percentage of our Derby winnings. He must know we can't lose the race."

"He already has a percentage, and so do the boys and just about everyone else." Jonesy cleared his throat. "If we promise any more of the purse, there won't be none left to promise. And then no jockey'll ride Black Diamond, no matter how good he is."

Will stared at his trainer in amazement. "Why didn't you tell me all this?"

"I did, sir. That note I wrote you weeks ago."

Note? What note? Will searched his memory. Yes, Jonesy had written to him. Something about how he should check the accounts. He should have done exactly that, immediately. But he'd been too busy— too wrapped up with Angelica Hamilton and her amber eyes. He'd let things go too long, and now he'd have to act.

"I can take some cash out of the household accounts," he said. "And I'll have to apply to my brother for more money."

"Will the duke come across for us, your lordship? He ain't done that much in the past."

Alice Chambers

No, George hadn't, and likely he wouldn't do much now besides giving Will the bare minimum. *Drat.* He couldn't dismantle everything and send the horses up to Brathshire so close to the race. They had to stay here, in London. This was his year to win the Derby—he could taste it. Perhaps if he could get *some* money from George and then manage to marry Angelica and her money quickly, the situation could be saved.

He put a hand on Jonesy's shoulder. "I know I've been neglecting you and the horses."

"I figured you knew what you were doing. We've come too far to get this close and give up."

"Don't worry. I have a plan."

Jonesy looked up at him. "You do?"

"A bit unusual, but a plan nevertheless."

"You ain't taken to gamin', I hope," Jonesy said. "I seen more good stables come to grief because their owners thought to richen up the stock with their winnings."

"I have a bit of a gamble in mind, but it won't happen at any gaming tables, and it won't cost any money if I lose." What it would cost was his heart if he lost, but he had no intention of losing.

Jonesy scratched his head. "You *have* been away too long, sir. Silly proposition, that—to gamble without money."

His idea was a silly one, just silly enough to work. Without thinking it through completely, he'd already put his plan in motion. He'd started the gossip mill by taking Angelica to a restaurant and then escorting her to Kent's ball. The logical extension was to compromise her completely, thereby forcing her to marry him.

So diabolical, so devious, so bloody unfair—he hated himself for even dreaming it up. How could anyone do anything like that to poor Miss Hamilton?

Still, he had to do it, if only for her own protection. If he didn't do something, she'd continue selling her

Taming Angelica

jewels for a fraction of their worth, and she'd keep approaching strange men to arrange passage to South America. Very likely she wouldn't be able to escape from the next man. That really *would* compromise her, and a whole lot worse.

"What are you thinkin', sir?" Jonesy said. "I ain't sure I like the look in your eye."

"Don't worry about my thoughts or my eye, Jonesy. Don't worry about anything. I have the situation well in hand."

Chapter Nine

As mornings went, this was a fine one for a betrayal—sunny and warm with a cool breeze that rippled through the trees. Just right for a private ride that would soon turn into a public display of illicit affection. Will hadn't had any practice *trying* to get discovered in flagrante delicto with a lady before, but his plan seemed sound. All he had to do was get Angelica off her horse near the bridle path and kiss her for all she was worth until some other riders came along. In this part of the park and at this time of day, that wouldn't take long.

The only real problem he faced would lie in keeping his own passions at bay while he waited for the appearance of observers to the ruination of Miss Hamilton of Boston. Merely thinking of kissing her had sometime in the night led to thinking of the shape and weight of her breasts in his hands. That had led to speculation of the color and texture of the hairs crowning her sex, and that had led to a very large, almost painful erection. One that plagued him again, now that she was actually nearby.

If he started to make love to her and they weren't detected promptly, he'd have the devil of a time keeping himself from seeking completion right there in Hyde Park. He didn't want to humiliate her. He only wanted to compromise her into marrying him.

He watched her out of the corner of his eye. She sat unsteadily on her mount, her hands clenched rather too firmly around the reins. "Are you quite comfortable, Miss Hamilton?" he asked.

She smiled, but that seemed uncertain, too. "Quite, Lord Claridge, but it is good to have you here."

"It is?"

"This sidesaddle is awkward."

"You're more accustomed to riding astride?" he asked. No proper English lady would ride astride, but who knew what they did in the United States?

"Actually, I'm not much used to riding on top of horses at all." Her smile broadened, all signs of uncertainty gone. "But I'm sure I'll be just fine with you here."

Splendid. She'd come around to trusting him, just when he'd decided to betray her trust. If he didn't know he was doing the best thing for both of them, he'd feel damned ashamed of himself.

"I'm very glad you asked me to ride this morning," she said. "In fact, I'm very glad I met you."

"You are?"

"Yes." She averted her gaze, and her cheeks took on that lovely flush they got when she was embarrassed. "I know I've been a trouble to you."

He stared at her face, at the glow to her skin, and images from his imaginings the night before crowded his memory. Angelica's expression as he entered her, as he thrust deep inside her and pushed them both to ecstasy.

"Hmm?" he said. "Oh, no. You're no trouble at all." Only a rock-hard sex that got jostled with every move of his mount.

"That's very sweet of you to say, but I know it isn't true." She reached over to touch his hand, and her horse chose that moment to stumble. She let out a little cry of alarm, but then settled herself back into her seat.

"Are you quite all right?" he asked.

She laughed. "Quite. Still, it seems much more secure to be seated as you are."

Seated as he was—with the horse between her legs, moving and rolling and rubbing at her thighs. Dear God, he had to get his thoughts under control.

"I've never really thanked you, you know," she said. "Not for finding Mr. Rush, nor for rescuing me from Mr. Montrose."

"You didn't need rescuing. You had the chap well in hand when I got there." *Well in hand.* Just the way he wanted the chap in his pants—well in her hand.

"Still, you were very understanding. You hardly even scolded me when I'd been so stupid."

What a hell of a time for her to become reasonable all of a sudden. If he truly understood her, he wouldn't be planning to trap her into matrimony, no matter how much the match would benefit them both. Still, he had to. It was his only hope of making her his and saving his horses in the bargain.

She smiled at him again, all innocence and openness. "You've been a good friend to me, and I've been an ungrateful wretch."

"Not at all."

"Yes, I have. I may be stubborn at times, but I've always been honest. You've been very good to me."

Stop it. Please stop. One more word, one more trusting look, and he wouldn't be able to go through with this. Where had these scruples come from? From loving her? Then why in hell couldn't he just crave her instead?

"You're a true gentleman, Lord Claridge, and I regret any difficulties I've caused you."

That did it. Will pulled his horse to a halt and turned in the saddle toward her. "I'm very sorry, but I'm not a gentleman, Miss Hamilton."

"I beg your pardon?"

"In fact, I'm a perfect scoundrel. You saw right through me the first time you met me."

"But I was wrong."

"No, you weren't." Damn it all, he'd make a full confession. Everything about everything. He'd tell her right now what he'd planned and how he regretted it. He'd tell her that he'd fallen in love with her and beg her to marry him, flaws and all. "Angelica, we need to leave here. This path isn't private, and I have a lot to tell you."

"Can't it wait until after our ride?" she said. "The morning is so lovely."

No, it couldn't wait. If he stayed with her, looking into her amber eyes and thinking of loving her and marrying her and having her in his bed whenever he wanted, he'd go quite mad. He'd pull her from her horse, pull off her clothes, and lose himself in her body, and they'd be discovered. "We need to go somewhere where we can be alone. Now, please."

Her eyes widened. "You seem upset. What have I done to upset you?"

"Nothing. You've done nothing. The fault is entirely mine. Only, please, let's go. Now."

"All right," she said. Just then her horse snorted and stomped, shaking it's head from side to side. "Oh, dear, what's he doing?"

Will glanced toward the side of the path and found the answer: a squirrel rising up on its haunches and chattering at the horse. Just enough to get the animal to bolt if she weren't careful. "Easy," he said. "Pull back on the reins easily."

"I can't," she cried. "The horse is too strong."

Will reached over for the reins, but it was too late. Miss Hamilton's mount reared up, whinnying loudly, and then took off at full speed, through the bushes lining the path and over the lawn. Will kicked his own horse into action, but he'd already lost ground. He watched in terror as her horse sped across the lawn with her hanging on for dear life and shouting for help.

He spurred his horse harder, trying desperately to catch up. The wind roared by his ears, deafening him to anything but the pounding of hooves and the rhythm of his own breath. Sunlight and shade went past him in a blur as he fought to keep the other horse and its precious rider in sight.

Dear God, protect her, don't let her be hurt. If anything happened to Angelica because of his stupid, selfish plans, he'd never forgive himself. She and her horse disappeared around a curve into a copse of trees. His own horse followed only seconds after, running into a dead end—a circular enclosure with no way out.

Angelica's horse stood there, lathered and breathing hard, the stupid animal. She was nowhere to be seen. He pulled his own mount to a stop and dropped to the ground.

"Angelica," he shouted. "Angelica, where are you?"

No answer. Where was she? Damn it, he'd get an answer out of the silly beast's hide if he could. "Angelica," he cried again. "Please, Angelica, where are you?"

A faint cry came from a shallow ditch at the border of the trees. He ran to it and found her. She lay in a heap of skirts, her eyes closed, her skin pale. He fell to his knees beside her. "Oh, my darling."

She opened her eyes, although they didn't quite focus, and smiled at him. "Why, there you are."

"Yes, my dearest, here I am." He didn't dare pull her into his arms until he knew what injuries she'd suffered. "Can you move? Gently, just your fingers."

She tried to sit up. She wobbled, but everything seemed to work. She looked around dizzily. "I guess the horse threw me."

Will steadied her, cradling her in his arms. "I would say so. Can you move your feet?"

She shifted her legs under her skirts. "Yes, but I don't think I want to take a walk right now."

Will let out a breath. "Thank God. I don't think I've ever been so frightened."

She looked up at him and smiled. "You were scared for me? You really are too sweet."

Not one bit. If he hadn't made his silly plans, she never would have been on that bloody horse at all. And it wouldn't have bolted and thrown her in a heap into this bloody ditch. "Angelica, listen. I'm not sweet. I'm a real cad. God, how I hate myself."

"I don't hate you," she said, still looking disconnected from reality. "In fact, I'd like you to kiss me. Right now."

Damn, his groin tightened just at the thought. "I don't think that's a good idea."

"I do," she declared. "I think it's a marvelous idea." She pulled herself up and pressed her mouth to his. Her kiss was sweet and innocent and incendiary. She moved her lips under his with a soft precision that went straight through him to his heart and below. Damn, how he wanted her.

He gave in to the hunger. After all, they had ended up in private. He kissed her back with all the yearning that had kept him awake the night before, with all the fire in his loins right now. He'd fought the need too long, and he couldn't fight it any longer.

She sighed into his mouth, and reality slipped away. He rested her back against the ground and set about loving her in earnest. He feathered kisses over her forehead, down her face, and to her jaw. Then for good measure, he dipped his head and nibbled at the soft skin of her neck. Drugged with passion, he pulled awkwardly at the buttons of her riding jacket—tiny, obstinate things. After much fumbling, he had them and the jacket open and could slip his hand inside to cup her breast.

She gasped, arching her back to bring her body to him. "Oh," she cried. "Oh, that feels so good."

"Oh, my darling," he murmured into her throat. "Yes, my darling."

"Yes," she answered. "Oh, yesssss."

He ought to stop. He had to stop, but God help him, he couldn't. He massaged her breast, feeling her nipple harden and rise even through all the layers of her clothing. She writhed beneath him, rubbing at his throbbing member. He pressed it into the softness of her belly, letting her feel what she did to him, letting her know how much he wanted her. He had never planned to make love to her like this, on the ground in a park, but if he didn't have her soon, he'd die.

And then a throat cleared just behind them. *Oh, no.* He stopped kissing her and held perfectly still, praying he hadn't heard what he knew very well he'd heard. Giggling followed, embarrassed female laughter. God help them both.

He lifted his head and found catastrophe. Not only had they been discovered, but they'd been discovered by half a dozen people, all still mounted on their horses. Reggie Montrose, still sporting the bruises Will had given him, and a few of his friends, and

Bertie Underwood and one of his young female cousins—the one with the bad skin. She'd done the giggling.

Montrose smiled his ugly smile. "We saw your horses running riderless and thought you might need help. Looks like you're doing just fine without us, Claridge."

"Oh, do shut up, Montrose," Will said.

The man laughed. "In fact, you've succeeded admirably where I failed. As usual. My hat's off to you, old fellow."

"Look away, Muriel," Bertie ordered his cousin. She didn't, of course, but just sat there giggling, her eyes wide.

"I just saw your aunt, Miss Hamilton," Montrose said, followed by an ugly chuckle.

Angelica sat straight up at that, apparently having recovered her senses. "Oh, no."

"Here she comes now," Montrose added.

An open carriage came into view. Lord and Lady Quimby and Minerva Hamilton and her friend, the solicitor. It stopped a few yards away, and both Quimbys' mouths dropped open. Minerva Hamilton stood up in the carriage, a look of pure horror on her face.

"Angelica!" she cried. Then her eyelids fluttered closed, and she swayed and fell back into her seat in a dead faint. Well, that was that. Angelica Hamilton's reputation had died a horrible death.

Aunt Minnie had her moments, and this was certainly one of them. She'd recovered fully from her fainting spell, it appeared. In fact, she seemed to have grown a few inches as she stood, regal and straight, by the sitting room fireplace. "Sit down, Angelica," she ordered. "You will remain standing, Lord Claridge."

The man looked pretty stiff himself as he cleared his throat. "Of course, Miss Hamilton. Whatever you say."

Alice Chambers

Angelica glanced from her aunt to Lord Claridge. Granted, she'd felt rather groggy after her spill from the horse, but she *thought* she'd recovered. Now she couldn't tell for sure. What on earth was Aunt Minnie doing ordering a peer of the realm around? And why on earth was he complying? He didn't return her gaze but looked squarely at Aunt Minnie, his jaw tight.

"Sit down, Angelica," Aunt Minnie repeated, sounding for all the world like the queen of England with all her authority. Angelica did as she was told, dropping into a straight-backed chair by Lord Claridge's side.

"Now then," Aunt Minnie continued, "I've spoken to both of you about your behavior. To you on more than one occasion, Lord Claridge."

"Yes, ma'am."

Angelica gaped up at him in wonder. *Ma'am?* He was going to call Aunt Minnie *ma'am?*

"Don't look to him for answers, Angelica. You hold more than a little responsibility yourself for this disaster."

"Oh, now, Auntie," Angelica said. "Surely this is no disaster."

Aunt Minnie's scowl fairly cramped her face. "You were found in each other's arms, rolling around on the ground."

"We weren't rolling on the ground."

"Rolling around on the ground," Aunt Minnie repeated, her normally soft voice thundering. "In front of half of London."

"That's a bit of an exaggeration, Auntie."

"The Quimby's," Aunt Minnie said, counting them off on her fingers. "Lord Underwood and his cousin and all those other people, whoever they were."

"Oh, blast them."

" 'Blast them' won't work this time, Angelica. You've disgraced yourself thoroughly this time. You'll have to pay the price, and so will Lord Claridge."

Taming Angelica

"Yes, ma'am," he said.

For heaven's sake, wasn't he going to say anything besides "Of course" and "Yes, ma'am"? They hadn't done anything wrong. Wasn't he going to defend himself? Wasn't he going to defend her?

Aunt Minnie folded her hands in front of her skirts and squared her shoulders. "I've told both of you that actions have consequences, and yet you chose to act. And in public. Now you'll have to suffer the consequences."

"Please, dear heart. You're taking this all too seriously."

Aunt Minnie took a breath so deep it was audible. "You will marry my niece, Lord Claridge."

"Of course," he said.

"What?" Angelica tried to rise from her chair, but he put a hand on her shoulder, holding her firmly in place. "What on earth are you saying?"

He didn't look at her but simply continued staring at Aunt Minnie. "I'd be honored to have Miss Hamilton as my wife."

The man had clearly lost his mind, but Angelica hadn't lost hers. "I won't do it," she said.

"You don't have any choice," Aunt Minnie said.

"Of course I have a choice. This is the nineteenth century. You can't just marry a woman off against her will."

"Your father has given me his authority over you," Aunt Minnie answered. "He would certainly order you to marry Lord Claridge, so that's what I'm doing."

"He can't marry me off against my will, either."

Lord Claridge's hand tightened on her shoulder. "It's for the best, Angelica."

She looked up at him. "How can you say that?"

He looked back down at her finally. "I've ruined your reputation, compromised your virtue. No other man would have you now."

143

"I don't care." Had they both gone mad? "I don't plan to marry anyone, anyway."

"I care," he answered. "Dear God, what kind of man do you think I am?"

Good question. She had thought she knew what sort of man he was—the sort who didn't give a fig for convention. The sort who respected a woman's right to choose whether or not to marry. The sort who realized she had dreams that didn't involve marriage and a husband to order her around. But now that she thought about it, had he ever actually *said* any of that, or had he just let her think he understood?

"No," Angelica said, pushing Lord Claridge's hand aside and rising from her chair. "I don't believe you. I don't believe any of this."

"You'd been warned," Aunt Minnie said. "And yet you walked in the park without your maid. You were seen in a restaurant without any chaperon. Heaven only knows what you were referring to the other night in the carriage."

"You were asleep. You didn't hear that," Angelica said.

"And now this," Aunt Minnie said. "The two of you playing nymph and satyr in a public place."

"We were doing no such thing."

"That's exactly what it looked like," Aunt Minnie replied.

"I'm afraid it did," Lord Claridge added.

Angelica spun on him. "Will you stop being so agreeable?"

He took both her hands in his. "Don't fight it, my darling. Your aunt is right about everything."

She pulled her hands from his. "I'm not your darling, and my aunt is not right about everything. This is insane, and I won't marry you."

"You don't have any choice," Aunt Minnie said.

Angelica turned toward her. "Stop saying that."

Taming Angelica

"All right." Aunt Minnie heaved a deep, loud sigh. "I'll give you a choice. You may either marry Lord Claridge or return with me to Boston on the next ship."

"No." Going home to Papa, to stultifying Boston? That would be even worse. He'd lock her in the house and never let her see daylight again. But she couldn't marry Lord Claridge or anyone else. For heaven's sake, she'd end up like her mother, always yes-my-dearing and no-my-dearing and whatever-you-say-my-dearing. She might as well go home to Boston. "Please, Auntie. That isn't any choice at all."

"Understand, Angelica. I love you as if you were my own child. But you can't have your own way in this. It's either marriage or Boston. Make up your mind."

Marriage or Boston. Prison or prison. There had to be some way out of this. *Yes, stay calm.* Ships didn't leave every day for the United States. She still had some time. She could sell some more jewels and run away. Yes, she could do that. Only *this* time she wasn't going to ask for any help from Lord Will Claridge.

"Tell me right now that you'll marry Lord Claridge, or I'll book passage for us home," Aunt Minnie said.

"Please, dear heart," Angelica said.

"And don't think you'll be able to sell any more of your jewelry. I've had Mr. Davidson put it all in a safe place."

Angelica turned to Lord Claridge. "You told her."

He shrugged and shook his head. "I didn't."

"I have my own ways of finding things out," Aunt Minnie said. "I'm not quite the doddering old fool you think I am."

Angelica just turned and stared at her aunt. The old dear had developed a sneaky streak, it appeared—pretending to be asleep in carriages and hiding jewels behind Angelica's back. How could she? And how could Lord Claridge just stand there and go along with everything Aunt Minnie said? If she didn't know better, she'd swear that the two of them had worked this plan out between them.

"As I said. You have a choice. Marriage or Boston," Aunt Minnie concluded. "Tell me which it will be."

So it appeared that Aunt Minnie had given her a choice between Lord Claridge's domination or her father's. Looked at that way, her decision was a simple one. With Lord Claridge she might enjoy some freedom. After her father heard about this "disaster" he wouldn't grant her any at all. Besides, if she stayed in London, she might still figure some way out of this mess.

"Marriage," she said. She turned toward Lord Claridge. "I will marry you, sir."

He smiled, the first real expression he'd shown since the look of horror on his face when they'd been found rolling around on the ground, as Aunt Minnie put it. He took her hands into his and gazed down into her eyes. "Miss Hamilton, you've made me the happiest man alive."

"Wonderful," Aunt Minnie exclaimed. She rushed to the two of them and placed her hands over their still-linked ones. "Lawrence will be so proud of me. You did it carelessly, sloppily, you two. But you did it anyway. You did it."

"Auntie, you sound as though we've just won a game of whist."

"But you have," Aunt Minnie bubbled. "Only more than whist, better than cards. You've won the game of love, you two darling children—forgive me, your lordship, but I am going to be your aunt now."

"Of course," he said, still grinning like an idiot. "Call me whatever you want. You might start with Will. That's my name."

"Will," she repeated. "Oh, my goodness. My nephew Will, the brother of a duke. Oh, my. Oh, my, oh, my, oh, my."

Taming Angelica

"Don't get into a state, Auntie."

"I've done it," Aunt Minnie said. "You've done it. Lawrence didn't think I could but I've done it. I must write to him right away. And then preparations. A small, simple wedding, under the circumstances, but still there are preparations."

"I'll do whatever I can to help," Lord Claridge said, agreeable as ever.

"Yes, I'll just go write to Lawrence," Aunt Minnie said as she headed toward the door. She stopped halfway there and turned around. "Be good, you two. Or I don't suppose that matters anymore, does it? Or it does, but not really. Oh, who cares? I'm so happy."

She left the room in a flutter of skirts and rose water, leaving Angelica standing with her husband-to-be still holding her hands and smiling at her. *Curse him.*

She removed her hands from his and stepped back. "You can stop the pretense now."

His eyebrows shot up. "What pretense?"

"That you want to marry me, of course."

"But I do want to marry you."

"No, you don't."

He put his hands on his hips. "Let's not play a game of 'yes-I-do-no-you-don't.' "

"Well, you don't."

"How could you know that?"

"You never asked me to marry you, for one thing," she said.

"Would you have accepted?"

She waved a hand at him. "No, of course not."

"Then why should I have asked you?" he said. "I do have some male pride, you know."

What a ridiculous conversation. Next thing she knew he'd be telling her he loved her. There wasn't any male pride involved, only lust. They'd both fallen victim to it, and they'd been caught. He didn't have to pretend there was anything more than that.

"I'll make you a good husband, Angelica," he said softly.

Exactly what she feared most—a good husband to take care of her, to plan her every move, to give her her every thought. "I'd rather you didn't, thank you."

He looked completely puzzled at that. "You're not making sense."

"You see, it's this way," she said, pacing in front of him. "What most people think of as good isn't what I think of as good. Especially what husbands think of as good. That's the worst."

"There's your problem, then," he answered.

"What?"

He reached out, caught her midpace, and pulled her into his arms. "You think too much," he whispered as he lowered his mouth to hers. "Don't think."

He kissed her then—not the desperate, crushing caress they'd shared in the park. This kiss was more about persuasion than hunger, honey rather than fire, but it sent flames rippling through her nevertheless. His lips tasted sweet, and his breath felt warm against her skin. She pulled herself to him, all along his solid length. Her breasts ached with the pressure, feeling tender and heavy. She craved his touch, the exploration he'd begun in the park. She wanted . . . she wanted . . . she didn't even know what she wanted, but he could give it to her.

He reached down and ran his palms over her buttocks, bringing her even more firmly against him. That bulge had returned to the front of his pants. It pressed up against her, hard and insistent as it had before, when he'd lain with her in the park. She moved herself, rubbing it, and he groaned—a sound halfway between pleasure and pain.

He pulled his lips from hers and rested his face against the side of her head. "Dear God, what you do to me, Angelica."

Taming Angelica

She moved just enough to give her room to place her hand against the hardness. The thing was part of him and truly enormous. She measured it with her fingers and squeezed gently.

He began to tremble. "Mercy, my darling," he said through gritted teeth. "You must stop."

She moved her hand, still feeling the memory of his hardness on her palm. His heat.

"I've been dying for you all day," he said. "Another moment of that and I wouldn't be able to wait for our wedding night. I'd take you right now."

The wedding night. Still such a mystery. She'd find out soon where all these intoxicating caresses led. That, at least, she could look forward to.

He straightened and looked down at her, a wicked gleam in his eye even though his breath still came raggedly. "It will be good between us, that I guarantee," he said. "I'll make you happy."

Chapter Ten

The skies let loose a torrent of rain on Will's wedding day, but even a flood of biblical proportions couldn't have dimmed his spirits. That night, or earlier if he could manage, he'd have Angelica Hamilton—Angelica Claridge—in his bed. Peter had dressed him immaculately that morning, not in formal attire, but in his most elegantly understated suit of day wear. He'd arrived at the Hamiltons' house at precisely the appointed time, and now he stood in the sitting room, gazing through the windowpane at the storm outside and waiting. All he needed was the vicar and his wife-to-be to make him the happiest man on Earth.

The door opened and he turned. Instead of Angelica or the vicar, Minerva Hamilton stood on the threshold. She looked at him—first up, then down—and twisted her hands together in front of her skirts. "My, but you are a handsome man, your lordship. I mean Will. I haven't made a mistake. I just know I haven't."

"Mistake?" he repeated. Dear God, he didn't have

Taming Angelica

time for any of her word puzzles just now. He wanted only to get married and take his wife home and make love to her until they both fell into a sated stupor. "What do you mean by a mistake?"

She stepped into the room and closed the door behind her. "I'm having an attack of conscience. Marriage even to someone as handsome as yourself isn't what Angelica wants, you know."

"You can't change your mind. Everything's been arranged. I won't hear of this marriage being called off, or even postponed."

She looked at him for a long moment, as if trying to look into him. "Would that break your heart?"

"Yes," he answered without hesitation, without even thinking. And that was the truth of the matter. Not having Angelica for his own would break his heart. *Extraordinary.*

"Yes," she said. "Yes, I had so hoped. But one never knows about these things, does one? At least, I never do."

"Please, Miss Hamilton, I must know. You haven't changed your mind about my marriage to your niece, have you?"

"No. That would be impossible, in any case."

He let out a breath. "Then where is Angelica?"

"She'll be along in a moment. I wanted to talk to you first."

He put his hands at his back and waited. She could talk about whatever she wanted. She could talk as long as she wanted. But when she was through Angelica had better appear, followed by the vicar and some witnesses. He had a cozy dinner planned back at his own house. Dinner in his bedroom in front of a roaring fire and then an afternoon and night spent in bed. He'd waited this long to have her, and he could wait through one more impenetrable conversation with her aunt, if he must.

Alice Chambers

Minerva twisted her hands together some more, searching for words, or so it appeared. "We've played a rather nasty trick on Angelica, you and I."

"I don't see how."

"You know very well she wouldn't be marrying you if we hadn't helped her into it."

"I don't know what you should have done differently," he said.

"I should have ordered her not to see you at all," she said. "Oh, but I couldn't do that. Well, yes, I could, but I shouldn't have. Or is it the other way around?"

"Please. I don't understand."

"It's very simple," she answered. "If I'd really wanted to keep you from her, I should have done it. But she really does care for you, I could see that, and you're so like Sean O'Malley."

"Sean O'Malley?" he repeated. Who in hell was Sean O'Malley? Some former beau of Angelica's? No matter—Angelica was his now, and he'd make her forget Sean O'Malley or any other man.

"What am I saying? You're not like Sean at all. But you're Angelica's Sean. I can feel that in my bones."

"Whatever you say, Miss Hamilton. I'll be her Sean. I'll be better than Sean, whoever he is. Was."

"I know you will." She reached into her bodice and pulled out a handkerchief, with which she dabbed at her eyes. "You're a good man. You'll make Angelica happy."

The last word came out on a sob, and she wept bitterly into the handkerchief. He walked to her and put an arm around her shoulders. "There, now," he said.

"It's just that I'm so happy for the two of you," she cried, her voice still catching on *happy* as though she couldn't bear to speak the word. "And Angelica's just as h-h-h-happy as I am. I know it."

"Has Angelica been crying?" he asked. Damn him if he'd made her cry. He'd make it up to her if he had. He kiss her twice for every tear she'd shed. He'd make her laugh. He'd tell her over and over again how beautiful she was. Anything.

"You will be good to her, won't you?" Minerva asked. "I won't regret helping you in your plan, will I?"

His plan? The woman had known what he was about all along? "I don't know what you're talking about."

She looked up at him out of watery eyes. "You kept putting yourself into questionable situations with Angelica. You were either very stupid or you were doing it on purpose. I didn't think you were stupid."

"I think I thought I was much more clever than I actually turned out to be." Good God, now he was talking like her.

She gripped his arm, pressing the wet handkerchief against his sleeve. "You will make Angelica happy, won't you? Please. If you don't I'll be just miserable."

At that she started sobbing again, and he patted her back. "I'll make her happy. I promise."

"Good." She dabbed at her eyes. "Oh, dear, I promised myself I wouldn't cry. I swore I wouldn't cry, and now look at me."

"It's only natural," he said.

She looked up at him, an expression of puzzlement on her face. "Hmm?"

"Don't women always cry at weddings?"

"Not me. Not today." She pulled away from him and straightened her shoulders. "I won't show Angelica a tear. This is going to be a joyous occasion."

Just then the door opened, and Angelica stood in the doorway. "The vicar is here, Auntie."

She caught sight of Will and smiled. His heart froze dead in his chest for a moment and then started up in a restless staccato. She was wearing something pale blue and innocent, layered in lace to the point that she resembled a doll in her perfection. She looked at him, a smoldering fire in her eyes.

"Hello, Will," she said, her voice coming out breathy. Everything male inside him responded, sending a shock through him. *Damn, what a woman.*

Beside him, Minerva began to sob again.

How odd to be coming home to a place she'd never been before. Angelica looked around the mammoth foyer and marveled at the opulence. An enormous chandelier hung overhead, dominating the parquet floors and the sweeping staircase lined with polished brass. It all made her feel very small, and very bedraggled and wet from the rain that had pelted her on the short walk from the carriage to the front door.

This was an English lord's house, and she was his wife. What an extraordinary turn of events. Weeks ago she'd been Miss Angelica Hamilton of Boston. Even this morning she'd been the same, and now she was the bride of Lord William Claridge. It was enough to make anyone's head spin, without even considering what would happen as soon as the two of them were alone together, and she was most definitely considering that.

Will took her wet cloak and handed it to a servant girl. The rest of the staff stood in attendance—butler, valet, cook, maids, footman, and scullery maids. All these people employed at nothing but caring for one person. Now two. And of course, she'd brought Mary with her to swell their ranks even further.

"Well," her new husband said into her ear. "Do you approve?"

"Approve?" she echoed. "It's all very beautiful, but I'm not sure I approve of such extravagance for just the two of us."

"It's the family house," he said. "My brother *is* a duke."

Taming Angelica

"Yes. How silly of me. I keep forgetting."

"Let me introduce the staff," he said, taking her arm and turning her toward the army of domestic uniforms. "This is Newsome, my majordomo."

The butler, an older man with clear blue eyes and a beatific smile, bowed deeply. "Honored, my lady." He turned to Will. "And my heartiest congratulations to you, my lord."

"Thank you, Newsome," Will said. "And thank you for assembling everyone."

"Our pleasure, sir."

"This is Mrs. Flowers, our wonderful cook," Will continued. The cook curtsied. "And everyone else," he concluded with a wave of his arm toward the staff.

A flurry of bows and curtsies greeted his declaration, and Angelica nodded in return.

"Everyone, this is my wife," he declared. He turned toward her, a light of tenderness and joy in his eyes. "Lady Claridge."

Her heart did a little dance—a hitch and then a flurry of beats. His wife, his lady. She'd never wanted to be a wife, but he did make it sound grand. And at the very least, he'd make a woman of her soon. This very night, most likely.

He turned toward the butler. "You've made everything ready, Newsome?"

"I've followed your instructions to the letter," the man answered.

"Good." Will extended his arm toward her. "We'll go upstairs, then. We're both"—he stopped and gave her a purposeful look—"tired."

She rested her hand on his sleeve. "Exhausted," she said.

She was anything but exhausted, of course. Every fiber of her being seemed alive with energy. All her senses had heightened, until she'd grown acutely aware of the warmth of the room, the late-afternoon light playing off the chandelier, the smell of rain still on Will's clothes.

The staff silently dispersed, leaving them alone in the foyer. "Lady Claridge," Will said to her softly. "Allow me to show you to my bedroom."

Her knees almost buckled at that. She looked into his face, at the deep blue of his eyes, at the regal slope to his nose, at the undisguised hunger in his expression. She wanted him more than anything she'd ever wanted before. Even though she had no good idea of exactly what would happen between them, her body told her still that she wanted him.

"Please," she said.

He smiled and escorted her to the stairway and up it to a long hallway lined with portraits.

"Your family?" she asked as they passed them, more to ease the silence than to get information.

"Various and sundry Claridges. Dukes and Duchesses of Brathshire. I'll tell you about them later." He stopped outside a door and opened it, revealing a large room filled with heavy, masculine furniture and an enormous curtained bed. "Right now there is one Claridge I especially want you to meet. He's most eager to make your acquaintance."

She couldn't tell what *that* meant. But the way he said it sent a shiver down her spine to the backs of her knees. She stepped over the threshold and walked to the hearth where a blazing fire sent heat into the room. Behind her the door closed quietly.

"Ah, Mary's been at work," he said.

She turned around and followed his gaze to the bed. Her new wedding set lay upon it. Underthings, gown, and robe. So many clothes. How was he to touch her through all that?

He nodded toward a doorway. "There's a dressing room in there."

Taming Angelica

She searched a bit before she found her voice. "Thank you."

"Don't be long," he said, more of a question than a command.

"I won't." She walked to the bed and bent to pick up all her garments. What she found lying next to them made her breath catch—a man's robe de chambre. Not exactly like her father's, nor like the one she'd imagined seeing Will in, but close enough. This was real, not the overactive imagination of a young woman after her first kiss. By the end of the day she would know her husband as she'd never known anyone before.

"Is something wrong?" Will asked quietly.

She shook herself mentally. Nothing would happen if she stayed staring at his dressing gown. She scooped up her own things and headed into the dressing room. "I'll just be a minute."

The little anteroom was hardly more than a closet, but lamplight brightened it enough so that she could find a hook for her nightclothes. She quickly draped them there and began in on the fastenings of her dress. With fingers made awkward with eagerness, she worked each one open slowly, one by one.

"I've ordered us a light supper," Will called from the other room. "I hope you like venison."

"I love it," she called back, slipping out of her dress and letting it fall to the floor. She untied the string to her petticoats and let them follow. Just the stays of her corset remained, and she started quickly on them.

"It's raining rather harder outside now," he called, as if they needed to be concerned with the weather. The dear man, could he have the same flutters in his stomach that she had in hers? She slipped out of the rest of her clothes until she stood naked in her new husband's dressing room. The air felt warm and comfortable against her skin, but still her nipples peaked and hardened. She looked down at them and at the flat of her belly. Would he find her beautiful? She knew only one way to find out.

She rejected all of her nightclothes but the robe, tossing them into the same pile with her dress, and then slipped into the garment. Then she walked to the door and opened it. Will was standing beside the fireplace, next to a table that held several covered plates—their supper—that had no doubt arrived while she was undressing. He had taken off his day clothes, too, in favor of his robe and a nightshirt that gleamed white at his throat.

He smiled at her, extending his hand. "Come and eat something. You'll need your strength."

She giggled—not at all the sound a grown, married woman would make—and went to him, seating herself with her bare feet tucked under her in a large, upholstered chair in front of the fire. He sat in the facing chair, lifted a cover from one of the plates at his elbow, and handed it to her.

The meal consisted of tiny medallions of venison, surrounded by a sauce that smelled of drippings and Madeira. She took the fork he offered and put a piece of the meat into her mouth. She chewed it slowly, savoring the rich but not too gamy taste.

He watched her eat, still smiling. "Is it good?"

"Wonderful."

"Good." He poured her a glass of claret and handed it to her and then poured another glass for himself. She took the wine and set the glass at the foot of the chair while she finished her venison.

He sat, sipping his wine and smiling at her, his legs stretched out in front of him, his gaze never leaving her face. He made such a splendid picture in the firelight, his elegant profile and dazzling blue eyes enhanced by the dimness of a rainy late afternoon. She studied his broad shoulders and long fingers, trying to memorize every detail. Soon she'd know him so completely—every gesture, every imperfection, every way he took a breath. If she worked very hard studying him at this exact moment, maybe she'd always have a memory of him from when his body was still a mystery.

She glanced down at her plate and discovered she'd finished every scrap. "Aren't you going to eat anything?"

"I'm not hungry," he answered. "At least not for food."

She handed him her plate. "Then neither am I."

He took it from her and set it on the table beside him. "Don't you want any wine?"

"No," she said, picking up her wineglass and handing it to him.

"Then neither do I." He put both glasses next to his untouched plate. That done, he leaned toward her and took her hands in both of his. "Angelica . . ."

"Yes, Will."

"Damn, I don't know how to say this." He rubbed his thumbs over her knuckles, back and forth, forth and back. "I know that you didn't . . . that is that you . . . oh, hell."

"What, Will?"

He looked at her, his gaze roaming her face as if searching for something. "There ought to be words," he said. "I'm usually rather good with words."

She didn't answer. She just watched his face, his dear, dear face. Whatever happened between them, however they worked things out, she'd always remember this afternoon and how he struggled to find the right words.

He took a deep breath. "I don't know what to say. I don't know how to tell you what I feel."

She pulled her hand from his and pressed her fingers against his lips. "Don't tell me. Show me."

"Oh, my darling." He leaned toward her, his eyes closed and his lips parted, inviting her to kiss him first. Inviting her to start the dance that would take her to a world of undiscovered sweetness. She complied. She pressed her mouth to his softly at first, moving her lips in a slow exploration.

He answered, kissing her gently. Giving and taking and giving some more, but never hurrying her, just teasing her into wanting him. She opened her mouth on a sigh, and his tongue sought entrance, touching her own. By now she knew his kisses and what they could do, so she leaned into him, resting a hand against his chest as she tasted him, taking his breath as her own.

He growled in the back of his throat, and before she knew what had happened to her, he'd grasped her bodily and lifted her into his arms, finally settling her into his lap. He slid his arms around her waist and kept right on kissing her until her head swam and she had to fight to breathe.

All the while his hands did things, wonderful things, all over her back and down to her buttocks. Rubbing, exploring, molding her to him. She pulled back from the kiss, rested her head against his shoulder, and let herself revel in the friction, the heat of his hands on her body. Over and down, sultry and demanding, like no way she'd ever been touched before. One hand moved to her front, cupping a breast, and a shock of pleasure raced through her, making her cry out.

"Did I hurt you?" he whispered, his voice husky.

"No," she barely managed to answer. "Oh, no, no, you didn't hurt me. Don't stop. Please."

He squeezed gently, running his thumb over the nipple until it was aching and hard. "Dear God," he said. "You're not wearing anything but this robe, are you?"

She couldn't find enough voice to answer, so she shook her head. He groaned in response. "You're com-

Taming Angelica

pletely naked under this. I swear, you'll drive me mad."

Mad? Yes, that was exactly what she wanted. She wanted him to feel the same hot urgency she felt, to drown in it and lose all reason as she was doing. Nothing short of madness could equal the pleasure he was giving her. "Touch me and see if I'm naked," she said. "Touch me. I dare you."

He smiled, a lazy curl to his lip. "Dare me, will you?"

She bit her lip and nodded.

"Well, then. I've always loved a challenge."

He reached down, caught the hem of her robe, and lifted it along her leg. His fingers swept along her skin, setting it on fire where he touched. An ache started deep in her belly, throbbing to the beat of her heart, the rhythm of his strokes. Up and up his hand came, closer and closer to the place where her legs met, where the pulsing built and built.

He moved farther, touching the sensitive skin along the inside of her thigh. She shifted, bringing herself closer to his fingers, but he continued stroking her thigh. Close to what she needed, but not close enough. She tried again, adjusting her position, but he held back. She moaned in utter frustration at having what she wanted and yet not having it.

"Not yet," he said. "You challenged me, remember?"

Remember? How could she remember anything when she couldn't even think? She didn't even know what she wanted, but he knew, damn him, and he wasn't doing it. "Please." She gasped.

"Hmm? Please what?"

"I don't know . . . oh, dear heaven . . . I don't."

"I think you do."

She just bit her lip and whimpered, moving her hips

once again. He touched her then, right at her core, and she nearly came apart. "Oh," she cried. "Oh, that, that."

"This?" he said and touched her again, this time lingering.

"Yes," she answered. "Yes, oh, yes."

"Yes, my darling," he whispered into her ear. "God, you're hot."

She couldn't answer, couldn't talk, couldn't breathe. She clutched his shoulders, the only solid thing in a world gone mad with throbbing. He brought his fingers even more firmly against her and rubbed at the exact center of her fire. Over and over, while she gasped and moaned into his shoulder.

Too much, too hot, too unbelievably good. She dug her fingertips into his shoulders and hung on. The feeling grew and grew, tightening inside her, building and building until she shattered. She flew apart in his arms, spasms rocking her, cries ripping from her throat. He stroked her for a moment, while the world spun out of control and the spasms took her to the brink of consciousness. Then he stopped and held her, just held her while her body rested, melting into a pool of liquefied flesh in his lap.

She rested her head on his shoulder and let herself drift into a perfect peace. Her body still thrummed with the aftermath of the storm—muscles she hadn't known she had clenching and relaxing at her center. Slowly she came back to Earth, to the sounds of rain and the beating of her husband's heart, to the smell of wood smoke and the warmth of the fire. Slowly she returned to a reality she'd never guessed of in her entire life.

"Did you like that?" he whispered.

"Yes," she whispered into his shoulder. "It was wonderful."

He chuckled, the sound coming right from his chest

Taming Angelica

into her ear. She snuggled closer to him, burying her nose into his neck.

"You're so delightfully responsive. More than any man dares hope for in a young wife."

She lifted her head and looked into his face. "I pleased you?"

"Oh, God, Angelica. Don't you know?"

She shook her head.

"Yes." He took a deep breath. "You pleased me."

"Are we . . ." She felt heat rise over her cheeks. "That is . . . did you . . . have you . . . ?"

"What, my darling?"

Curse her ignorance in these matters. She didn't even know what to ask him. "What happened in my body—did it happen in yours, too?"

"Not yet."

Thank heaven. "Then you aren't finished? There's more?"

He laughed outright at that. "Bless you," he said, slapping a hand on her bottom and squeezing. "Bless you for a lusty one, my wife."

"I don't see what's funny."

"Oh, you don't?"

"No." She did her best to pout, but she'd never been very good at it. "And I don't think you ought to laugh, anyway."

"Then I'll have to show you what's funny," he said, taking her hand and slipping it inside the front of his robe, so that only his nightshirt lay between his body and her fingers. Under the soft cotton she found that bulge she'd felt before, the long, thick ridge of hard flesh.

"I've been like this all day wanting you, and as long as I'm like this I'm not through with you. I imagine I'll get like this more than once before morning, and I'll want you every time."

"What is it?" she asked.

"Men have dozens of names for it—Priapus, rod, member—it's my sex, you magnificent innocent, and it will soon seek its own satisfaction inside yours."

Dear heaven, how could that be possible? Such an enormous thing could never fit inside her. "How?" she whispered. "Where?"

He slid his hand along her thigh to the newly sensitive spot between her legs. He stroked her again, and slipped a finger into her most secret place. Moisture collected where his finger probed—hot and languid—and that delicious pressure built again in the pit of her belly.

"Would you like me here?" he asked softly. He stroked her some more, coaxing pleasure from the center of her until her back arched of its own accord, bringing even more contact with his hand. "Do you want me inside you?" he asked.

"Yes," she heard herself answer and wondered at the words. "Yes, Will, please."

He pressed his face to hers and groaned into her ear, the sound reverberating down her spine. "Then you'd best release me," he whispered, "or I don't know how I'll manage to be gentle with you."

Oh, my. She was still holding his sex. Without even knowing what she'd done, she'd somehow curled her fingers around the length of him. She let him go and pulled her hand from his robe. He smiled and rose, lifting her up into his arms. Without removing his gaze from her face, he covered the distance to the bed and laid her gently upon it. He kissed her once, gently, and then straightened, pulling at the belt of his robe. He had it off in a moment and then his nightshirt, until he stood naked, still smiling at her.

She propped herself up on her elbows and drank in the sight of him. He was sleekly muscled from his broad shoulders, over his chest, and down to narrow hips and strong legs. His sex stood straight out from his body, surrounded by a patch of curly, dark blond hairs. All that size, all that hardness, all that power would soon be inside her, or so he said. The thought frightened her and fascinated her all at once. But something inside her body responded without thought. Where she'd been wet, she grew wetter. Where she'd been hot, she grew hotter. Her body didn't fear him. Her body only wanted him.

"Now then, my turn," he said.

"Hmm?"

"You've seen me as my Maker made me. Now it's my turn to see you."

Her cheeks warmed again, but she sat up and shrugged out of her robe, finally tossing it onto the floor. She forced herself to remain uncovered for his gaze and lay back against the pillows.

His eyes widened, and his nostrils flared at he stared at her. "My God, Angelica, you're beautiful."

Her cheeks flamed even hotter. She'd probably turned bright red to the roots of her hair, but she returned his gaze without flinching. "You find me pretty? Really?"

" 'Pretty' is inadequate to describe you."

She extended her arms to him. "Then come to me."

"Oh, Angelica." He joined her on the bed and pulled her into his arms. He kissed her, deeply and hungrily, while his hands moved over her naked skin—from her shoulders, down her arms, and back up. He slid her onto her back and covered her with his own body, still taking her mouth with his while she held his face between her palms.

He pulled away from the kiss and nibbled along her jaw and then down her throat. Everywhere his mouth touched her, tiny sparks of pleasure ignited. His tongue dipped into the hollow above her collarbone, and her heart lurched in her chest. His teeth nipped at the flesh of her breast, and her breath came out in a sigh. His lips closed over her nipple, and her sighs turned into pleasured cries.

He suckled, stealing her sanity with his mouth, until she clasped his head and held him to her breast. Shameless, throbbing need. Hunger, hot and urgent. He switched to the other nipple and she twisted beneath him, her thighs rubbing together over that sensitive spot. She needed him there, needed the completion of having all his hardness there.

As though sensing her need, he shifted and pressed his hand to her sex, his fingers separating the sensitive flesh and probing inside her. She writhed and twisted and cried out, all words gone but one. "Please," she said with a moan. "Please, oh, please."

"Yes, my darling," he answered in a growl. "Yes, I understand. God, I understand."

He separated her legs and positioned himself between them. The tip of his sex pressed against her where she most craved it. Hard and smooth, it moved her closer and closer to the madness. He pushed, and she strained against him, trying to take all of him inside to where the throbbing built. Pain started somewhere inside, but nothing penetrated the haze of pleasure in her brain.

He moved again, and more heat flared in her belly, drowning out the pain. Just another movement, just a bit more pressure, and he'd be fully inside, where she wanted him.

But he stopped. He held himself over her, his whole body trembling with the effort. He looked down at her, his face twisted in passion and agony. "I can't," he said in a gasp. "I can't hurt you."

"Please," she cried.

He didn't answer, but put his face next to hers and whimpered.

That was no answer. She wouldn't accept that as an answer while her body throbbed and burned for him.

She clasped his shoulders and wrapped her legs around his torso, trapping him against her. And she surged upward, pulling him into her.

He roared and pushed forward, ending the pain and filling her completely. She dug her fingers into his back and held on while he moved, hard and fast, sliding in and out of her wetness. Her breath came with the rhythm of his thrusts. Her heart beat with it. And deep inside her the pressure climbed, coiling, tightening. She rode the crest of his passion, of her own white-hot need, until it shattered her. Until wave after wave of pleasure washed over her and the spasms rocked her again.

He moved even faster, even harder, taking her even higher. One more powerful thrust, one more maddening surge into her, and he shuddered in her arms, helpless and gasping. Then he collapsed on top of her, his breath labored and ragged, while she floated back to reality.

"I love you, Angelica," he whispered. "Dear God, how I love you."

Chapter Eleven

When Will awoke, naked and tangled in the sheets of his well-rumpled bed, his first sight was of his new wife standing beside his bedroom window, gazing out. The weather had cleared overnight, and an early morning sun slanted in, bathing her in light.

Her hair hung in a sleep-tousled cascade around her shoulders, the sun streaking her sable curls with gold. The silhouette of her form barely showed through the cotton of her robe, reminding him of the curves and hollows he'd explored so thoroughly the night before. Damn him if he couldn't make love to her again, right on the spot; she was that beautiful.

"Good morning," he said in a voice rough from sleep.

She turned and looked at him, her expression unreadable. He'd seen that look in a woman's eyes before. It always promised trouble—even if no poor male could ever hope to know in advance exactly what kind. She stood there for a moment, studying him as though he were a particularly interesting insect specimen, before turning and walking toward the hearth.

Someone had built the fire up and brought in a tea tray. Angelica poured him a cup, put something onto a plate, and brought them both over to him. She sat on the edge of the bed as though she'd always done exactly that in the morning, and held the cup out to him. He sat up and took it from her. She set a small plate with one of Mrs. Flowers's scones and some marmalade onto the sheet that barely covered him.

"Thank you," he said.

"Your man Newsome is very efficient," she answered, somehow making the word *efficient* sound like a vice rather than a virtue. "He seemed to know exactly when to come in. I suppose he's brought morning tea to you and other women here before. Often."

"No," Will answered.

"He's never brought you and a woman refreshments here before?"

Ah, so that was what had put the burr under her blanket—jealousy. He knew how to handle that. "No," he said. "Never."

She didn't say anything, but merely raised an eyebrow as if she didn't believe him.

"You know that I haven't lived like a saint, but I've always been discreet."

"You've really never had another woman here?"

"Really. You're the first and the only. You're my wife." He reached out with his free hand and stroked her cheek. "This is your home now, Angelica. At least while we're in town."

A tiny smile threatened to creep over her lips before she pulled away from his touch and very deliberately set her mouth into a straight line. "You own a lot of property, do you?"

"My family does. That is, my brother does."

"For example . . ." she prompted.

Alice Chambers

"Well, let's see." He took a sip of his tea. "There's the family estate in Brathshire. That's the biggest holding, of course."

"Is it ridiculously large?" she asked.

"Positively obscene. Most of a forest, with an entire park cleared out for the main house, stables, formal gardens, and long gravel drives."

She crossed her arms over her chest. "All for two people?"

"Three now, including you."

"And there's more?" she asked.

"A house on the Cornish coast, and a hunting cottage in Scotland, only a dozen or so rooms there." He set his teacup into the saucer. "I say, isn't it a bit late to be inquiring into my ability to support a wife?"

"I just want to understand how things are between us," she answered.

Now it was his turn to stare at her. "How things are?"

"Your family doesn't need money," she said. "So you didn't marry me to rescue the good name of Claridge."

"I didn't marry you to rescue anyone."

"But you did marry me for money. We both know that."

"You certainly have a low opinion of yourself," he said. "And an even lower one of me, it appears."

"I'm only being honest. You don't have to act like that."

"Like what?" he demanded.

She threw her hands into the air. "I don't know. Wounded. We entered into a financial deal, and it seems you got the better part of it."

"That's all our marriage means to you?" he said.

She didn't answer but just put her hands on her hips and stared at him.

Taming Angelica

"I am wounded," he said after a moment. "I had lots of reasons for marrying you."

"Fine. What are they?"

"Your reputation, for one thing. Or have you forgotten that we were discovered making a public spectacle of ourselves in Hyde Park in the middle of the morning?"

"You married me because you'd disgraced me?" She made a nasty little snorting sound in the back of her throat. "Don't be ridiculous."

"I don't think that's the least bit ridiculous." In truth, he'd had better reasons than her disgrace, as she put it. But he could hardly ignore the fact that he'd utterly and thoroughly ruined her reputation. What sort of cad did she think he was? "Your aunt insisted, and she was entirely within her rights. After the way I'd behaved, I had to marry you."

Her eyes widened. "You had to?"

"Oh, Angelica." He reached for her, and the action turned his teacup over on the bedding.

"Damn this mess," he said in a growl as he scooped up the cup along with the plate holding the scone and set them both on the bedside table. He reached for her again, and this time he managed to rest the palm of his hand against her cheek. "I didn't have to marry you. I *wanted* to marry you."

"What reason could you have to *want* to marry me except for my money?"

"There were lots of reasons."

She rose from the bed and paced to the fireplace. "You needn't have married me to satisfy convention," she said. "I don't give a fig for convention."

"One of your most admirable traits, in my opinion." Or one of her most irritating, depending on the circumstance.

"You needn't have married me just because Aunt

Minnie said you had to. I can get around her very easily."

"You weren't having much success at getting around her, that I could see."

She glared at him for a minute then walked to the window and stared out. "I could have talked her out of it if you hadn't just stood there agreeing with her."

"Angelica, she was ready to load you onto a ship like so much cargo and send you back to Boston."

She turned toward him, her hands on her hips. "I would have gotten away, just as I'd planned to before I met you."

"You weren't having any success with that either, as I recall."

"And who's fault was that?" she demanded.

"Certainly not mine," he answered, glaring back at her. "Or am I now to blame for what happened to you *before* we met, too?"

She didn't answer but let out a petulant little huff and looked down at her hands. "So why did you marry me?" she asked quietly after a moment.

He took a deep breath and searched his brain for just the right answer. He didn't want to lie to her—at least not much—but he didn't want to make any blunders in his phrasing either. He'd told her the night before that he loved her, but perhaps she hadn't heard him after the storm of passion they'd just shared.

Perhaps she'd heard him but hadn't believed him. Lots of men declared their love without really meaning it under those circumstances. Although as a virgin, she couldn't know that. He'd certainly never lied about loving someone, but she couldn't know that, either.

He could try again now to tell her he loved her. But that sounded too simple right this moment, when she seemed so unwilling to believe anything he said at all. No, for now he'd remain quiet about love and keep to the obvious and undeniable—that he'd married her out

Taming Angelica

of lust. Later, when he absolutely couldn't avoid the topic any longer, he'd admit that her money had attracted him, too. But for now he'd stick to lust.

He cleared his throat and did his best to look embarrassed. "You remember my telling you about a man's needs, I trust."

She turned a very appealing shade of pink and glanced at him out of the corners of her eyes. "Yes."

"You should understand about that a bit better today, I think."

Her skin colored even more, as her blush traveled over her throat to where her nightgown parted just enough to hint at the swell of her breasts. She didn't say anything but merely bit her lower lip and giggled in a way that hardly suited an intrepid world explorer.

"To be perfectly honest," he continued, "I'd gone quite mad with wanting you. I think I would have taken you right there in Hyde Park if the others hadn't happened along."

She still didn't look at him, but she smiled. "I would have let you, too."

"I'd never felt that way about an innocent before. All my liaisons had been with experienced women."

Her head shot up at that, and she stared at him with what looked like a combination of defiance and hope.

"I want to be perfectly honest with you about my past love life so that you can trust me completely with your heart."

The moment those words left his mouth, he realized how utterly true they were. He'd lied about a lot of things in his life, but not about his feelings. He bloody well wasn't going to start lying about them now, especially not with the woman he'd married.

"A woman's innocence is far too important a thing to toy with," he said. "If I was going to take yours, I'd do it only as your husband."

He meant that, too. God help him, every word of

that impossible proclamation was true. When had he sprouted a conscience? And how much was it going to cost him on down the road?

"I believe that," she said.

"Good." He breathed deeply again, and his shoulders relaxed. Amazing how much it meant to him that she believed him. "We have something quite remarkable between us. Something very precious and rare."

She looked at him straight on, but he could still read uncertainty in her face. "So you married me because you wanted to make love to me."

"Desperately." There were other reasons, honorable and less than honorable, but he'd remain silent about them for right now.

"And was I worth it?" she asked, smiling shyly and biting her lower lip again. A few days before, the gesture would have excited him. Today, after spending the night lost in her scent and learning how she sighed and moved and cried out in her release, the gesture inflamed him. She wanted to know if he thought their lovemaking was worth marrying her for. Very well, he'd show her.

"My dear Lady Claridge, why don't you come over here and get your answer?"

"My dear Lord Claridge," she answered. "You can't mean to have your way with me again."

"Why in heaven's name not?"

"But it's daytime, and the sun is out."

He patted the bed beside him, indicating she should join him. "The sun has seen lots of men having their way with women in its many long years. I hardly think we'll scandalize it."

"You're sure about that?" she asked.

"I have it on the best authority. In fact, the last time I asked the sun about this very subject, he told me that he delights in helping the newly married to explore each other."

She made a sound of sweet and evil laughter in the back of her throat. Dear God, she made him hot.

"Would you like to explore me further?" he asked, and held his breath waiting for her answer.

"The light was rather dim last night," she said finally. "And I do need to further my study of . . ."

He let himself breathe, and the sound came out like a groan. "Of?"

"Anatomy," she said as she gave him a wicked smile. "In the interest of my education, of course."

His anatomy was all too happy to further her education. It responded to the merest suggestion by getting hard and ready until it pressed upward against the sheet. "Then come over here, wife," he said huskily, "and let me educate you."

She walked to the bed, unfastening her robe as she approached. She dropped it into a puddle of linen at her feet, and Will let his gaze adore her body. Her breasts were small but perfect, and her hips and thighs lushly plump. The perfect female form.

He tossed back the sheet to let her see exactly what she did to him. Her eyes widened as she looked at his erection, but in contrast to the day before, her expression held no fear but only delight. He held out his arms to her, and she came to him. He held her tight as he rolled her onto her back and set to teaching her about love in the daylight.

Reggie Montrose had never found Bertie Underwood particularly appealing, despite the fact that the man had helped him to gain entrance to the prestigious Traveller's Club. Bertie always did things that he found in his own best interest, and he'd performed that particular favor for the reason he did everything—money. Reggie's family had more wealth than prestige, so he was always willing to relinquish some for Bertie's help when it suited him. If only he didn't have to spend so much time in the company of the annoying little twit to do so.

Right now he was spending seemingly interminable hour with the twit in the exact club the twit had helped him to join the year before. And the twit was pouting, damn him, which made him even twittier than usual, if that was a word. As Reggie watched, Bertie took a long swallow of the cognac Reggie had ordered for him and sighed like a man who'd lost his best hunting dog.

"Buck up, old fellow," Reggie said with a friendliness he truly didn't feel. "Things can't be that bad."

"She broke my heart, Reg," Bertie said.

"Reggie," he corrected. He didn't even like "Reggie" much, as he found it only slightly less repulsive than Reginald. He would *not* be called Reg, especially by a twit.

Bertie didn't acknowledge the correction but only sighed again. "Yes, indeed. She broke my heart."

"The Hamilton woman?" Reggie prompted.

"One and the same."

Reggie snorted. "You fared better than I. She almost broke my shin, and Claridge almost broke my nose."

"It served you right. You shouldn't have toyed with her," Bertie declared, and drained his glass.

"You've toyed with a few women in your day," Reggie answered. "You would have toyed with Hamilton, too, if she'd given you the chance."

Bertie set his glass loudly on the table between them. "You're talking about the woman I love."

"Oh, stop, Bertie. This is Reggie Montrose you're talking to."

Bertie gave him a wounded look but didn't object when he signaled for Bertie's glass to be refilled. A waiter in the club's livery appeared with the decanter, silently poured Bertie another drink and added a splash to Reggie's glass, and disappeared again with-

Taming Angelica

out a word. Reggie picked up his glass and took a swig. Damned good stuff, this cognac, and what you'd expect at a place like the Traveller's.

"So," he said after a moment, "I assume the wedding came off without a problem."

"Wedding?" Bertie repeated.

"The wedding. Claridge and Miss Hamilton. The one you've been sulking about all afternoon." Damn, but the man could be annoying.

"Oh, yes. The vicar's wife told their daughter, who told my cousin Muriel. It's official. Man and wife and all that rot."

"Well, cheer up, old man. Another American with lots of money will come along. They seem to be popping up everywhere." Reggie took another sip of his drink. "In the meantime, would you like to enjoy a bit of revenge against the man who stole the love of your life?"

Bertie's eyebrow rose. "Revenge?"

Reggie shrugged. "Nothing too serious. Some sport. Disrupt his wedded bliss a bit."

"I'd love nothing better." Bertie put his hand over his heart. "But alas, I'll be leaving London for some time. Pressing business, I'm afraid."

Running away from his debts and unsavory creditors as usual. "Pity," Reggie said. "I was sure you'd enjoy watching Claridge struggle to keep his new bride."

"A pity, indeed."

"I don't suppose I could help you with your business. A small transfer of funds, perhaps?"

That lifted Bertie's spirits, from the look of it. For the first time he lost the glum expression that had been grating on Reggie's nerves all afternoon. "How much?" he asked.

"Whatever you need to take care of your pressing business," Reggie answered.

Alice Chambers

"I say, that's decent of you," Bertie said. "But what would I have to do to help you with this revenge?"

"Just what you'd ordinarily do as a matter of course—find things out."

Bertie's eyes narrowed. "What sort of things?"

"Oh, I don't know. Anything that might make Claridge's married life difficult. Things he does that his new wife doesn't like. Problems he might have putting his hands on her money. Anything. When you hear it, you'll recognize it."

Bertie put his hand over his heart again. "I hope you don't think that I'd pry into anyone else's business."

"Of course not." *You bloody little twit.* "But everyone finds out everything about everyone else sooner or later. Just let me know what you've found out—sooner rather than later."

"I suppose I could do that. And who knows? I might even exercise some charm on Lady Claridge while I'm there."

Reggie almost choked on that. Charm? The charm of Bertie Underwood would be lost on any woman with functioning eyes and ears. He could hardly imagine Bertie's own mother finding him charming. "Why don't you leave charming Lady Claridge to me?"

"To you?" Bertie chuckled at that. At least it sounded like a chuckle. "After you tried to force yourself on her? I doubt she'll find you welcome, let alone charming."

"I'll apologize for that. After all, she came to my house unescorted and uninvited in the middle of the day. What was I to think except that she was looking for a bit of fun?"

"Your idea of fun and a woman's idea of fun don't exactly agree, Reg," Bertie said.

"Reggie."

"Who knows why women do the things they do?" Bertie added. "Especially a woman like Lady Claridge. But if she'd been looking for your idea of fun, she wouldn't have let loose with a kick to your shin, would she?"

Reggie gripped his glass tightly and took another swallow. "I made a mistake."

"Mistake?" Bertie grinned smugly. "Major blunder, old boy."

"All right, all right. You needn't natter on and on about it."

"So sorry," Bertie said. But he didn't look sorry. He managed to stifle his smile only long enough to take a hefty draft of his cognac.

"I'll apologize. I'll throw myself at the woman's feet if I must. I'll appeal to her sense of fairness. All Americans have a sense of fairness, don't they?"

"Never having been to America, I wouldn't know," Bertie answered.

"Of course, they have." And if they didn't, he'd somehow convince Lady Claridge that they did. "The whole bloody country's founded on the principle of giving a man a second chance, isn't it?"

"Whatever you say, old boy."

"Of course it is."

Bertie smirked at that. *Damn the man.* The only thing worse than an annoying twit was a smirking twit. "Besides, I have the one thing Lady Claridge has that her husband won't give her."

That at least got the insufferable smile off Bertie's face. "I say, what could that be?"

Reggie hadn't planned on revealing his trump card to anyone—except to Lady Claridge, of course. But it wouldn't do any harm to tell Bertie. Anything to get the man to stop smirking. He leaned toward Bertie and gave him a conspiratorial wink. "I have passage on a ship to South America."

"South America?" Bertie repeated. "Why on earth would she want to go to South America?"

Alice Chambers

"Damned if I know, but that's why she told me she showed up at my house that day."

"She told you that she wanted you to take her to South America?"

"That's what she said," Reggie answered. "After an overture like that is it any surprise that I expected a roll in the hay as part of the bargain?"

Bertie whistled softly between his teeth. "Do you think Claridge knows about that part of the visit?"

"I don't know. But I suppose you could make sure that he knows. As part of our transaction."

"I could at that." Bertie laughed a very evil laugh. He'd gone back to smirking. But at least this time it was at Claridge's expense, not Reggie's. "Say," he said after a minute. "Aren't you expected to be on that ship as part of some sort of exile?"

Damn, was there nothing that could be kept private from Bertie Underwood? "I managed to delay the departure."

Bertie straightened in his chair. "You managed to delay one of Her Majesty's ships?"

"I persuaded the cartographer—for a healthy sum—that his best interests lie in leaving for South America when I say it's time. No survey expedition accomplishes much without a cartographer."

"You clever dog."

Reggie set his glass down on the table between them and gently fingered the lip. If things went as planned, he'd soon be fingering the soft skin of Lady Angelica Claridge's bosom in much the same manner. Or at the very least, he'd convince her husband he was.

"So you plan to use the promise of a trip to South America to get La Claridge into your bed?" Bertie asked.

Reggie shrugged. "Either that or I'll help her to escape London and her husband altogether. In either case, Claridge is made miserable."

"You're a hard man to cross, Reg."

"Reggie." *Damn the twit.*

"Why do you hate Claridge so much, anyway?" Bertie asked.

"I'm tired of sucking hind teat because of him. I'm tired of taking his leavings. I'm tired of losing out to him in the race into a desirable woman's bed."

"The two of you have crossed paths before, I take it," Bertie said.

"More than once," Reggie answered. "Too often I've finally made it to a woman's boudoir only to find out that he's been there before me."

"Claridge is good with the fairer sex; I'll hand that to him."

"But he's never had a wife before, and now he does. That makes him vulnerable, by my estimation."

"And so we'll use her to have our revenge." Bertie raised his glass in a toast. "Mine for stealing my intended."

Reggie raised his glass to Bertie's and gave it a tap. "And mine for that thrashing he gave me."

Bertie tossed back the rest of his drink and laughed. "He'll regret the day he crossed us."

Reggie finished his own cognac and set the glass on the table with a clunk. "That he will."

Chapter Twelve

Only a transfer of accounts. A mere passing of the purse strings from a guardian to a husband. This little family meeting seemed innocent enough on the surface—only the newly wedded Lord and Lady Claridge having tea with the lady's maiden aunt and her solicitor. But Angelica knew perfectly well that this pleasant soiree sealed her fate more securely than the formal wedding ceremony had.

Her husband was about to receive total control over the money that furnished her day-to-day living. She would now depend on him for the very food she ate—not that he was going to enjoy that control, if she had anything to say about it. Besides, if she had read her loving husband correctly, he had a little surprise coming. She'd settle for letting him have this small victory now while she won the greater victory later.

"Now if you'll sign here, your lordship," Mr. Foxworthy said, indicating a spot on yet another set of papers. Will signed it in a firm hand. Mr. Foxworthy turned a few pages. "And here, sir."

Will wrote his name out with the determination of a man set on shouldering some heavy responsibility or other, when in reality all he was doing was accepting money he'd done nothing to earn. Of course, men made a great noise about what a burden marriage was to them, but who really benefited from the arrangement? It surely wasn't Angelica in this instance.

Mr. Foxworthy gathered up all the papers into one neat pile in front of him. "That's done, then," he said. "Lady Claridge's accounts are all in your hands."

"Thank you," Will answered, smiling broadly. *Curse the man.* He hadn't invented this system of female indenture, but he didn't have to enjoy it so blasted much.

"And may I take this opportunity to congratulate the two of you on this happy state of affairs," Mr. Foxworthy said, and followed it with a deep blush. "That is, the happy state of your marriage." He cleared his throat. "Oh, dear."

Aunt Minnie giggled and placed her hand over Mr. Foxworthy's. "We're all very pleased with the happy state of affairs and marriages, I'm sure."

Mr. Foxworthy turned an even deeper red as he gazed down at Aunt Minnie's hand.

"That we are," Will declared as he reached over and placed his hand on Angelica's shoulder. She didn't respond. They could all be as pleased and happy as they wanted. Their celebration didn't hide the fact that she'd just been handed from one owner to another like so much acreage.

But she still had a little surprise for her new owner. She smiled at Will, but took his hand from her shoulder and set it back firmly on the table. "Thank you for all your help, Mr. Foxworthy," she said. "I do have a question, though."

"Certainly, your ladyship."

"Those accounts are still to be held in trust, aren't they?"

"Why, yes," Mr. Foxworthy answered.

"So no one, not even my husband, may touch the principle, is that correct?"

"That's correct," Mr. Foxworthy answered. "Although the interest alone is quite a substantial yearly amount. You and his lordship will want for nothing." He stopped and cleared his throat again. "You wouldn't have wanted, in any case. Not with Lord Claridge's holdings, I'm sure."

She watched her husband closely for any sign of surprise or alarm at this news. His handsome features didn't reveal anything beyond a newlywed's bliss, the scoundrel. If he'd had any plans to run through his new wife's funds, he didn't give it away with his face. Neither did he betray the fact that his own personal holdings amounted to little more than what it took to keep food on his table and oh-so-elegant clothing on his back.

At least, that was how she'd understood his finances. Now she had to wonder if he didn't have a better understanding of her situation than she did of his. Honestly, what a way to embark on a life together—a life that was supposed to be full to overflowing with shared affection and trust. *What a farce.* She really ought to laugh.

"As you say," Will answered, that insincere smile still firm on his face. "Between my wife's funds and my own, we'll want for nothing."

She crossed her arms over her chest and stared at him. Was he truly going to be content with a comfortable life, or did he have grander designs for getting money out of this marriage? Would he say something

Taming Angelica

now, with Mr. Foxworthy sitting here ready to discuss finances? Or would he bide his time so as not to appear too eager?

"Still," he said. "I did have a vague idea that Angelica came into an inheritance of some sort upon her marriage."

Well, there was the answer to *that* question. "Oh, yes," she said, smiling at him sweetly. "I almost forgot my inheritance."

"Not that we'll need it," he added quickly.

"Of course not," Mr. Foxworthy agreed.

"But I should understand everything if I'm to be a good steward to my wife's interests."

"Certainly," Mr. Foxworthy answered. "I'm sure Lady Claridge would have it no other way."

"Certainly," she echoed, still smiling—although the effort made her back teeth hurt, as if she'd bitten into something too sweet.

"Mr. Hamilton will explain all the details to you, your lordship," Mr. Foxworthy said.

That finally caused a crack in Will's serenity, or at least in his smile. "Mr. Hamilton?"

"My father, dearest," she said. "You've heard of him."

"Of course, my love," he answered. His expression looked as though the pain in her teeth had moved to the spot just between his shining blue eyes.

"He'll have to approve of you before he transfers the money my grandfather left me," she added. "That shouldn't be too difficult for you, seeing that you're the brother of a duke and all. But somehow you'll have to accomplish it with you here and him in Boston."

"No, he won't," Aunt Minnie said. "Lawrence wrote to me the minute he heard the two of you were engaged. He'd booked passage for himself and the whole family on the next available ship."

Angelica straightened and gaped at her aunt. "He's coming here?" she demanded. "Now?"

"He couldn't let his younger daughter get married without meeting her husband, now, could he?" Aunt Minnie answered.

"But he's always so busy at the factory," Angelica said. "How could he leave it all to come to England?"

"I'm very sure I don't know about those things, but he's coming all the same," Aunt Minnie declared.

Oh, wonderful. All her wedded bliss needed was the addition of her father. "And he's bringing the rest of them?"

"Your mother, of course," Aunt Minnie said. "And Penny and that husband of hers. What is his name?"

Papa and Mama and Penny and John. All of them would soon arrive whether she wanted them or not. Heaven knew Will deserved this punishment for trapping her into marriage, but she didn't. She'd managed to get herself to England to get away from them, and now he'd brought them all down on her head again. Well, he could handle them—he owed her that.

She turned to Will. "There you are, then. My father will explain everything you have to do to get your hands on my inheritance."

Will finally dropped the pretense of perfect harmony and sent her a warning glance.

"That is to gain access to my inheritance," she amended. "So that you can manage it wisely. For my own benefit. I couldn't possibly manage it myself, helpless female creature that I am."

Mr. Foxworthy looked embarrassed again, and Aunt Minnie made some disapproving sounds in her throat. "Angelica, really. Sarcasm doesn't become you."

"Neither does responsibility, it would appear." She rose from the table and paced across the room to where sunlight spilled through the window onto the Oriental carpet. "I've been handed from father to aunt and now from aunt to husband without ever having my destiny in my own hands for even a moment. And now my father's coming here to see that the transfer has gone off without a hitch."

"We only want what's best for you," Aunt Minnie said.

"And you all have such definite ideas what that is, don't you?" She turned toward Will. "Prepare yourself, my dearest, because the person with the most definite ideas in the world about what's best for everyone is about to descend on you to tell you exactly what those ideas are."

"Angelica, that's no way to talk about your father," Aunt Minnie scolded.

"I look forward to meeting my father-in-law," Will said pleasantly, his composure back in place after the tiny slip. "I'm sure we'll have a number of ideas in common."

Aunt Minnie let out a tiny gasp and stared at him. "Do you really think so?"

"Absolutely. We both want to make Angelica happy. It's that simple."

"Yes, if you say so," Aunt Minnie sputtered. "I'm sure my brother means well, but he doesn't succeed often. At making Angelica happy, that is." She fiddled with her teacup and then her napkin. "Not that that should always be a parent's goal, mind you. Children don't always know what will make them happy, even if they're certain they do. In fact, sometimes you have to make them miserable to make them happy. It's a parent's duty, after all."

Angelica walked to Aunt Minnie and placed her hands on the old dear's shoulder. "Save your breath, Auntie. My husband has no idea what he's talking about."

Will glared up at her, for once honestly angry. *Fine. Let him simmer.* He'd brought her father down on them with his silly marriage idea, and now he could suffer the consequences. With any luck, just once—just this once—he'd listen to her for a change, and maybe they could come out of this mess with her father back in Boston and with a great deal of money right here.

When Mr. Foxworthy and Aunt Minnie had gone, Angelica walked to the sideboard and poured a quarter-inch of scotch into each of two crystal tumblers. Will stood in the doorway, where he'd returned from seeing the couple out, and watched her with a clear look of amusement in his eyes.

"I see I've married a drinker," he said. "I'm not sure I approve."

"I don't care whether you approve or not," she said. She raised one of the glasses to her lips and tipped a swallow of liquor into her mouth. She barely managed to gulp it down before she started coughing. The stuff burned. People drank it for pleasure?

She straightened and did her best to ignore what sounded like suppressed laughter coming from her husband. Holding the other glass out to him, she stared him in the eye. "Here. You'll need this."

He walked to her and took the tumbler. "Thank you. But surely your father won't arrive for some time yet."

"We might as well start getting ready for him now."

"Come now, Angelica. He can't really be the ogre you make him out to be."

"You don't think so?"

"No one could be," he answered.

"Sit down and I'll show you."

He stood where he was, his drink in his hand and a bemused expression on his face.

She molded her features into her best impersonation of Papa's squinty-faced scowl and glared at Will. "I told you to sit down, young man. Or are you hard of hearing?"

"No. I heard you."

"Then sit down," she thundered.

He jumped and looked at her as if she'd lost her mind. But he pulled a chair away from the table and sat in it.

"Yes . . . sir."

"That's better." She paced in front of him for a moment. "Put that drink down. I can't talk to a man who's drinking."

Will did as he was told and settled his hands into his lap.

Angelica swallowed the rest of her scotch and coughed it down. Then she set the glass firmly on the table and continued her pacing. "I don't know what's the matter with you English, anyway. What use is a man who drinks in the middle of the day? You ought to be at work—good, honest work." She stopped for moment and thumped her chest with her forefinger. "I've worked all my life, young man, whether I wanted to or not. No one gave me anything."

"Excuse me, Mr. Hamilton," Will said. "But I understood that you inherited your business from your own father."

"Don't interrupt me," Angelica ordered. "When I want your opinions, I'll ask for them."

Will fell silent, but a distinct smile threatened to steal across his face.

"Now, then. Where was I? Ah, yes, hard work," Angelica continued. "It was good enough for my father, and it's good enough for me. But not for the nobility, with your high-living ways, eh?"

"I'm sure I'm very sorry, sir."

She grunted at him, put her hands behind her back, and returned to pacing. "So you disgraced my daughter, did you?"

"I wouldn't put it quite like that," Will answered.

"Then how would you put it? The way my sister

tells it, the two of you were found making yourselves disgusting in front of God and the queen."

"I hardly think Her Majesty was there."

"Be quiet, young man. This is no joking matter." She stopped and scowled at him some more. "Young people didn't do those things in public in my day. We did them behind closed doors, where we could be properly ashamed of ourselves."

For good measure, Angelica placed an imaginary Mama in one corner of the room and turned toward her. "Be quiet, Katherine," she ordered. "This is between the boy and me."

Will made a strangled sound, and Angelica turned to discover that he'd turned bright red with suppressed laughter. She crossed her arms over her chest and glowered at him. "Well enough, you've married my daughter, and that'll have to be your punishment."

"Punishment?" he repeated, as he wiped tears of laughter from his eyes.

"Of course, a punishment. What do you think marriage is?" She pounded her fist into her open palm. "I expect you to take my daughter in hand. Chase these crazy ideas out of her head. Make her into a wife, young man. Do you think you can do that?"

"But she already is my wife."

"Don't play stupid with me."

Will straightened, and his eyes grew wide, as if he was finally going to take this seriously. "I'm not playing anything. Angelica is my wife, and I like her the way she is."

"Nonsense," Angelica barked. "She thinks she can make decisions for herself, say anything she wants. That's no way for a woman to behave, and if you're any kind of a man, you'll crush it right out of her."

"I'll do no such thing," Will objected. "I admire her spirit."

"Then you're a bigger fool than you look, Claridge."

"Now see here, Hamilton," Will answered, almost in a shout.

Angelica put her hands on her hips and stared at her husband. "For heaven's sake, Will, that's not how to do it."

"Well, I won't let him make me into a bully," he said. He appeared to mean it, too. She was beginning to understand Will Claridge, or at least she thought she was. This new knowledge buoyed her spirits. Did she dare hope he'd turn out to be an ally, after all?

"All right," she said. "You're not to become a bully."

He crossed his arms over his chest and managed to look offended. "I should hope not."

"But you have to pretend that you'll take his advice. You have to convince him that you'll do your best to turn me into a docile female just as he's done with my mother."

He harrumphed. "I don't like it."

"But you have to do it so that he'll give me . . . you . . . my inheritance. Then, once he gives it to you . . . us . . . he'll go away again, and we'll still have the money. Don't you see?"

"Very well." His eyes got an indecent twinkle in them. "And are you willing to pretend, too?"

"I?"

"You. Are you willing to play the dutiful wife in order to get the money?"

Good question. She hadn't figured on that part of it—only on Will's convincing her father that he could make her into a younger version of her mother. Things probably would go better if she played her part, but how galling that would be after resisting his domination all these years.

"All right," she said finally. "Yes. I'll play the dutiful wife."

He smiled, and the twinkle in his eye flashed into something hotter. "Then why not start practicing now?"

She knew what that look meant, and she always enjoyed its consequence. But she was in no mood to start surrendering so easily, at least not yet. She lowered her lashes and gazed at him out of the corner of her eye. "What do you mean, 'practicing'?"

"Come over here and sit on my lap."

"I don't think that's what my father means by obedient."

"I don't give a fig what your father means. I want you on my lap."

She toyed with the idea for a moment, biting her lower lip in a way that she knew aroused him. Then she walked slowly to him and sat on his knee. He turned his face up to hers to be kissed, but she hesitated. "May I ask you something?"

"Of course."

"Did you know that the money for my living expenses was held in trust?"

"I assumed as much."

She ran the backs of her fingers over his cheek and felt the beginnings of the stubble of his beard. "You knew that you'd be able to use only the interest on that money and not the principal?"

"That's how it's usually done in wealthy families, isn't it?"

She shrugged. "I just wondered."

"I wouldn't bankrupt you, Angelica, even if I could."

"I know that." And she did—now.

"I care for you," he said, looking up at her out of deep blue eyes. "More sincerely than you know, I imagine."

His words sent a little shudder of joy through her. It raced down her spine and set her heart to fluttering.

Taming Angelica

She ran her fingers through the golden silk of his hair. "Do you, Will?"

"Kiss me and find out."

That she did, and happily. She bent and pressed her mouth to his and tasted him. He slid his arms around her waist, circling her in his warmth, all the while his lips and tongue explored hers. Over and over until her heart beat frantically in her bosom and she could scarcely catch her breath.

He'd take her upstairs and love her now. He'd take off every scrap of her clothes and possess her, body and soul. Until she ached and cried out her pleasure, riding wave after wave of ecstasy. And once he'd sated both of them and they lay on a rumpled bed with their limbs entwined, she'd figure out how best to use him to get to South America.

Will sat in the chair by the fireplace in his bedroom and watched Angelica sleep in the aftermath of their passion. He'd tried lying next to her and watching her from there, but he couldn't maintain any sort of objectivity when he lay close enough to feel the warmth of her body and hear her even breathing. That near to her after making love to her, all his poor, male soul could manage was to lie there in awe of this magical creature he called his wife—to look on as the late-afternoon sun slanted across her forehead and made shadows of her eyelashes against her cheeks.

No, he needed to be able to think. So he'd arisen and taken up watch from the chair safely across the room.

What an ass he'd been. What a perfect fool. He'd thought he understood this marrying-into-money business, when he'd had no idea what he'd been about. One didn't simply find an heiress and marry her and expect the money to show up somewhere among her small clothes on the wedding night. Young women didn't come with satchels full of banknotes. Women of

Angelica's station didn't own their own money any more than he owned the family estate in Brathshire. Someone else controlled their purse strings, and the new husband had to dance to their tune to take over.

Still, all in all, as he looked at it now, he had to admit that he'd had a bit of luck with his marriage. Angelica's money truly was hers—left to her by her grandfather—not her father's. He'd have to talk Lawrence Hamilton into relinquishing it, but the man wouldn't have to be persuaded to give up anything of his own.

Angelica's father sounded like a perfect bastard, though, a bully of the worst sort. But his type usually had a blind spot where flattery was concerned. They thought themselves so exemplary, so infallible, so superior in every way that they could scarcely believe that any praise they received might be insincere. They took every compliment—no matter how outlandish—as gospel truth.

So if Will seemed eager to follow his father-in-law's instruction in marriage, Hamilton wasn't likely to doubt his motives. He'd just assume that Will had wisely taken his advice.

Angelica certainly seemed to believe that they could fool her father into thinking that Will would crush her spirit. Of course, they'd have to handle him more carefully than simply aping the roles of traditional husband and wife. The man wasn't likely to be stupid. But with any sensitivity at all, they ought to manage getting access to her money.

The real problems would arise after they'd obtained her inheritance. Angelica still harbored dreams of seeing the world—long ocean voyages and treks among the tortoises. He had nothing against such travel except for one thing: he had the Derby to win. This year.

It wasn't often that one had the right horse at the

peak of his performance at just the right time. Black Diamond was all of that and more. Black Diamond was Will's best chance at winning the Derby, and that would win his breeding program something money couldn't buy—a reputation. With a Derby winner, he could make a small fortune selling stud services and breed some damned good horses himself.

All that would take time. Time to win the Derby, time to find the right spot in the country for his stables, time to build the facility, and time to start making tomorrow's winners. Years perhaps. He'd happily take Angelica anywhere she wanted sometime after that, but no doubt "sometime" wouldn't satisfy her.

She rolled over in her sleep until she faced him, her hand tucked under her pillow and her chin jutting toward him. How like her the pose was. How full of defiance and pride. If he wouldn't agree to spend her money the way she wanted to spend it, would she feel he'd betrayed her? And if she felt betrayed, would she try to escape him the way she'd escaped her father?

Perhaps she wouldn't try deception or escape but would instead appeal to fairness. Perhaps she'd offer to split the money—let him keep some while she took the rest and went on her adventure. Not many husbands would accept a bargain like that, but she no doubt realized that he wouldn't hold her back just because of convention.

In principle, he understood equality and independence for both sexes, and in principle, he supported them. Practice, however, was quite another matter. In practice, equality and independence meant that she would leave him. He couldn't tolerate that, even if he knew she'd be coming back.

The truth was that he'd become so completely smitten with her he couldn't bear to be away from her for more than a heartbeat. Her smile in the morning brought out the sun. Her laughter sweetened his tea.

Their sparring kept him constantly amused. And at night he fell asleep awash in the warmth of her body.

He hadn't even let her use her own bedroom yet. He'd kept her with him even on nights when he'd already exhausted himself making love to her during the day and all he could do was hold her as she drifted off.

No, feeling as he did, he couldn't let go of her during this lifetime. Somehow he'd have to convince her to stay with him for a year or more while he got his business settled. Only how would he do it?

Chapter Thirteen

A fantasy place like Vauxhall Gardens was the last thing Angelica had expected to find in stuffy London. One had to take a little boat to get there, traveling with dozens of similar boats across the Thames as the sun set. When you arrived in the dimming light, it seemed you'd stepped off into a different world—one filled with music and laughter and garden paths that disappeared into the gathering dusk.

By the time Will and Angelica had taken their seats in their box, darkness had settled over the gardens, and the grove filled with clusters of people promenading underneath the flickering light of hundreds of lanterns. An orchestra in a garlanded rotunda started up a schottische, and Angelica's toes began to tap as if of their own volition.

She put a hand on Will's sleeve. "Let's stroll out there with the others."

"We'd lose the box and perhaps our supper as well," he answered, indicating the basket he'd carried from the landing. "You wouldn't hear of bringing any servants, remember?"

"Whoever heard of taking servants to a pleasure garden?" she demanded.

"Everyone but puritanical Bostonians who frown on any sort of indulgence."

"I'm not puritanical," she objected.

"Not where it counts, I'll admit. But you do have peculiar, democratic views about servants, my dear wife."

"I don't see what's so strange about my views," she said. "Why should I be treated like nobility?"

"Because you *are* nobility, Lady Claridge."

"Oh, yes," she said, waving a hand at him. "Well, I forget sometimes."

"Besides, servants can be very convenient." He glanced across the grove. "There, for example."

He pointed to where a man in livery pushed his way through the crowd, headed toward a box with several young ladies, their chaperons, and assorted servants. The man quickly and unobtrusively passed a piece of paper to one of the ladies, one who appeared to have been waiting for him to do exactly that. Then he disappeared again into the crowd.

"That fellow's just delivered an invitation to a tryst, if I read servants right," Will said.

"A tryst?" she repeated. "Where?"

"In the garden walks away from the light. It's done all the time."

"Oh, my."

"You needn't sound shocked," he answered. "We did much the same among the Duchess of Kent's marrows."

She blushed to remember that evening, when she hardly knew Will and his kisses were quite new. Things could certainly change quickly.

Taming Angelica

He bent and rummaged in the basket they'd brought, finally pulling out a parcel wrapped in linen napkins and setting it on his lap. "We should eat before the fireworks get started."

"Fireworks?" she asked.

"The highlight of the evening. They make quite a display."

Just then Angelica caught sight of a familiar figure in the crowd. The woman was strikingly beautiful, with hair just red enough to capture the eye but not so red as to be garish. She walked in a small cluster of people, all wearing the most elegant clothes imaginable. When she turned, Angelica caught the green of her eyes and suddenly recognized her—the woman she'd surprised with Will on the first night they'd met.

He chose that exact moment to look up from the cooked hen he'd been unwrapping, and he glanced from Angelica to the promenade before them. Was he looking for the woman? Had he seen her?

Angelica scanned the crowd again, but the woman was gone. She turned back to Will and found him smiling at her as though nothing out of the ordinary had happened.

Angelica shook herself. What a silly goose she'd become. Nothing *had* happened. That woman was bound to cross their paths again, and why not here?

"Did something upset you?" he asked.

"No."

"Good, then. Let's eat." He handed her a napkin and a plate with some roasted chicken.

Before Will had a chance to serve himself, another familiar figure appeared in the throng. Only this one headed right for them. Bertie Underwood.

"Well, well," Will commented dryly. "It appears we're to be honored with a visit."

"Must we?"

Bertie approached the box and tipped his hat to Angelica. "Lord and Lady Claridge, what a pleasure."

"Hello, Underwood," Will replied. "Out chasing down the latest scandal, are you? On the trail of some errant husband? In search of lonely heiresses, perhaps?"

Bertie placed his hand over his heart. "Why, Claridge, you cut me to the quick."

"No doubt. No doubt you've been cut there before once or twice," Will answered.

Angelica nudged Will's ribs with her elbow. Bertie was an insufferable little fellow, but she saw no reason to ridicule him. Maybe if they just ignored him, he'd go away.

"I only wanted to congratulate the two of you on your marriage," Bertie said. "I say, you both look radiant."

"Do we really?" Will looked toward Angelica with mock concern. "You are giving off a bit of a shine, my love. Are you quite well?"

"Honestly, Will," she chided, but she couldn't stifle her laughter completely.

"I've never seen Lady Claridge looking lovelier," Bertie added. "And she's never failed to look less than ravishing."

"Thank you, Lord Underwood," she replied.

"And so I'll give you my heartiest good wishes, Lady Claridge, even if your husband doesn't care to hear them," Bertie concluded.

"Thank you for that, too," she said. "From both of us."

"I'll just be off, then." Bertie walked a few paces toward the crowd and then turned around and came back. "Oh, I almost forgot. A friend of yours was looking for you, Claridge."

Will stiffened almost imperceptibly. "A friend?"

Taming Angelica

"The friend hasn't seen you for some time and would like to have a word."

Angelica looked from Will to Bertie and back. Bertie might be talking about that woman, or maybe about someone else. Whoever he was referring to, Will seemed to understand, and he wasn't overly pleased.

"Where did you see this person last?" Will asked.

"In that part of the grove, I think," Bertie answered, indicating an area near the rotunda with a wave of his arm. "I think your friend was going to wait for you there."

Will glanced in that direction, but his expression didn't reveal whether he recognized anyone there or not. "Would you stay with Lady Claridge for a bit, Underwood?"

"Happily," Bertie replied.

He turned to Angelica. "I'll be right back, my dear."

She didn't relish the idea of spending time alone with Bertie, but objecting would only make her seem silly and jealous. "Of course," she answered.

Will kissed her forehead and left the box, headed toward the spot Bertie had indicated. She watched him go and then turned back to find Bertie grinning at her in that insipid manner he had. "Would you care for something to eat, Lord Underwood?"

"No, thank you," he answered, still smiling. "I have everything I want. For now."

Something about his expression made her lose her appetite. She held her plate out to him. "Please. I wouldn't want to think I was keeping you from your supper."

"Oh, I say," he replied, placing his palm against his cheek in an expression of alarm that wouldn't fool a child. "How stupid of me. I quite forgot Muriel."

"Muriel?"

He continued his display with a bulgy-eyed show of

worry. "My young cousin. I should have been back by now."

Whatever reasons he had for dissembling suited Angelica just fine. If she could just convince him to go away, she might enjoy the spectacle of the gardens in peace. She might even enjoy her supper. "Then you should go quickly, don't you think?"

"You can manage on your own?" he asked, now feigning concern for her.

Really, the man was preposterous. "Lord Underwood, I'm a woman, not a child. I think I can sit here quietly by myself for a while without coming to harm."

"Just what he said you'd say," Bertie declared.

"He?"

He laughed nervously for a moment—covering up something *else*, no doubt. "Your husband. Says it all the time. 'My wife sits quietly by herself.' "

Will had never said anything of the kind. Who would? And he hardly said anything to Bertie at all. But discussing the point with the fellow would only keep him here. "My husband's quite right. I'll be just fine."

"Good evening, then. I'm off," he said. She nodded to him, and he disappeared into the crowd.

She looked back down at her food. Maybe with Bertie Underwood gone, she could find the stomach to eat it.

"Good evening, Angelica," a masculine voice said nearby.

Now, who could *that* be? She looked up to find Reginald Montrose standing at the edge of the box. Before she had a chance to send him away, he entered the box and took Will's seat.

"Lord Montrose," she said. "What are you doing here?"

"Why, thank you." He took her plate from her hand. "I think I will."

"I didn't invite you to join me, and I didn't offer you my food."

He gave her that smile of his—the one that made his very ordinary features seem perfectly repulsive. "Splendid evening. I can't for the life of me understand how your husband could leave you alone on an evening like this."

"He didn't. He'll be back in a moment, and I'd like you gone by then."

"Now, now, Angelica."

"And don't call me Angelica."

Montrose picked up the leg of chicken in his fingers and bit into it with a great show of gusto. She crossed her arms over her chest and watched him eat. With any luck he'd choke on a bone, and she wouldn't lift a finger to help him. After a moment he'd finished, and she handed him her napkin. Maybe now he'd leave.

"That was delicious," he said finally. "Aren't you having any?"

"Oh, for heaven's sake. That *was* mine."

"And thank you for sharing it with me," he said.

She raised an eyebrow and glared at him.

"Lady Claridge," he amended. "I didn't come here to make you uncomfortable."

"Then why did you come here?"

"Direct as always." He chuckled. "I came here for several reasons. One was to apologize."

She didn't answer, but sat staring at him.

"I behaved very badly the day you visited me at my home. For that I'm truly sorry."

"Thank you," she answered. "Will that be all?"

"But you must understand the picture you presented." His eyes got a nasty gleam in them. "We'd only just met—hadn't even been properly introduced.

And you appeared at my house, unescorted and looking good enough to eat. Under those circumstances, what's a poor fellow to do?"

"Why, jump on me, by all means," she said. "If a woman's had the audacity to visit you, she deserves whatever she gets."

"I've told you I regret doing that," he said, managing to look contrite. Or something like it. "But you must admit that your story about wanting to go to South America sounded fabricated. Why on earth would anyone want to go to South America? Especially a tender young thing like yourself."

"I'm neither tender nor a thing, Lord Montrose. And I'm through trying to convince you that I want to go to South America. You can believe me or not, as you choose."

"I do believe you. Now." He sat studying her for a moment, his ordinary features trying entirely too hard to look pleasant. "In fact, I've come to try to make amends."

Amends. What sort of amends could a man like Reginald Montrose offer for attempting violence toward her? From the look in his eyes, she probably didn't want to know the answer to that question. "I accept your apology, Lord Montrose. No further amends are necessary."

He lifted an eyebrow. "Really?"

"Really."

He leaned toward her—not much, just the subtlest inclination of his head. "I do hope so. Because I still admire you very much."

"I don't need your admiration," she said quietly.

"But you have it nevertheless. It would pain me greatly to think you harbored some ill will toward me."

What a ridiculous conversation. She'd told the man she accepted his apology. Why couldn't he just go away? "No ill will, Lord Montrose. Truly."

Taming Angelica

"Good, then. I've spoken to the captain of the survey expedition. A word from me and he'd be willing to find you a place on board."

She felt her own eyes grow wide at that news. "You could get me on a ship to South America?"

"It's the least I could do for treating you so badly."

Oh, dear heavens. The very last thing she'd expected him to offer and the one thing she could hardly find it in herself to refuse. But going to South America would mean leaving Will behind, and she wasn't ready to do that. Not if she didn't have to. It would hurt him too much; she could tell.

Then there was the matter of her inheritance. Her father was on his way from Boston to measure the worth of her new husband. If Will won his approval, they'd have enough money to buy a ship and head to South America on their own.

Still, if none of that happened—if it turned out that Will had married her only for her money, if her father refused to turn over her inheritance—where would she find herself then? With a man who didn't love her and no money to escape from him. And with her only opportunity—this opportunity from Reginald Montrose—gone.

Blast Montrose. Why had he, not Will, offered her this?

"I'll have to think," she said. "I can't decide such a thing on the spur of the moment."

He smiled broadly, clearly pleased at her indecision. "The ship won't wait forever," he answered. "Survey expeditions to South America are rare, and captains who'll take women are even rarer."

"The captain who brought Aunt Minnie and I here seemed happy enough to take our money."

"This is a Royal Navy ship, a ten-gun brig converted for scientific work. It's not a passenger ship and not meant for women at all."

Alice Chambers

"And yet you could get me onto it?" she asked.

His smile broadened. "As an effort to make peace between us and a token of my regard."

"Still." She took a deep breath. "I'll have to think about it."

"By all means, do," he answered. "Consult your husband, while you're at it."

Curse the man. He knew exactly what sort of challenge that was. "I make my own decisions, Lord Montrose."

He laughed, not pleasantly. "I'm sure you do, Lady Claridge. Only bear in mind that this offer won't stand indefinitely."

"Thank you. I will."

He put the napkin onto his plate and handed the whole to her. Then he rose and bowed to her. "When you've made up your mind, you know where to find me. Good evening to you."

"Good evening."

He left the box and joined the promenade. Angelica looked down and discovered she still held the plate, complete with napkin and bones from the chicken. Dear heavens, the man was rude.

She bent to place them in the basket and discovered something that looked like another napkin but of a different linen. After stowing the remains of what would have been her supper, she picked up the cloth from the floor of the box. It was a handkerchief. She turned it over and found an unfamiliar coat-of-arms embroidered on the other side. Lord Montrose's handkerchief, no doubt. He must have dropped it.

She looked up and scanned the crowd for him, but he was gone. At a loss for anything else to do, she quickly stuffed the handkerchief into her reticule and waited for Will to return.

* * *

Taming Angelica

Underwood had led Will on a merry chase, it seemed. Elizabeth Gates had been nowhere near the rotunda, and neither was anyone else who might have wanted to speak to him. He had seen Elizabeth earlier among the throng. If she truly needed a word with him, she'd find a way to contact him without Bertie's help.

Not that they had anything to discuss, of course. He hadn't even seen her since Lady Kimball's party. But still, after all they'd been to each other, he'd be a perfect cad to ignore her entirely. Happily, it seemed she didn't need him for anything tonight, and he could get back to his wife.

As he approached the box, he discovered another person sitting with Angelica, and not Bertie Underwood. He quickly stepped into a shadow so that he could watch unobserved. The man turned toward the light. *Bloody hell, Reginald Montrose.* What was that bastard doing with his wife?

Eating her supper, for one thing. In one hand he held the plate Will had prepared for Angelica. From the other hand, he was devouring the roast chicken. For her part, Angelica seemed even less pleased with Montrose's presence than Will was, as she watched the man with obvious disgust.

He ought to go over there and rescue his wife. Order the fellow out of his box with all the husbandly outrage he could muster. But Angelica could take care of herself, as she'd proved at Montrose's house the day she'd gone to see him. Besides, there was something about this particular conversation that seemed to hold her attention, and with more than just astonishment that the fellow would have the effrontery to approach her in a public place.

In fact, her posture—arms crossed defensively over her chest, back ramrod straight and inclined away from her visitor—demonstrated clearly that she found the man an unwelcome intrusion. But still, she didn't send him away, and she seemed quite engrossed in what he had to say.

There was only one subject on this Earth that could rivet her attention to a man who so obviously repulsed her—South America. She'd gone to Montrose's house that day in hopes of gaining his cooperation for her escape. Montrose wouldn't have forgotten that, and he was no doubt using it to make his way into her favor.

Will would put a stop to that. Now. But just as he was about to step out of the shadows and confront them, Montrose handed her the plate and rose. After a few more words, he departed, mixing into the crowd.

Angelica bent to do something, and Will strode up to the box. She was doing something with her hands in her lap when he got there, and she didn't see him until he was quite on top of her.

"There you are," she said, and gave him a smile that held a hint of worry in it—her eyes just a bit too wide and a slight crease to her brow.

"Underwood left you alone?" he asked as he entered the box and took the seat next to her. He sat and studied her for a moment, giving her every opportunity to tell him about Montrose's visit.

"Really, Will," she said instead. "I'm a grown woman. I don't need a caretaker."

What she needed was a conscience that forbade her to lie to her husband. But then, he was hardly anyone to lecture someone else about honesty.

"It's a husband's duty to fret over his wife." He took her hand in his and pressed his lips to the glove that covered her palm. "I hope I always perform my husbandly duties to your satisfaction."

She blushed and smiled honestly at that. "You always exceed my expectations."

He set her hand into her lap. "Good, then. Let me serve you some more supper."

Taming Angelica

She put her hand over her stomach. "Thank you, no. I'm quite full."

Another lie. He'd watched Montrose eat every scrap of food he'd given her before. "Angelica," he said. "Is there something you want to tell me?"

She paused for a heartbeat and then gave him the same worried smile. "No, Will. What would there be?"

"Please, my love—"

Just then the fireworks started. A rocket flew up from somewhere with a screech and a hiss and then exploded loudly, sending a shower of golden sparks out over the crowd.

Will spent the trip home in a fever of male territorial rage. Montrose had approached his wife in his absence, and although Will trusted Angelica's fidelity implicitly, he had no such faith in Montrose's character. Quite the opposite. Hell, he'd been in Montrose's position himself, and he knew all too well what a temptation a young, comely wife could prove.

The more he thought about it, the more his fury grew. The bastard had sat looking down the front of Angelica's dress. Just as Will was doing in the dim light of the carriage right now. Montrose had stared at her bosom, just as Will was doing right now—curse the fashion for low-cut bodices. Montrose couldn't have helped but notice how soft and plump her breasts were, just as Will couldn't help but notice right now. How they'd fit exactly into his palms, how the nipples would be wet and puckered after he'd run his tongue over them and taken them into his mouth to suckle.

Damn, who would have thought jealousy would make a man so randy? Perhaps it *was* territoriality, no more than a natural male desire to claim this female as his. Whatever it was, it had made him as hot as a schoolboy who'd found some naughty pictures.

Angelica turned from where she'd been looking out

the window as a darkened London went by. She caught the way he stared at her, and she took a sharp breath. The action pushed her breasts against the fabric of her dress. They seemed to swell as he watched them, rising and falling in an effort to be free. Calling to him, begging him to massage them until they blossomed in his hands.

"Will?" Angelica said, her voice already taking on the husky contralto of passion. And he hadn't even touched her. Yet.

He would need to go slowly. He would need to take utter and total possession of her. To do that, he had to take his time—strip away her every defense as he took off each piece of her clothing. Carefully and methodically, making her beg for more at each step of the way. He'd start by kissing her gently, sweetly, reverently.

He leaned toward her, and she responded by sliding over in the carriage until she was almost sitting in his lap. She parted her lips and closed her eyes and raised her face toward his. He kissed her softly, running his lips and then his tongue over her lips.

She twined her arms around his neck and opened her mouth to allow his tongue entrance. Groaning in the back of his throat, he acquiesced. He took her mouth hungrily, while she pulled herself against him, pressing her breasts into his chest.

He rubbed her back, knowing that the action would push her bosom even more firmly against him—and distract her from the fact that he'd started unhooking her dress. He pressed his face to her ear and blew hot breath into it. She uttered a little cry, and he nibbled at her earlobe, all the while still working at the fastenings under his fingers.

"Oh, Will." She gasped. "Should we?"

"Hush, my darling."

"But we're . . . the carriage," she whispered. "Oh, that feels so good."

Taming Angelica

"Hush, hush," he murmured into the skin of her throat. He kissed her all along her neck to her collarbone, pulling her sleeves over her arms to bare the flesh there. He nipped that gently and then buried his face into the valley between her breasts.

"Will," she cried. "Will, we can't. Not here."

He slipped his fingers into her corset and freed one soft breast, finally pulling the nipple into his mouth.

She moaned and ran her fingers into his hair, holding his face against her as he sucked and licked and teased her nipple into hardness. "Oh, dear God." She gasped. "Not here. We'll be found. Oh, dear."

But she didn't let him go, and he had to pull against her hand to move to the other breast, free it, and plunder it with his mouth.

She stopped all pretense of protest but arched her back, pressing herself into his mouth as she grasped at his head and made helpless noises in her throat.

He slid his mouth up the other side of her neck and groaned into her ear. "Do you want me to stop, Angelica?"

"No," she cried. "No. No-no-no-no, don't stop."

The devil could take reverence, and he could jolly well take gentleness, too. They'd already gone too far to take things slowly. He was going to have her in this carriage, just as soon as he thought of some way to get around all the clothing.

He took her hand and pressed it against the front of his pants. He'd grown so hard—so impossibly hard and aching and throbbing. She pulled her hand away only long enough to tear off her gloves, and then her fingers were back on him. Only the fabric of his trousers lay between her hand and his erection as she stroked his shaft and nuzzled at the tip with her thumb.

He slid his hands under her dress and sought frantically between skirts and petticoats for her hot flesh.

Just as he'd found the inside of her thigh, the carriage came to a stop.

Angelica sat bolt upright, her eyes wide, and her naked breasts rising and falling in a frantic rhythm. What a sight she made with her moist nipples and the flush of passion on her skin. "What are we going to do?" she asked.

"I can think of a number of things."

"Blast it, Will." She took his shoulders in her hands and shook him. "What are we going to do about getting out of this carriage?"

Good God, she was right. The footman would open the door at any moment. He searched the seat until he found her shawl. "Here, cover up with this. Quickly."

She'd just managed to put the shawl over her shoulders and naked breasts when the door opened, letting in a blast of cool air.

She raised her chin, tossed her head, and did her best to laugh. The sound came out more like a croak. "Well then, here we are," she proclaimed too loudly. "Home at last."

She allowed the footman to help her from the carriage, all the while still trying to laugh. Will found his hat and climbed out after her, only to find her grinning like an idiot at the footman.

"What an excellent job you do," she said, trying for a light tone and failing miserably. "Tom, isn't it?"

"James, my lady," the footman answered. James glanced nervously at Will, and Will placed his hat in front of his pants. Probably too late to keep the young fellow from noticing his condition, but hell, any man would understand.

He took Angelica's elbow and led her toward the house.

"My, it's late," she said, and gave a huge yawn. "I'm tired."

"Never mind all that," he muttered under his breath. "Come inside."

The foyer was dark and deserted, thank God. The minute he closed the door behind them, he tossed his hat to the floor and ripped her shawl from around her shoulders. Then he pinned his wife against the door, pressing himself against her everywhere.

"Upstairs," she whispered hotly into his ear. "Hurry."

"Too far," he grumbled as he grabbed her hand and guided her across the foyer and down the hall. He opened the first door he came to and led her into the center of the room until he bumped into something. He reached down and found the billiard table. Fine, the billiard room was where they'd ended up, and the billiard room it would be.

He pulled her against him and started in on the rest of the fastenings of her dress. She slipped her fingers between them and unbuttoned his pants, fumbling in her haste and making him wild with the pressure against his already throbbing hardness.

In a moment she had his member free, and she stroked it and petted it until she'd driven him quite mad. Under that assault on his senses, he could do nothing but stand, clutching her to him and trying to still the shaking in his knees. She'd undo him with her fingers. Somewhere, somehow, he had to find control.

A light appeared in the doorway, bringing with it rescue—and torture—as her fingers stilled. He held her against his chest, burying himself in her skirts to hide his state. He brought the edges of her dress together with his hands and glanced toward the doorway.

Newsome stood there, a candle in his hand. "You're home, my lord."

Yes, you bloody dolt, I'm home. Now go away. "As

you can see, Newsome. We're home. You can go to bed now."

Newsome stood there, the perfect butler and the perfect obstruction to the coupling and the release Will's body craved.

"I was checking on things, my lord, before I retire. I haven't secured this room as yet." The man made as if to step into the room. *Good God.*

"No need, Newsome. I'll lock up," Will said. "Now go to bed. As you can see, her ladyship is . . ." What? Her ladyship was what? "Indisposed."

Angelica laid her head on his shoulder and coughed. Newsome did enter the room at that. "Perhaps her ladyship would like a hot toddy?"

"Thank you, but no," Will replied.

"At least let me light some candles for you," Newsome said.

"My eyes," Angelica whimpered. "The light. It hurts my eyes."

"There, you've heard her ladyship. You're hurting her eyes. Now, good night," Will nearly shouted.

Newsome bowed. "Quite so, sir."

"And close the door behind you."

Finally Newsome obeyed, leaving them alone. Any other servant who entered would just have to watch them in the act because, Lord help him, he couldn't stop again.

He kissed Angelica frantically, and she responded with equal ardor as they pulled and twisted and tore at each other's clothing. His jacket came off and then his waistcoat. He finally got her dress undone, and it dropped to the floor, followed by her petticoats. She slid his shirt over his shoulders and pushed his pants down his legs. He left her just long enough to bend and remove his shoes so that he could be free of the trousers altogether.

When he rose again, he found that she'd scooted up

onto the billiard table and waited for him, her shift pulled up to her knees and her legs parted. Dear God, what a sight she made in the moonlight.

He walked to the table and caught her hips in his hands, bringing her to the edge so that he could drive himself home. She was hot and wet and so wonderfully tight as he entered her that he almost spent right on the spot. Somehow he found the strength to hold himself in check so that he could thrust into her, deep and long and hard. Over and over.

She moved against him, straining and raising herself up to meet his thrusts. She was a wild thing—driving him past endurance. Her cries came faster now, and louder. She was nearing her own fulfillment, and he needed only to hold on for her sake so that he could give her the earth-shattering release that promised to overcome him. He put a hand at their joining and found her sex—the bud between her legs that swelled for him.

He stroked her there and felt her muscles clasp him. *No more.* He could take no more. He rubbed her fast and hard as she moved with him, gasping and sobbing. And in a moment it was on her. She tightened all around him and her spasms started. Sucking at him, pulling him.

She released a hoarse shout just as he finished inside her. He gave himself to the pulsing waves of heat that started at the base of his spine and moved out. His body jerked as he emptied his essence into her. *Oh God, now. Now. And again.*

Extraordinary. Unimaginable joy. He rested his body on the table over hers, holding his weight on his elbows as she sighed and stroked his back and whimpered his name.

Chapter Fourteen

No matter how much it tried Will's patience, Angelica still hadn't volunteered the story of Reggie Montrose's visit to their box at Vauxhall. Now, three days later, he had to conclude that she didn't plan to tell him at all. While he found it a damned shame she didn't trust him with the information, he couldn't very well force the story from her, either. If he did, she'd surely bring up the subject of South America, and that was the last thing he cared to discuss with her.

At least the rest of the Boston Hamiltons had arrived, and they would prove a diversion from thoughts of sea travel. Angelica couldn't very well expect him to take her to South America if they were engaged in winning her inheritance right here. They'd have that battle later, and God help him if he couldn't convince her to stay in England.

For now he'd have Lawrence Hamilton to battle, and quite a fellow he was, too. No sooner had he set foot inside the house than he started bellowing orders. Newsome and the others were already scrambling to keep up with the man's barked commands when Will and Angelica stepped into the foyer to meet him.

Hamilton didn't look at all as Will had expected. From the way Angelica and Aunt Minnie talked about the man, Will had expected a burly fellow, capable of dominating everything around him with his physical presence. In fact, Angelica's father wasn't much taller than she was. They resembled each other in the color of their eyes and hair, too, although Hamilton had little of his hair left.

Angelica walked across the foyer to her father with a sort of grim resolve and planted a kiss on his cheek. "Hello, Papa. I hope your crossing was a pleasant one."

"Never mind the chitchat," Hamilton answered. "Where's the husband?"

Angelica made a little gesture in Will's direction, and Will joined them, extending his hand toward his new father-in-law. "Will Claridge, sir. I'm glad to meet you."

"So you're the blueblood." Hamilton took Will's hand and shook it, rather more firmly than necessary, all the while studying Will the way one scrutinized a stock animal. "Not bad, I guess, considering how much of my money it cost finding you."

"Thank you, sir. I've always aspired to cost a great deal."

Hamilton appeared to ignore that remark, if he'd even heard it, as he looked around. "Where has my wife gotten to?"

"Did you have her a moment ago?" Will asked. Angelica nudged him in the ribs.

"That woman could lose her way in a broom closet," Hamilton said, now ignoring both Will and his own daughter. On the one hand, Will really ought not to use sarcasm with the man who held dominion over a small fortune. On the other hand, Hamilton hadn't even seemed to notice.

"Katherine," Hamilton bellowed. "Where in hell are you? Don't you want to meet the Englishman your daughter married?"

More people appeared at the doorway—a tall man who didn't look like Angelica or her father and a pair of perfectly matched porcelain-doll women.

"There you are," Hamilton said. "What took you so long this time?"

"I'm sorry, my dear," one of the women said. On closer examination, the speaker appeared quite a bit older than her twin. She had to be Angelica's mother and the other delicate beauty Angelica's sister. "I wanted to see that the trunks were handled properly," Mrs. Hamilton said. "You know the clasp is loose on one of them."

"Good," Hamilton said. "Servants in England don't seem any better than the ones we have at home. You can't find good help anymore, can you, Will?"

"My people are excellent, sir," Will answered. Hamilton could act rudely to him all he wanted, but he'd better treat the household staff decently. Some of them had been with the family since before Will was born.

"Yes. Well," Hamilton huffed. "Let's get all the hellos and howdy-dos out of the way so I can see my room. It was a damnable trip."

Angelica stepped forward and embraced her mother, bending over to do it. "Hello, Mama."

Mrs. Hamilton held her daughter close and smiled. "Well, well. You're quite the grown and married woman now, aren't you?"

"I missed you," Angelica said.

"And I you." Mrs. Hamilton pulled back and held Angelica at arm's length. "You look wonderful. And what a lovely place this is. You must be very happy."

"Of course she is," Hamilton said. "She has a husband, doesn't she? And this big house. You probably have a castle somewhere, eh, Will?"

"Ah, no."

Angelica took her mother's hand and turned toward Will. "Mother, this is Will Claridge, my husband."

Mrs. Hamilton smiled. "Oh, my, am I supposed to curtsy?"

"Don't be silly, Katherine. Americans don't have to curtsy to anyone," Hamilton said.

"I'm sorry, my dear," Mrs. Hamilton said.

Angelica indicated the other couple. "And this is my sister Penny, and her husband John."

The younger woman did curtsy, and Will found himself staring at her. She was honestly and truly stunning, with wide-set eyes of an almost midnight blue, pale skin, and dark hair with golden highlights. But perhaps the most striking feature about her—and her mother's—was her size. Both of them standing on each other's shoulders wouldn't come near to the ceiling, they were so tiny. Their petite stature would make a lot of men feel protective, he supposed, but he'd only worry about breaking something if he touched one of them. Perhaps Angelica felt herself large compared to her mother and sister, but he'd happily take the larger Hamilton woman over either of the smaller versions.

Angelica cleared her throat, bringing Will back to reality. He bowed to Penny and extended his hand toward her husband. "Delighted. And welcome to London."

"All right, all right, all right," Hamilton snapped. "Next thing you know we'll get my sister into the act, and we'll never get out of this foyer."

"Aunt Minnie?" Will asked.

"Minerva," Hamilton answered. "You have her here, don't you?"

"She's not actually here, Papa," Angelica answered. "She stayed in the house we rented by the park."

"Not here?" Hamilton scowled. "You left your aunt all alone?"

"Aunt Minnie has a houseful of servants," Will said. She had the solicitor, Mr. Foxworthy, too, but Will didn't mention him. "She'll be fine."

"Don't tell me about my own sister, young man," Hamilton said. "She ought to be here with her family."

"She's enjoying her independence," Angelica said. "For once in her life."

"Ha!" Hamilton declared. "I can see you haven't drummed that nonsense out of my daughter's head yet, Will."

"I've only just started with nonsense drumming, I'm afraid."

"You have a lot to learn about being a husband, then."

"No doubt you'll have some hard-earned lessons to share," Will answered.

"Damned right I will."

"Dear," Mrs. Hamilton said with a gasp. "Your language."

"Never mind my language." Hamilton looked up at Will. "Now show me to my room so I can get out of this damned collar. And order me a bath. Your servants can manage that, can't they?"

"I'm sure they can find a tub and some water somewhere."

Hamilton made a disapproving noise in his throat, halfway between a harrumph and a grumble. "I'll be upstairs. Come along, Katherine."

He headed toward the staircase with Penny and her husband behind him. Mrs. Hamilton held back, still looking at Angelica. "I want you to tell me everything," she said to her daughter. "How you two met, what the wedding was like, everything."

"There's not much to tell," Angelica answered.

"But it's all so romantic," Mrs. Hamilton gushed. "The brother of a duke, and such a handsome man."

"Come along, Katherine," Hamilton bellowed from halfway up the stairs.

"I'll be right there," she called back. "I haven't seen Angelica for months."

"She'll be here when you get back down. Come along, Katherine. Now."

"Very well, my dear," she answered. "I'm coming. I'm sorry." She followed obediently after her husband, and the lot of them trooped up to the second floor, leaving Angelica and Will alone.

"Well, there you are," Angelica said. "My father."

Will crossed his arms over his chest and stood gazing up the staircase to where Hamilton would be ordering the furniture about by now. "Your description hardly did him justice."

"I tried to tell you what he was like."

"It seems mere words can't capture the true spirit of the man," Will answered. "What an ass."

Angelica took Will's arm and turned him around to face her. "You're going to have to stop doing that if we hope to get my inheritance."

"What?" he demanded.

"That," she repeated. "Sarcasm, insults, defiance."

"I?" He stared at her. "*I* have to refrain from defiance? This from Little Miss Insolence herself."

"Oh, really. You should have heard yourself. 'I haven't started nonsense drumming,' " she said, mimicking him. " 'I've always aspired to cost a great deal.' "

"You're the one who told him his own sister was enjoying her independence. How am I to convince him that I've dominated you if you persist in saying things like that?"

She huffed. "I suppose you're right."

"Of course I am. From now on we'll have to behave ourselves," he said. "Both of us."

"But Will . . ."

"Both of us," he repeated. He waited for a moment. "Angelica?" he prompted finally.

She waved a hand at him. "Yes, yes, yes."

Angelica had to behave herself, but she didn't have to enjoy it. In fact, she probably wouldn't even manage to enjoy her dinner. No matter how delicious the cook's dishes were, they'd probably taste like ashes by the time Papa was through with ruling everything and everyone around him.

Will sat at the head of the table—much too far away for her to be able to kick him if he decided to engage in a battle of wits with her father. She could only hope that he'd play his role, and she'd do her best to play her own.

Papa began before they'd finished their soup. He put his spoon down and stared at Will. "So, young man, what do you do?"

Will's spoon stopped halfway to his mouth. He set it back into his bowl. "Do?"

"Yes, what do you do?" Papa repeated. "Your occupation. Every man needs an occupation."

"Will's a lordship," Aunt Minnie said. "He does lordly things, I'm sure."

Angelica looked at the dear. Aunt Minnie had moved in under her brother's instruction, but Angelica would see to it that Mr. Foxworthy would call just as often as he wanted. No matter what happened with her and Will and the inheritance, Aunt Minnie would be happy, even if Angelica had to murder her father to accomplish it.

Now there was an idea. Oh, dear heavens, what was she thinking?

"Will can speak for himself," Papa said. "Can't you, Will?"

"Of course," Will answered.

"So then, what do you do?"

Angelica stared at Will. If he answered that he raised and trained racehorses, she'd die on the spot. Being Irish and owning a dry-goods store, as Aunt Minnie's poor Sean had, couldn't compare with the sin of having anything to do with horse racing. Why hadn't she thought of this and warned Will?

Will smiled pleasantly at Papa. "I do . . . animal husbandry. Yes, animal husbandry. That's my occupation."

"What in hell is animal husbandry?" Papa demanded.

"Please, my dear," Mama chided.

"Well, it doesn't sound decent, Katherine."

"Of course it's decent, Lawrence," Aunt Minnie said. "It's . . . well . . . something to do with animals. You explain it, Angelica."

Wonderful. She set down her spoon and turned toward her father, smiling sweetly, no matter how much it cost her. "Animal husbandry is an old and honored profession. It involves, um, breeding animals. For their desired characteristics."

"Not more of that natural selection nonsense," Papa said. He glowered at Will. "You aren't one of those Darwinians, are you?"

"No, sir. I'm a Claridge."

Angelica took a breath. Very well, she couldn't kick Will now, but she could do it later. "People in agriculture have practiced animal husbandry for years, Papa," she said. "Farmers, cattlemen, sheepherders—they simply mate the animals that have the traits they find useful. There's nothing sinister about it."

Alice Chambers

Papa looked at her as if he didn't believe a word she'd said. But how could he question something so obvious? Instead he turned to Will. "So what kind of animals do you husband?"

"Horses," Will said.

"What kind of horses?" Papa demanded.

"The four-legged kind," Will answered evenly. "So, Lawrence, what do you do?"

Papa's head came up at the sound of his name, and his eyes widened in surprise. No one called him Lawrence but Aunt Minnie, and she could hardly call him anything else. Even Mama called him "my dear," as in "yes, my dear." Angelica would have to kick her husband twice for that one. Swiftly and painfully in the shin.

"I manufacture corsets," Papa answered. "I have the largest corset manufacturing concern in the northeastern United States. We employ three hundred souls manufacturing our corsets, and you won't find a better corset anywhere for love or money. Isn't that right, John?"

"Yes, sir," John answered.

Mama put her hand on Papa's sleeve. "Do you really think we should be discussing corsets at dinner, my dear?"

"Corsets are what put the clothes on your back, Katherine," Papa answered. "They're what paid for passage here so that Angelica could find a husband. Corsets, not polite sensibilities."

"I'm sure you're right," Mama said. "But they're hardly pleasant dinner table conversation."

"We're all men of the world here, and those of us who aren't are women," Papa said.

"Impeccable logic, Lawrence," Will said.

Papa bristled at the use of his name again, but didn't comment on it. Will leaned back to allow the footman to remove his soup dish and replace it with the fish

Taming Angelica

course. When the footman was gone, he picke[d up his] knife and fork and smiled at Papa. "So you make tho[se] whalebone things that pinch women's waists and bruise their ribs."

Angelica looked at her husband in amazement, and—despite her best intentions—awe. No one had ever questioned her father or criticized him, that she knew of. And the expression on Will's face was as pleasant and serene as if he'd just made a comment about the climate.

The weather at Papa's place at the table grew stormier as he leaned forward, fork in hand. "The modern corset is a miracle of design, young man. Proven beneficial to the woman who wears it."

"If she doesn't want to breathe too deeply, I imagine," Will answered.

Dear heavens, she was going to have to do something to stop this or bid farewell to her inheritance.

"Will, *dearest*," she said, trying to make the endearment sound like the threat it was. "You needn't be so disagreeable."

Will raised his wineglass in her direction, and he smiled. Or maybe he was only gritting his teeth. "But, *darling*, you've often said exactly that to me."

She leaned across her plate and glared at him. "Yes, *my love*, but that was in private conversation."

"But *precious*," he replied, setting his glass down rather harder than he should, "you know you can hardly stand to wear one of the accursed things."

"Angelica!" Mama exclaimed. "Is that true?"

Aunt Minnie raised her own glass. "I should hope so," she declared. "In my day I stayed out of corsets as much as I could, too. They're horribly uncomfortable."

Mama gasped audibly. "Minerva! How could you say such a thing, and in front of other people?"

"It's true," Aunt Minnie answered. "And it's about time someone said so."

225

Mama huffed loudly. "Well, I don't think a little discomfort is too much to endure to look one's best," she said. "And my husband and John make the best corsets in the United States."

"Yes, they do," Penny said, easily doubling the words Angelica had heard her utter since she arrived.

"What feels best isn't always best for the body," Papa said. "Medical experts have found that a good corset improves the posture and straightens the alignment of the internal organs."

Will looked pointedly down the length of the table at Angelica. "And do you agree, *sweeting?*"

Oh, but she was going to have to murder him. He knew how she felt about corsets. He'd listened to her rail against them as unnatural, unhealthful, and oppressive. Now he was going to force her into defending them, all for the sake of a game she'd proposed. For heaven's sake, he was the one who'd made her swear to behave herself, and now look where it had gotten her.

"Well?" he prompted.

She took a breath. "If my father says so, *turtledove*, then it must be true."

Something crashed, and Angelica looked over to find that Papa had dropped his fork onto his plate. He'd dropped his jaw, too, and his mouth hung open wide enough to draw flies. She smiled sweetly at him and then picked up her fork and stared at the fish someone had put in front of her during this ridiculous charade.

"I expect you'll be wearing a corset more often then, *lambkins*," Will said.

She didn't raise her head but sat clutching her fork and staring at her fish. As soon as she was alone with Will Claridge she was going to throttle him with her bare hands.

Taming Angelica

* * *

"You two made quite a spectacle of yourselves tonight," Aunt Minnie said when the rest of Angelica's family had gone to bed.

Angelica watched Will walk to the table that held the decanters Newsome set out every night. He poured himself a stiff whiskey, took half of it in one swallow, and grimaced. For heaven's sake, how could he act like the aggrieved party? He'd made her promise to behave like a docile female and then gone on to make a perfect fool of himself.

"If this is your plan to win my brother over and get Angelica's inheritance, I must say I don't understand it," Aunt Minnie said.

"There's nothing to understand, dear heart," Angelica said. "My husband merely behaved like the product of a spoiled English upbringing that he is."

Will turned and glowered at her.

"He's still doing it," Angelica continued, "or he would have offered us some sherry. Heaven knows we could use it."

He managed to look ashamed of himself at that. "I say, I am sorry." He lifted the sherry decanter. "Aunt Minnie?"

"Oh, yes, please," Aunt Minnie gushed. "What a delightful idea."

He set his own tumbler on the tray and filled two tiny glasses with sherry, then crossed to the settee and handed them to Angelica and Aunt Minnie.

Aunt Minnie took a sip of hers and closed her eyes in appreciation. "All the things I've missed. Teetotaling is highly overrated, let me tell you."

Will walked back to the tray and picked up his whiskey again. Aunt Minnie opened her eyes. "Now, to the problem at hand," she said. "How to get Lawrence to relinquish your inheritance."

"We had a plan, or at least I thought we did," Angelica said, staring daggers at Will. "We were both going to behave ourselves so that Will could show he's made me into a proper automaton—pardon me—wife."

"Oh, dear me," Aunt Minnie said. "Is that how you act when you're behaving yourself, Will?"

"I'm sorry," he said. He downed the rest of his drink and put his glass onto the tray. "The man nettled me."

"I told you how he is," Angelica said. "I even showed you."

"I know you tried, but the man is so"—Will paused, apparently searching for the right word—"irksome."

"And yet you expected me to kowtow to him," Angelica said.

Aunt Minnie put a hand on her arm. "You must forgive Will, Angelica. He hasn't had the advantage of the constant browbeatings that you and I have had."

"Yes, please," he said, gazing at her out of his sparkling blue eyes. "I made a colossal mess of things, and I'm very sorry."

"Then I don't have to wear a corset if I don't want to?"

He looked positively sick. "Good God, did I really say that? I'm sorry for that, too."

Homicide would have to wait if he was going to look so handsome and so contrite. "Papa can be quite overwhelming," she conceded.

"And your baiting him was so much fun," Aunt Minnie added. "I've never stood up to him before. I had no idea how exhilarating it could be."

"You were magnificent, Aunt Minnie," Will said.

She giggled, quite pleased with herself. "I thought I'd die when you deferred to his opinion, Angelica," Aunt Minnie declared. "And on corsets, of all things. I've never seen my brother so astonished in my life. So speechless."

Angelica slipped an arm around her aunt's ample

waist. "If you enjoyed yourself, then the evening wasn't a complete loss."

"Well then, that brings us back to the original problem," Aunt Minnie said. "How to get your inheritance. As much fun as tonight was, you'll have to do better, Will."

He made a little bow. "Your servant, madam."

"I have an idea on that score, if you'd like to hear it."

"Of course, dear heart," Angelica answered.

Aunt Minnie's eyes took on an absolutely evil gleam. "You two shall have to surrender me."

"Surrender you?" Will repeated.

"Give me up. Discover me in the act of misbehaving and hand me over to the forces of decency and ladylike behavior," Aunt Minnie said, waving a finger in the air. "Turn me in."

"I don't understand, Auntie."

"I'll arrange for a secret meeting with Mr. Foxworthy, right here in the bosom of your good, upstanding home. You two will catch me enjoying myself and turn me over to be punished."

Angelica looked at Will. "Is this making any sense to you?"

"Some," he answered. "I think."

"It's very simple," Aunt Minnie said. "If Lawrence can be convinced that the two of you detest happiness of any kind, he'll willingly turn your inheritance over to you. As long as he thinks you won't get any enjoyment out of the money, or anything else for that matter."

"That settles that," Will said. "I have no idea what you're talking about, Aunt Minnie."

"Neither do I," Angelica added. "Why don't you just describe, a little bit at a time, what you'd want us to do."

Aunt Minnie set her glass on the table at her end of the settee and turned toward Angelica. "Well, I'd arrange for Mr. Foxworthy to visit me here, right in this sitting room. You could arrange for Lawrence to discover us kissing each other."

Angelica set her own glass aside and took Aunt Minnie's hands in hers. "Auntie, you've progressed to kissing?"

"Oh, my, yes. A long time ago. But don't interrupt me."

"That's right, *lambkins*," Will said. "Don't interrupt your aunt."

Angelica sent him a warning glance and then turned back to her aunt. "So we would discover you kissing Mr. Foxworthy."

"All three of you. Katherine, too, if you can manage it," Aunt Minnie answered. "Then you and Will would denounce me loudly, proving that you've become just as stuffy as Lawrence is."

"And you think that would convince Papa?"

"We'd all play our parts to the hilt," Aunt Minnie said. "You two demanding that I marry the man who's ruined me, and me demanding my independence."

"The exact reversal of when you ordered Angelica to marry me," Will said. He chuckled. "What delicious irony."

"But poor Mr. Foxworthy," Angelica objected. "It would break his heart for you to refuse him."

"He'll understand what we're doing." Aunt Minnie waved a hand. "He asked me to marry him long ago, and I accepted."

"Dear heart." Angelica threw her arms around her aunt and hugged her. "How absolutely wonderful. But you should have told us."

Aunt Minnie pulled away, a definite twinkle in her eye. "We would have soon. But we've so enjoyed having a secret. I declare, I've had so little mischief in my life, and now I shall have as much as I want."

"Of course you shall," Will said. "Congratulations, Aunt Minnie. Well done, indeed."

"Do you think Papa will believe we're a properly married couple if we insist that you marry Mr. Foxworthy?"

"He will if you make it clear that marriage is my punishment," Aunt Minnie said. "You see, to the properly moral person these days everything must be a punishment and a burden. Or it isn't . . . well . . . proper."

"That's what you meant about getting no enjoyment from the money or anything else," Will said.

Aunt Minnie clapped her hands together with glee. "Exactly. If I were to ask Lawrence's permission to marry, he'd most certainly turn me down. But if he can make marriage into a punishment, he'll insist on it."

"How perfectly devious," Will said. "And exactly what the man deserves."

"But surely you don't need Papa's permission to marry," Angelica said.

"Of course not, my dear. I'd marry Mr. Foxworthy if the archangel Gabriel himself denounced the match. But don't you see? Tricking Lawrence into giving his blessing makes the victory that much sweeter."

"Aunt Minnie, you have my undying admiration," Will declared. "What do you say, *lambkins?* Shall we give the plan a try?"

"Of course. If nothing else, it will get Aunt Minnie married to Mr. Foxworthy," she said. "But for heaven's sake, stop calling me that."

Chapter Fifteen

Angelica would love Black Diamond. Will would make sure the stallion captured her heart. Somehow. Or if not her heart, exactly, perhaps her imagination. Once she'd seen the horse run, she'd have to understand why their future lay here, in England, at least for the next several years.

He took her hand and raised it to his lips as, out on the practice track, his jockey guided his finest thoroughbred up to the starting line. He glanced over Angelica's head to Jonesy. "Ready, Mr. Jones?"

"Yes, my lord."

"Then let Black Diamond run."

"Yes, sir." Jonesy raised a pistol over his head and fired one shot into the air. Black Diamond didn't even need a touch of the whip, but took off at the sound of the gun, running as though the devil were chasing him. The jockey needed only to keep his seat to have the ride of his life.

Horse and rider rounded the first curve and bore

down on where Will and Angelica stood. Black Diamond's nostrils flared and his hooves thundered, kicking up clods of the track and sending them flying in his wake. Will slid an arm around Angelica's waist and pointed toward the horse as it flew by. "See how long his stride is. That's how he covers ground so quickly."

She followed the horse with her eyes. "He's very beautiful."

"There's more than beauty involved. There's soul. There's spirit."

"Very, very beautiful," she said.

"His sire and dam were both champions," Will said. "He comes from a long line of champions, but he's the best of the lot."

Angelica didn't answer but watched in silence as Black Diamond approached the far turn. Will pulled her closer, as if he could imbue her with his enthusiasm by holding her tightly.

Black Diamond negotiated the turn and headed back toward them. Will pointed to him again. "See how broad his chest is. That means he has a large heart."

Angelica looked at him out of the corner of her eye. "He's kindhearted?"

"His heart is big," Will corrected. "It pumps great quantities of blood. It has to if he's to maintain this pace."

"Oh." She looked back down the track and watched Black Diamond running back toward them at an impossible speed.

"He's the perfect Derby horse, and he's in the perfect condition at the perfect time."

"He's very, very, very beautiful," she said. "Indeed."

Will studied her. She was either being obstinate, or she'd missed his point altogether. His wife wasn't stupid, so he'd have to settle on obstinate. Only why? Perhaps she could sense that only this—his hopes for the Derby and continuing Black Diamond's line under his ownership—posed any opposition to his taking her to South America.

He did plan to take her to South America, of course. But not for some years. South America and the finches and the tortoises would still be there. She'd have to see the reasons he needed to stay here for the time being. She'd just have to.

Black Diamond crossed the finish line, and Jonesy checked his watch. "Two minutes and twenty seconds, sir," he called.

"Well done," Will shouted. "His best time yet."

"Congratulations, sir," Jonesy added.

"Thank you." Will watched as the jockey led Black Diamond back to where they stood. The horse was lathered and wide-eyed, but still he danced as though he could escape his rider and do it all over again.

"He is magnificent," Angelica said softly.

"He'll do even better in a field of horses," Will said.

She cocked her head. "He runs better in a crowd?"

"He's a terrific competitor. Can't stand to have another horse beat him. What spirit. What intelligence."

"He's a horse, Will."

"Animals have sensibilities," he answered. "You talk of your tortoises as though they have purpose."

"*I* mean it figuratively when I say it."

"Well, I don't. Black Diamond's a winner, and he knows it better than the rest of us." Will looked up at the jockey. "Good job. Take him in and rub him down."

The jockey nodded and walked Black Diamond off toward the stables. Will turned Angelica toward him and gazed into her face. "I want you to understand something, my wife. I do have dreams of my own. I know you think me a shallow, spoiled fellow—little more than a scoundrel. But this is important to me. As important as freedom to explore is to you."

She touched his cheek. "I know, Will. And as soon

Taming Angelica

as we've seen the world, we'll come right back here. You can start up the most extravagant, expensive stables in all of England."

"But you don't understand, my darling," Will said.

"There you are, Claridge," a male voice said from nearby. "And with your new bride, too."

Will glanced along the fence and found Reggie Montrose lounging against the planks, only a few yards away. He had an insolent, indecently self-satisfied look on his face as he pushed away from the boards and approached Will and Angelica.

Angelica stiffened immediately. She stepped away from Will and turned to watch Montrose approach. The man walked straight up to her and reached down to take her hand, even though she hadn't offered it.

"Lady Claridge," he said, holding her fingers close to his lips. "You look lovelier every time I see you."

Angelica pulled her hand away. "Lord Montrose."

"I thought I might find the two of you here," Montrose said.

"Bertie Underwood keeping you up-to-date on our whereabouts is he?" Will asked.

Montrose's eyebrows rose, making his aspect even more insufferable, if that was possible. "Underwood?"

"The two of you have been quite thick of late," Will answered. "Just the other night at Vauxhall I left my wife with him, only to have you visit her instead."

Angelica's head shot around, and she stared at him wide-eyed. Clearly she hadn't known he'd seen her with Montrose. Keeping the knowledge from her any longer served no purpose. And he wasn't about to let Montrose think she hadn't confided in him.

"Lady Claridge told you of our little tête-à-tête?" Montrose asked.

"My wife keeps no secrets from me."

"Then I'm sure she told you I left something behind in your box," Montrose replied smoothly. He smiled down at Angelica. "My handkerchief, Lady Claridge, if you're quite done with it."

"Done with it?" she repeated. "I didn't use it for anything. You dropped it."

"Perhaps you've forgotten," Montrose said and then stopped suddenly. "But of course, you're quite right. I dropped it."

Will didn't say anything but just watched the man maneuver. If he hadn't seen their interaction at Vauxhall that night, he'd swear that Angelica was now hiding some secret use of Montrose's handkerchief. He knew damned well she wasn't, so obviously Montrose had calculated to make Will jealous. How he'd love to give the bounder another black eye.

"I don't have it here, in any case," she answered quickly. "It's at the house."

"Perhaps some afternoon I could call on you to retrieve it, Lady Claridge."

"Send a footman around for the thing," Will answered. "We'll happily surrender it."

"As you say, Claridge." Montrose turned to Angelica and gave her another of his oily smiles. "Good day, Lady Claridge."

"Good day to you, sir," she answered, clear dismissal ringing in her tone.

Montrose walked away, and Angelica watched him until he was well out of earshot. Then she turned on Will. "You knew he visited me at Vauxhall."

"I saw the two of you together."

She put her hands on her hips. "And you said nothing?"

"You didn't say anything either. Why is that, I wonder?"

"I didn't see any need to upset you." She was lying. He could tell from the way she dropped her hands to her sides and avoided his gaze.

Taming Angelica

"You didn't think the fact that you'd keep secrets from me would upset me?" he demanded.

"I didn't know you'd seen him with me." She looked up at Will finally. "The man seems intent on making you jealous for some reason. I didn't want to give him the satisfaction."

"That bastard can't make me jealous," Will answered, peering down into her face. "Unless I have reason to think you're keeping things from me."

She narrowed her eyes as she studied him. "What things?"

"Why don't you tell me?"

"You're a fine one to talk about secrets," she said, lifting her chin. "Who was it you went to see that night?"

"See?" he repeated.

She crossed her arms over her chest. "Your friend. By the rotunda. A lady, no doubt."

"There was no one there. Underwood sent me off after no one. He and Montrose are working together; I can feel it. Don't trust either of them."

"But you thought someone was waiting for you there, didn't you?" she said.

"Yes."

"A lady?"

"It wasn't to be a tryst, if that's what you're thinking," he said.

"But it was a lady you went to meet."

"Damn it all, yes."

"I don't trust either of the Lords Montrose or Underwood," she said. "I'd like to think I can trust you."

"You can, Angelica." *Oh, hell.* Somehow this had started out to be about her secrets and ended up his fault. How had she managed it?

"Take me home, Will. Please."

Alice Chambers

* * *

Angelica had had quite enough of racehorses, arguments, and men named Montrose, thank you very much. And she'd had enough of Will's questioning, too. Really, if she could trust him enough to let him run off after former lovers, he could trust her enough to keep her own confidences about visits from loathsome people like Reginald Montrose.

Besides, it was time to catch her maiden Aunt Minerva in the act of disgracing herself. Rather past time to catch them, actually. The two of them might have been kissing for several minutes now, and who knew what state they'd be in if she didn't find her sulking husband soon?

Really. Aunt Minnie and Mr. Foxworthy being intimate with each other. What a picture they'd make. *How perfectly delightful.*

She tiptoed up to the sitting room door and tapped softly on it. She gave Aunt Minnie and Mr. Foxworthy several seconds to compose themselves and then opened the door a crack.

She didn't look inside, but merely put her face up to the opening. "Pssst. It's Angelica. Are you two ready?"

"My, yes," came Aunt Minnie's answering warble. "Proceed."

"Not so loud," she whispered. "Papa can't know we planned this."

"We're ready," Aunt Minnie said, more softly this time.

She eased the door shut again and looked around. Will finally appeared from the other end of the corridor, and she waved her hand to him.

"Where have you been?" she demanded in a hoarse whisper.

"Preparing," he answered.

She placed her fingers over his lips. "Shh. Do you want Papa to hear you?"

Taming Angelica

He took her hand in his and removed it from his mouth. "You're being a little melodramatic, don't you think?" he whispered.

"This has to work. Both for our sake and for Aunt Minnie's."

"Well then, let's get on with it."

"All right." She took a breath and flung open the door. "Oh, Aunt Minnie," she cried. "How could you?"

Aunt Minnie and Mr. Foxworthy were together on the settee, their arms draped around each other. Mr. Foxworthy made as if to pull back, but Aunt Minnie held on to him firmly. "Edward," she declared loudly, "we've been discovered."

Mr. Foxworthy blushed furiously, but he held his head high. They all waited for the clatter of footsteps, Papa shouting, anything, but the only sound came from the ticking of the grandfather clock in the hallway.

For heaven's sake, Papa never let anything get by him in Boston. Where was he now?

She looked over to Will for help and found him shaking his head and trying not to laugh. She frowned at him and motioned with her hands for him to do something. He straightened and wiped the smile off his face—almost. "Yes, Aunt Minnie," he shouted. "Lawrence will be shocked."

Curse him. He knew he shouldn't call Papa by his first name. She put her hands on her hips and glared at him.

"That is, Mr. Hamilton," he said. He walked to the door and stuck his face into the corridor. "Mr. Hamilton," he bellowed toward the staircase. "Your brother. I'm glad he isn't here to see this."

Will stepped back inside the sitting room and shrugged. "If he didn't hear that, he's deaf."

Sure enough, a flurry of footsteps sounded from

upstairs. Angelica stood and straightened her skirts, waiting for her father to arrive.

It didn't take long. Lawrence Hamilton barged into the room, followed by his wife. He took one look at his sister and her beau tangled around each other and came to a complete halt. His face registered surprise and then fury. "Unhand my sister, you cad," he shouted.

Mr. Foxworthy removed his arms from Aunt Minnie, but she caught his hands and held them in her lap. "There's no reason to upset yourself, Lawrence."

"No reason?" Papa sputtered. "No reason to upset myself? I come in here to find this man molesting you, and I'm not to upset myself?"

"He wasn't molesting me," Aunt Minnie said calmly. "He was kissing me."

"Kissing?" he repeated as if he didn't understand the word. "Kissing? Dear God in heaven." He turned toward Angelica. "This is your doing, I suppose. You put her up to this."

Angelica opened her eyes as wide as they would go, trying desperately to look like the wounded innocent. "No, Papa. Truly."

Papa spun and glowered at Will. "You did this, then."

Will straightened to his full height and looked down his nose at Papa. "Certainly not, sir. We have a decent, upstanding household here."

"Well then, it was his idea," Papa said, pointing to Mr. Foxworthy. "And I'm going to beat the tar out of him."

"Now, Lawrence," Mama said quietly.

"Who in hell are you, anyway?" Papa demanded.

"Edward Foxworthy," Aunt Minnie's beau said, rising from the settee. "And I intend to marry your sister."

"Not until I've flattened your face, you won't," Papa

answered. He shrugged out of his jacket and held it out to Mama. "Take this while I pound him into a pulp."

"I'll do no such thing," Mama answered.

Papa huffed and slipped back into his jacket. "Just count your blessings that my wife is here, Foxworthy."

Angelica flew to Will's side and tucked herself under his arm, the very picture of feminine helplessness. At least she hoped so. What did she know about such things? "Oh, it's too horrible," she said. "My own aunt in my own sitting room. Such behavior."

"Don't exert yourself, my dear," Will answered in the most patronizing manner possible. If he ever did that in earnest, she'd have to box his ears.

"But whatever will we do?" Angelica wailed. "Aunt Minnie's disgraced herself, and marriage at her age would be so unseemly."

Papa watched her while she did her utmost to simper. She'd watched Mama and Penny do it over the years, so she had some idea how a virtuous woman was supposed to act in this sort of situation. Still, this was a decided change from her past behavior. Would Papa believe it?

She smiled at him and then turned toward her mother. "What do you say, Mama? Can we allow Aunt Minnie to be a disgraced bride at her age?"

Mama looked uncertain, and no wonder. The way Angelica had put it, neither alternative—disgrace or an unseemly marriage—could hold much appeal. "I don't know," Mama said. "We may not have a choice in the matter."

"Well, I do," Aunt Minnie declared with a wave of her hand. "I don't intend to marry anyone. I've finally discovered my freedom, and I plan to make the most of it."

Mr. Foxworthy looked at Aunt Minnie in feigned alarm. At least Angelica hoped it was feigned. The

Alice Chambers

whole idea behind this plan was to join the two of them in matrimony, and there was no point in upsetting the poor man.

"Minerva," he declared, placing his hand over his breast. "We had an understanding."

"Don't worry, Edward," Aunt Minnie said. "We'll simply carry on as we have. We don't need to be married to express our love."

Angelica put the back of her hand to her forehead and let her eyelids flutter open and shut. That was what one did before one fainted, wasn't it? Will cleared his throat beside her and gave his head the tiniest of shakes. Maybe she was overdoing her act a little.

"That settles it," Papa said. "If you're going to carry on, Minerva, you're going to have to pay the piper. I insist you marry this man." He turned to Mr. Foxworthy. "What was your name again?"

"Foxworthy, sir. Edward Foxworthy."

"You just got yourself a wife, Foxworthy," Papa said.

"I won't get married just because you tell me to, you bully," Aunt Minnie said. "I won't do it, and you can't make me."

Angelica watched her aunt in amazement. Had she herself ever sounded that obstinate? She'd resisted marrying Will in much the same manner, but she'd had good reason. Oh, well, she had no time to worry about that now. Just one more touch to her performance and the scene would be complete.

"Papa's right," she said. "You must marry Mr. Foxworthy or the whole family will be humiliated." She glanced over at her mother. "Won't we, Mama?"

Mama looked uncertain, but she could always be counted on to echo Papa's sentiments exactly. "Yes, Minerva," Mama said after a moment. "You've made your bed and now you must lie in it."

Taming Angelica

"Katherine!" Papa exclaimed. "Watch what you say."

"Only a figure of speech, my dear," Mama added. "I'm very sorry, I'm sure."

"Very well," Aunt Minnie said, hanging her head. "I will marry you, Mr. Foxworthy."

Well, that was that. They'd accomplished Aunt Minnie's purpose—to win Papa's permission to marry, something he'd never have given of his own free will. Now if only he'd surrender Angelica's inheritance, too.

Every bone in Angelica's body told her that as people, women were at least equal in worth to men. But a few hours in the company of the women of her family invariably made her wish for the solace of a monastery. And now for an entire week, she'd had to act exactly like the rest of them. If Papa didn't volunteer her inheritance soon, she'd have to demand it out-and-out. She couldn't tolerate much more sweetness and light without screaming.

This morning she could only hope that this "pleasant cup of tea and chat" would convince her mother of her conversion to the feminine way of things and thereby hasten the end of her ordeal.

"If you must do this, Minerva," Mama was saying, "at least do it properly."

"I don't know why you insist on making this marriage sound like a disgrace," Aunt Minnie said. "I'd think it much more a disgrace if I weren't to marry Edward."

"Yes," Angelica tossed in. "In this case, marriage is certainly the lesser of two evils, don't you agree, Mama?" *God forgive me for that one. And while you're about it, Lord, please bring an end to this farce.*

"I suppose it must be," Mama said, but she didn't

look convinced. In fact, she looked like she smelled something that wasn't quite right. How dare she sit in judgment on Aunt Minnie's happiness like that?

"It's either marriage or Edward and I will live in sin," Aunt Minnie added. "You've never favored fornication before, Katherine. Have things changed back in Boston?"

"How can you even speak of fornication?" Mama demanded.

"Yes," Penny chimed in. "A woman of your age."

"Oh, we plan to fornicate." Aunt Minnie lifted her teacup and looked sweetly over the rim as if she were discussing the weather. "We plan to fornicate morning, noon, and night. We may not even wait until the wedding."

"Please, Auntie," Penny begged. "Stop."

"When a woman reaches my age, she must fornicate as much as she can or miss the opportunity. I've already missed too many opportunities."

"But, Auntie," Angelica said. "I'm not sure it's considered fornication if you're married."

Aunt Minnie hoisted her cup in a toast. "Whatever it's called, then, we plan to do it. Often."

Penny set her own cup on the table and raised her palm to her forehead. "How perfectly distasteful even to contemplate. You and Mr. Foxworthy, doing . . . that. How perfectly unpleasant."

Angelica clutched at her teacup. Maybe that way she could keep her hands from reaching across the table and slapping her sister silly.

"Whatever Minerva and her husband do in private is their business," Mama said. "Their wedding is quite another matter. It needs to be done correctly."

"We'll be married by the vicar here and then return to Edward's house," Aunt Minnie said. "What more needs to be done?"

Taming Angelica

"What more?" Mama rolled her eyes toward heaven. "A great deal more. You're a Hamilton, and the proper conventions must be observed."

"Oh, my, yes," Angelica said. At least that protestation didn't carry any content.

"I don't see why I should observe any convention," Aunt Minnie answered.

"Because otherwise people will think something has gone amiss. You don't want people to think you've been disgraced, do you?" Mama asked.

"I was married quickly and quietly," Angelica pointed out.

Mama turned toward her, fire in the depths of her dark blue eyes. "You *were* disgraced, Angelica. All that saved your marriage was the fact that you'd caught such a desirable husband."

"I'm very sorry, Mama, I'm sure," Angelica said, as a headache started up behind her left eyelid. What a staggering impossibility that Angelica might have succeeded in trapping a desirable husband. Angelica, not Penny, of whom such female triumphs were to be expected.

"Well, I'm sick of talking about disgraces," Aunt Minnie proclaimed. "I don't want to hear the word again for the rest of the day. Then maybe we can find more pleasant things to discuss. And maybe not, but at least we will have tried."

"That's all very well for you to say," Mama replied. "We can agree not to discuss England if you want, but that won't make the place disappear."

"Mama's right," Penny said. "We need to face reality."

"Reality." Aunt Minnie snorted. "What did reality ever do for me, I'd like to know."

"But you've always had a lovely home with us," Mama said. "You've always been so happy."

Alice Chambers

"I was content," Aunt Minnie corrected. "There's a difference. My own father and brother saw to it that contentment was all I ever had. Now I plan to be happy, and I'd thumb my nose at anyone—even my father, God rest his soul—who tried to keep me from it. Happiness, that is."

Mama let out a little grunt of disapproval, and Penny made a face.

"I want to ask your forgiveness, Angelica," Aunt Minnie said.

"Why, whatever for?" she answered, simpering to the very best of her ability.

"I tried to keep you from your dream. I didn't understand about freedom until I'd found it for myself," Aunt Minnie said.

"Really, Minerva," Mama said.

"Yes, really, Aunt Minnie. I've forgotten all that nonsense about travel." That did it. Now the Lord would strike her down on the spot for such lies. If He didn't, her best hope lay in someone less august putting her out of her misery.

"Don't ever forget about your heart's fondest dreams," Aunt Minnie said. "No one must own you, ever. You must remain free to follow your dreams."

"Sweet merciful heaven, Aunt Minnie's a suffragist," Penny declared. "My own aunt has become a suffragist. How will I ever live this down?"

"Just don't tell anyone, and they'll never know," Angelica answered. Blast, she shouldn't have done that, but she'd taken all she could. Aunt Minnie reached over and squeezed her hand. Hard.

"All right." Mama placed her hands palms down on top of the table. "We'll all be quiet for a moment and take a few deep breaths. Then we'll calmly discuss the matter at hand—how to get Minerva married without disgracing us all."

"You said that word," Aunt Minnie said, pointing at

Taming Angelica

Mama. "Can't we get through five minutes without your using that word?"

"Calm," Mama said. "We will all be very calm and quiet."

Just then the morning room door opened, thank heaven. Will stood on the threshold. He smiled pleasantly. "Well, there you all are."

"Yes, please do come in," Angelica said. Mama glared at her, not happy for masculine company while planning how to avoid Aunt Minnie's downfall, no doubt. But Angelica sorely needed help in containing herself.

"I don't want to interrupt anything," Will said. "If I could have a word with you in the corridor, Angelica."

"Please join us, dear boy," Aunt Minnie said. "We need some male perspective on our discussion."

Mama tried for a smile but failed. "No, we don't, Minerva. We're doing very well on our own."

"Well, there you are, then," Will said. He gestured toward the hallway. "Please, my own dear wife. A word."

Angelica rose from the table. "My husband wants me, Mama," she said. "I must obey him as you obey Papa."

Dear heaven, much more of that and she really would have a headache. She squeezed Aunt Minnie's hand, giving the old dear as much strength as she could, and then headed for the doorway.

"Hurry back," Mama called.

"Of course, Mama." Not until she absolutely couldn't avoid returning any longer.

Will smiled as she approached and opened the door wider so that she could step around him into the hallway. He'd only just closed the door behind them when she stepped into his arms and smothered his mouth with a kiss. She pushed him against the wall and kissed him until she couldn't breathe.

Alice Chambers

After a moment he put his hands on her shoulders and eased her away from him. "My dear Lady Claridge, to what do I owe the honor?"

"For rescuing me from that."

"That?" he repeated.

"That." Angelica gestured toward the morning room door. "I don't know how much more I can stand."

"Behaving yourself doesn't sit quite right, eh, lambkins?"

She swatted his arm. "Stop that."

He laughed. "With any luck you can revert to your usual upstart self soon."

"It couldn't be soon enough."

"Then let's go plan how to wrest your inheritance from your father, shall we?"

Chapter Sixteen

The day of reckoning came less than a fortnight after Lawrence Hamilton and his brood's arrival in England. One splendid morning, Will's father-in-law ordered him—and as an afterthought, his wife, the man's own daughter—into the library as if he owned the house. Even Angelica's mother wasn't invited to observe. It seemed no female but the particular one whose fate was to be decided ought to attend.

No wonder Angelica regarded society's treatment of women with such venom. Will could work up a healthy outrage at the proceedings, too, if he weren't about to receive a huge sum of money.

Hamilton stretched out in a wing-back chair, looking like a ridiculous little potentate, and fixed them both with a stern eye. "You've done it, Will," he declared. "I didn't think anyone could tame my daughter, but you have."

From the chair beside him, Angelica made a soft but nasty noise in the back of her throat. Will reached over and squeezed her hand, and she gave him a too-tight smile.

"I could hardly have believed it," Hamilton continued, seemingly oblivious to his daughter's displeasure, "but it looks like women are better behaved in this country than in America, even with your queen."

"What does the queen have to do with anything?" Angelica asked. Will squeezed her hand again, a bit harder this time, and Hamilton eyed her with some suspicion.

"That is, I'm sure the queen was a dutiful wife, too," she said quickly, "before her husband died, of course."

"Right you are, my dear," Will said. He smiled at his father-in-law. "The female sensibility is a remarkable thing, isn't it? The most accomplished women so often make the most obedient wives."

Angelica made that noise again, and Will held on to her hand for dear life. She could box his ears later, when they were alone. But right now she'd better hold her tongue, for both of their sakes.

Again, Hamilton seemed to take no notice but leaned forward in his chair. "Women in charge. That's what you get with nonsense like a monarchy," he said. "You'll never see a female president of the United States, I guarantee it."

At that, Angelica clasped Will's fingers in her own, tightly enough to cut off the flow of blood.

"It's damned unnatural for a woman to govern an entire country, if you ask me," Hamilton concluded.

"I'll share your views with Her Majesty when I next see her," Will replied. Of course, his sovereign wouldn't recognize him if she ran over him with her carriage, but his father-in-law couldn't know that.

In any case, the remark shut Hamilton up, as he sat straight up, his eyes wide. He recovered quickly, though, resting back against his chair and assuming once again the air of a man in control of things.

Taming Angelica

Will wasn't about to satisfy the pompous bastard by asking directly about the inheritance or why he'd been summoned into his own library, so he sat quietly, smiling at his father-in-law and holding on to his wife's hand.

After a long moment, Hamilton cleared his throat. "I suppose you're wondering why I asked to talk to you."

"It had entered my mind," Will said. "But I'm sure you have a good reason for everything you do."

"Yes, Papa," Angelica said. "I'm sure you didn't mean to keep me away from my wifely duties."

Hamilton shook a finger at her. "We'll have no talk of that sort of thing, young lady."

"I only meant ordering the servants around or embroidery or something like that, Papa."

"Of course," Hamilton huffed. "I knew that."

"So, then, sir . . . you were saying," Will prompted.

Hamilton rested back against the upholstery of his chair again. "Will, you're aware that Angelica's grandfather left her a large sum of money to be turned over to her husband on the occasion of her marriage."

"Yes, sir."

"At my discretion, of course."

"Yes, sir."

"You've done a fine job with Angelica, young man," Hamilton said as he reached into the inner pocket of his jacket. He pulled out some papers and turned toward Angelica. "You're satisfied with this marriage, are you?"

Will gripped her hand tightly. She looked over and gave him a rather pained smile. He eased up the pressure of his fingers over hers, and she turned toward her father. "I'm very happy, Papa."

"I didn't ask if you were happy," Hamilton replied. "What in hell does happiness have to do with marriage?"

"Whatever you'd like me to be, then, I am," she said. "I'm very sure of that, Papa."

"Good." Hamilton handed the papers to Will. "I had those drawn up in Boston. You now possess everything of my daughter's, including my daughter herself."

Will slipped the documents into his own jacket pocket. "Thank you, sir. I'm very proud to have your trust."

"See you earn it," Hamilton said. "Minerva will be staying here if she insists on marrying that Foxworthy fellow. She'll let me know if you mistreat Angelica."

Good God, mistreat Angelica? Did the man think he was stupid? "I won't, sir."

"Well, go on, go on," Hamilton said, waving a finger toward Will's pocket. "Don't you want to read them?"

"Should I?" he answered. "I'm sure everything is in order."

Hamilton laughed. "I guess I don't understand you blue bloods. Any ordinary man would have *some* reaction to being given five million dollars."

"Five?" Will managed to say before his throat closed up tightly. *Million? Five million? Dollars?* The ground beneath Will's chair moved; he could swear it. *Five million dollars?*

He could build the most modern stables imaginable and hire the best trainers money could lure. He could buy breeding mares of the very best bloodlines to set Black Diamond upon. For the love of God, Black Diamond could have every bloody mare he bloody well fancied. Five million dollars.

He glanced at Angelica and found her looking back at him, her brow furrowed in concern. "Are you all right?"

"Yes," he said, or rather croaked. He cleared his throat. "Of course. I'm fine. Why wouldn't I be?"

"You look rather odd," she answered.

Hamilton laughed again. "Five million dollars got your attention, did it, young man?"

"I rather think so."

"You won't be sneering at corsets anymore, I guess," Hamilton said.

"I rather think not."

"You earned it, young man," Hamilton said, smiling like a well-fed cat. "Most men wouldn't even have a woman as willful as Angelica is . . . was."

Then most men were bigger bloody fools than most men . . . well, were. Marrying a beautiful, passionate, intelligent woman ought to be enough reward in itself. And he'd just been paid five million dollars for the privilege. What a world.

"I'm honored to have Angelica as my wife, and I'll do my utmost to make her happy, sir."

"Happy, satisfied, whatever you call it," Hamilton said. "She's yours now. Don't let me hear any bad reports."

"I won't."

Hamilton rose from his chair. "We'll be leaving England, then."

Will and Angelica stood, too. "Leaving?" she asked. "You can't mean to take the long trip home already."

"I wish we were," Hamilton said. "But your mother has some crazy idea she wants to see France. Probably just another excuse to spend my money."

Angelica put her hand on his arm. "You will let her see what she wants, won't you?"

"I suppose so," he grumbled. "But I don't know what she thinks they have in France that we don't have in Boston."

"Oh, nothing," Will answered. "Paris, Provence, the Riviera."

"Rubbish," Hamilton said.

"As you say, sir."

"Well, I'll be off for now." Hamilton kissed Angelica on the forehead, then clapped Will on the shoulder. "Keep her in line, Will."

"As you say, sir."

Hamilton left the room. Angelica stood almost on tiptoe, waiting until his footsteps had disappeared well down the hallway. Then she threw herself into Will's arms. "We did it," she declared. "I don't think I could have endured another day of behaving myself, but it was worth it."

He held her and buried his nose into her hair. "You were magnificent, my darling."

She put her hands on his forearms and pushed herself away from him, gazing up into his face with a flush of triumph coloring her features. "At first I wasn't sure we could convince him I'd reformed. I'd spent my entire life in his house in a state of rebellion."

"I'm sure you're right," he said. "Angelica, listen. There's something we need to discuss."

"And you," she said, taking his face between her hands. "You almost overplayed your part. 'Lambkins,' for heaven's sake. No one would believe anyone would call me lambkins."

"I don't see why not. But that doesn't matter right now." And it didn't. What did matter was that she had to understand how they were going to spend the money. At least for the next several years. Maybe they'd never manage to spend *all* of five million dollars. *Good God, five million dollars.*

"You're right. That doesn't matter." She pushed herself out of his arms entirely and began to dance around the room. "What does matter is that we got the money and my father will be off for France. We can start planning our journey immediately."

Oh, dear. He'd known this moment would come sooner or later, and now it had. She wouldn't like it when he told her that South America would have to

Taming Angelica

wait, but somehow he'd have to convince her that the stables and the horses would have to come first. "Angelica, darling, listen."

"We'll need the right kind of clothing," she said, waltzing to the fireplace and back. "Trousers for me, I think. I can't very well climb around in crinolines. They'll have to be made."

"But, dearest."

She stopped and looked at him. "Maybe you're right. Maybe I can find some boys' trousers that will fit me." She started moving again, this time to the window. "And we'll need foreign currency, lots of it. South American *pesos,* or something like that."

"I think you mean Chilean or Argentine. South America isn't a country, you know."

She laughed. "How silly of me. We can approach the right embassies or consulates. Now, the ship." She walked back toward the fireplace. "With all this money, we can probably hire a ship if we can't find one that will take us on."

"Angelica, please."

"Oh, Will, I can't believe it. I've wanted this my entire life, and now it's coming true."

"Your entire life? Even before you'd heard of South America?"

She stopped and laughed again. "That can't be true, can it? It just feels like it."

Will walked to her and put his arms around her. "Angelica, please listen to me."

She gazed up at him, still flushed with excitement. "What is it, Will?"

He studied her face, all the joy there. He'd make her dreams come true. Only not right now. "I'm not ready to go to South America just at present, my darling."

She clapped her hand over her mouth. "The Derby!" she cried. "How could I have been so thoughtless? We'll wait until after the Derby, of course."

He put a palm against her face. "Not then, either, I'm afraid."

She pulled back and eyed him suspiciously. "Then when will you be ready?"

"There are facilities to be bought and built. Stables, practice tracks, and the like. Then I'll have to buy breeding stock. The best mares to breed with Black Diamond."

Her eyes narrowed. "And then?"

"The foals will have to be culled, some sold off, the best kept for training."

"And how much time will that take?"

"Oh, no more than a few years," he answered. "At most."

"Years?" she repeated, her eyes growing wide. "Years?"

"Not many."

"Years!" she shouted. "Oh, no. I don't believe you. You wouldn't ask me to wait years, not after all this time. Not after all I've been through. You wouldn't. You couldn't."

"It only sounds like forever," he answered. "The time will fly by."

"No, Will. The time won't fly by. Not after all this waiting. I want to go now."

"I know you do, dearest, but try to understand. After Black Diamond wins the Derby he'll be a very desirable commodity. I can't leave now. I just can't."

She crossed her arms over her chest. "Fine, then. I'll go without you."

"I can't let you do that, either. What would I do if something were to happen to you? There are wild animals in South America and even wilder people, if you can believe the stories. I can't let you go unprotected. What kind of husband would that make me?"

"The kind who grants his wife some independence,"

she answered. "The kind who gives a woman credit for having some strength. And a mind."

"I know you have all those things," he said. "But think of it, please. How could I sleep at night worrying about you catching some dreadful disease or falling off a cliff or something?"

She stood and stared at him, hurt warring with disbelief in her eyes. "Then come with me."

"I will. Truly. South America will still be there in three years' time. I promise you."

"Three years?" she repeated in a tiny voice. She swallowed and then stiffened her back. "No. I'll go now. I must insist on it."

"And I must refuse," he answered.

Her eyes grew wide, as she stood and stared at him as if she'd never seen him before. "You'd forbid me to go?"

He took a breath. "Yes."

"I don't believe it." She gasped. "You'd actually forbid me to go?"

"I don't want to," he answered. "I'd rather you agreed to wait until I can leave."

"But if I insist on going now, you'll forbid it."

"Yes. You give me no choice."

Her hands clenched into fists by her sides, and her whole body shook. "Curse you," she said after a moment. "You're as bad as the rest of them. No, worse. You gave me reason to hope."

"Angelica, you don't mean that."

"Yes, I do. Every word. You tricked me into marrying you," she shouted.

"I did no such thing," he shouted back. Damn it, he had to get control of himself. She had every right to feel he'd betrayed her, and getting angry with her would only make things worse.

"You tricked me into marrying you," she repeated.

"Then you let me think you cared about my dreams."

"I do."

"No, you don't," she answered, and her chin began to tremble. "That was just trickery, too."

"It wasn't," he reached for her. "Angelica, please."

She batted at his arm, pushing it away. "You don't care about me. You never have. But blast you, you've made me care about you."

She started crying in earnest at that, although she pretended not to. She bit her lip and held her chin high, all the while wiping at her eyes.

"I do care about you, my darling," he said, reaching for her again. "I love you."

That did it. Whatever misery he'd seen in her eyes disappeared, followed by the most murderous fury he'd ever seen. "Don't lie to me." She pushed him away from her. "Don't touch me."

"Angelica!"

"Don't even talk to me." With that, she turned on her heel and flew from the room as if Satan himself were after her.

He started to follow her but then thought better of it. There was no point talking to her until her rage had calmed a little—at least to only white-hot. He'd let her fume and cry for a while, until he could talk reason to her.

She had every reason for her anger, of course. He hadn't told her he had no plans to leave England for the next few years. So naturally she was disappointed. He'd explain things to her. He'd make her see that he had to take care of his business here now, while everything was right. She needed only to wait a little while, and then they'd both have their dreams. He'd make her see that.

He looked toward the doorway where she'd just left, and he remembered the sight of her rustling skirts as she'd run from him. The image of her unhappiness—first the tears and then the anger—came back to him. He'd seen her upset before, but not like that. Hell, he'd never seen anyone that upset.

But he'd fix things between them somehow. Only how?

Angelica sat at her dressing table, staring at her red-eyed reflection in the mirror. How the woman looking back at her could hold so much rage and hurt without exploding was a mystery. She was about to burst with it all.

Damn Will. Damn him. He'd played her like a master from the moment they'd met. As though she were some kind of stringed instrument.

Pluck. He'd let her think he'd help her escape London, when instead he'd planned to marry her to get her money.

Twang. He'd maneuvered them into being caught in an intimate embrace in the park. She'd probably never figure out how he'd gotten her horse to bolt, but he'd done it somehow.

Pluck, pluck. Then he'd gotten her to agree to marry him. He'd made her agree to her own betrayal, the cad.

Twang. He'd made love to her until she didn't know sometimes what day it was. He'd drugged her senses, overloaded them, until she'd forgotten all his machinations to get her to this point to begin with. The scoundrel had made her enjoy her own confinement.

And then, to add insult to injury, to make her humiliation one hundred percent complete, he'd made her play her part in this latest charade. He'd convinced her to simper and smile and bend and scrape—to play the docile little wife. And for what? So that he could get her inheritance and then keep it from her.

She was going to kill him. Really. She was going to murder him with her bare hands. Slowly and horribly. While he screamed and begged for mercy.

Oh, blast, she didn't know how to kill anyone. Besides, if she did, her father would probably just take her back to Boston.

Dear heavens, what was she thinking? She put her elbows on the tabletop and rested her face in her hands. Think, she had to think. And breathe, too, before the weight of her fury crushed the life right out of her.

What to do? What to do?

She sat back up and looked at her reflection again while she composed her face into some semblance of rationality. She could still go to Papa and tell him about their ruse—that all her good behavior had been a sham, a trick to get the money from him. That wouldn't win the inheritance for her, of course, but at least Will wouldn't get any benefit from it.

She could go back to Boston with her family. *No, not Boston. Anything but Boston.*

She'd stay here and live comfortably enough. Will would be terribly angry with her, but she would only have given him the treatment he deserved. Staying here with an unhappy husband and no inheritance certainly wasn't what she'd always dreamed of, but she could manage. Maybe.

Or she could leave things as they were. She could continue to demand that Will take her to South America or give her the money to go on her own. He probably wouldn't agree to either, but she could keep at him until he relented. At the very least, she might get him to sign an agreement to leave after some specified time. Such a document wouldn't have any weight in a court of law, but maybe she could use it to shame him into keeping his word.

Taming Angelica

Shame? For heaven's sake, Will Claridge had no shame. He might sign, say, or do anything to make her content, only to betray her once again. She couldn't stand that again. Besides, the one thing she'd make damned sure of was that he wouldn't get away with this. No, her dear husband had played his last trick on her and her family. He was going to pay.

That left only one possibility—her plan from the very beginning. Escape to South America on her own. She'd been planning to escape from Aunt Minnie. Very well, now she could escape from Will.

She opened the dressing table drawer and pulled out her jewel case. She lifted the lid and peered inside. Her sapphire ring and matching earrings lay inside, as did the diamond-and-ruby brooch, and numerous other pieces. She wouldn't sell her jewels for a pittance this time. She'd use them for money. She'd need to do business in several different countries, and jewels were small and easy to carry.

She rose and crossed to "her" bed, the bed she hadn't once slept in since moving here. That would change now, too. She'd played the fool in his bed for the last time, as he'd soon find out. She set the jewel case onto the coverlet and walked to the wardrobe. Inside, she found the cherry wood case that held her other jewelry—the long strings of pearls and the pendant with the single emerald so large she'd always felt it too gaudy to wear.

After checking that all those were in order, she closed the case and rummaged around in the bottom of the wardrobe until she found a small satchel—just big enough to hold both jewel cases. She took them to the bed, deposited both cases into the satchel, and bent to hide the lot under her bed. Later, when everyone had gone to sleep, she'd sneak downstairs and hide everything where no one but she could find it.

Alice Chambers

She straightened and looked around the room. She had a lot more to do before she could make good her escape, but that could wait. Right now she planned to go into her husband's bedroom and remove from it any sign that she had ever been there.

Chapter Seventeen

Will left for the track, finally, some time after two in the afternoon. Angelica didn't actually see him go, as she'd carefully avoided him—and everyone else—since their argument the day before in the library. Along with her newfound female sensibilities came the privilege of taking to her bed with a headache for hours on end, it appeared. At least as far as her family was concerned. As for what Will thought of her absence—she knew nothing and cared even less.

But she heard his voice as he left, talking to Newsome in the foyer. She waited for almost half an hour after that—as long as she could force herself to wait—to make sure his leaving wasn't a hoax to draw her out. Then she'd crept quietly down the stairs and left alone to walk the short distance to Hyde Park.

Now it seemed she'd been here for hours, although it couldn't possibly have been for that long, walking up and down, here and there, hoping for a chance meeting with Reginald Montrose. For heaven's sake, the man had seemed so intent on popping up, first at Vauxhall and then at the track; why wouldn't he pop up now when she wanted him to? She certainly didn't intend on visiting his house again, no matter how desperate she got.

Finally she spotted her quarry. Not Lord Montrose but Lord Underwood. He was walking on the other side of a sun-dappled meadow. His ever-present cousin, Muriel, walked on one side, and another young lady and a maid on the other. Both of the ladies wore the very latest fashions and carried parasols, to protect themselves from the scourge of freckles, no doubt. Angelica nodded to them all, and Lord Underwood tipped his hat.

She slowly moved on, letting him follow with his gaze. If Will's suspicions were correct, Lord Underwood would soon produce Lord Montrose. If not today, then tomorrow or the day after. She'd make it a habit to come every day at the same time until Reginald Montrose happened by.

But she didn't have to wait that long, as it turned out. Only a few moments after she'd spotted Lord Underwood, Lord Montrose appeared at her side. He tipped his hat to her.

"Lady Claridge," he said.

She didn't face him directly but nodded as she kept on walking. "Lord Montrose."

"Delightful afternoon, no?"

"Yes," she answered. "Quite."

"Your husband was unable to accompany you today?" he asked.

She glanced at him out of the corner of her eye and found the smuggest of smiles on his very ordinary features. "I don't need my husband to take a walk."

"Of course not."

"I'm a grown woman and now married, too."

"Certainly," he said, the very picture of agreeability.

"I can make my own decisions, Lord Montrose, run my own life."

"My dear Lady Claridge, I meant no offense. When one sees a wife it isn't unusual to ask after her husband."

She stopped briefly and turned to him. "I am sorry. I'm afraid I'm a bit on edge today." He smiled, and she turned and began walking again. "My husband's at the track this afternoon," she said.

"Ah, yes, his hopes for the Derby. Still, I don't see how he could choose his horses over your company."

Neither did she, but then, therein lay the crux of the matter, didn't it? If Will hadn't chosen his horses over her plans for her very own money, she wouldn't have had to sneak out of the house this afternoon in search of a man who'd attempted violence on her person in the past. She wouldn't be walking through the park trying to think of the right words to ask that same man to take her away to South America.

Well, she'd never been very good at roundabout ways of asking things. She might as well just come out with it. "Lord Montrose, that ship you mentioned."

"The *Peregrine?*"

"Is that the name?"

"Of the survey ship I told you of. Yes."

The *Peregrine*—even the name conjured up images of travel, of swift flights to new and exotic lands. She could keep a journal, as Darwin had on the *Beagle*. "The Flight of the *Peregrine*," sounded even better than "The Voyage of the *Beagle*." Dear heavens, she was so close to her goal of travel, she could almost reach out and grasp it.

"The *Peregrine*," she said, trying the name out on her tongue. It felt good there. "Is the captain still willing to take a woman along?"

"I could make it worth his while to be willing," Lord Montrose answered.

"Then I'd like to go." The minute the words were out of her mouth, she realized the right of them. She would go on the voyage of her dreams. Now, not years from now.

"My dear Lady Claridge." Lord Montrose stopped in his tracks and took her hand in his.

She withdrew her hand immediately. "You must understand that I hope to join you in exploration of the world and nothing more."

"Of course."

"I cannot emphasize this enough, Lord Montrose. I want no more misunderstandings between us on this score. I'm a married woman and plan to keep my wedding vows."

"By running away from your husband?" he asked.

"I'm not running away," she objected, lying through her teeth.

He raised one eyebrow. "You're not?"

"It's just that . . . well . . . Lord Claridge can't leave right now to accompany me."

"But he gave you his permission?"

"I don't need his permission or anyone else's, Lord Montrose. I'm a grown woman and may do what I please."

"I'm sure of that," he replied. "Still, isn't there some marriage vow about cleaving yourself to your husband? I should think it would be rather hard cleaving to him from that distance."

Blast, the man had her there. "Well, I won't worry about that vow for a while."

"Did you not vow to obey him, too?"

She waved her hand at him. "Not that one, either. I don't plan to obey anyone but myself ever again."

"Then, may I ask . . . which vows do you plan to keep?"

Really, that ought to be obvious. She put her hands

Taming Angelica

on her hips. "There will be no more encounters between us of the . . . well, personal sort."

He didn't say anything but stood looking down at her, pretending not to understand what she meant, curse him.

"We will not have any intercourse of a sexual nature, sir," she said finally. "I hope I make myself clear."

He chuckled. "Perfectly, Lady Claridge. Nothing could be further from my mind."

Now that was perfectly preposterous. She stared up at him in exasperation.

"Very well," he conceded. "Very few things are further from my mind."

"Thank you." She began walking again, for the first time truly tasting her freedom. "Now then, we'll need to work out the details. I'm afraid all my money is tied up in jewelry right now."

She glanced at him out of the corner of her eye, half expecting him to make some remark about her lack of hard currency. He could hardly doubt that she was a rich woman, but if he found it odd she didn't have any wealth except for her jewels, he didn't show it. Instead he simply smiled at her. "Don't worry about money," he said. "I have enough for both of us."

"I won't take anything from you, sir," she said. "I couldn't bear to be in your debt."

"We'll use your jewelry where it's handy, then," he answered. "Or you can sell it to me or use it as assurance that I'll be paid back when we return. Does that meet with your approval?"

"Fine."

"Good. I'll send a carriage for you. Say, next Friday afternoon?"

Afternoon? Oh, dear, that wouldn't work. Will would see her leaving and try to stop her. Or one of the servants would tell him of her departure, and he'd follow. She'd confront him if she had to, of course. But things would go so much more smoothly if no one saw her go at all.

"How long will it take to get to the ship?" she asked.

"Portsmouth's several hours' ride."

"Then could you come for me at night? Say, two in the morning?"

That did make him look at her oddly. "Two in the morning?"

"Oh, yes, then we'd get there shortly after dawn, ready for our voyage."

He smiled—or rather smirked—again. "Certainly. Ride all night. Splendid idea."

So he knew she was running away, after all. Oh, well, he could hardly think anything else. No point arguing with him. She stopped and turned to him, extending her hand. "Two o'clock, then. What day did you say?"

He took her hand and shook it. "Next Friday, or rather, Saturday morning."

The day of the Derby. *Oh, dear.* She'd have to leave without seeing Will's horse run and knowing if it won.

But then, that day would do quite well, after all. Will would be so busy with preparations, he wouldn't notice that she'd gone. "Next Saturday morning," she repeated.

"Until then." He dropped her hand. "And pack lots of clothes. We'll likely be gone for a year or two."

A year? Or two? He tipped his hat again and left her. A year. She'd be gone a year. Or two. *Oh, my.*

Will caught Angelica trying to slip back into the house unobserved. She couldn't see him where he stood in the doorway of the sitting room, but he could watch her as she tiptoed into the front foyer and turned to

Taming Angelica

close the door silently behind her. He stepped out of the shadows. "Where have you been?"

She jumped and turned around. "You startled me."

"Where have you been?" he repeated.

She lifted her chin and looked at him. "Out."

"I can see that. Where?"

"What's all this?" she said, looking around at the luggage Newsome had placed in readiness for the other Hamiltons' departure.

"Your family is leaving for France soon," he answered. "They'll be back for Aunt Minnie's wedding."

"Oh," she said, as she headed toward the stairs.

He moved to block her way. "Where have you been?"

"Is this another rule for wives I have to learn?" she asked, glaring at him. "Am I supposed to tell you my whereabouts every moment?"

"Am I out of line to want to know where my wife has been?" he asked.

"Are you going to order me to tell you?"

"No, of course not," he said.

"Good." She moved around him and headed toward the stairs again.

"Don't you at least want to say good-bye to your parents and your sister?"

That stopped her. She stood for a moment and then walked back, headed toward the sitting room door. This time he caught her physically, putting his hands on her elbows and turning her to him. "Angelica, stay a moment and listen. I know you're angry with me."

She didn't say anything but just glared at him. He took a deep breath. "Please try to understand. I'm not saying we'll never make the voyage you want, just that we won't make it now."

She still didn't say anything, but she did try to twist

out of his grasp. He held on. "Very well. We won't talk about that now."

She greeted that with silence, too. He'd expected her to rant and rail about the unfairness of how he'd treated her. He'd expected arguments, shouting, even tears. He hadn't expected stony, cold silence. If only she'd say something. Anything.

"I missed you last night, Angelica," he said finally. "Today, too. But especially last night. I want you to come back to my bed."

"Will you order me to do that, too?" she replied.

"Damn it, no," he said. So much for wanting her to say something. "I want you to *want* to come back to my bed."

"Fine. When I want to, I will."

"Don't stay away long, please."

She tried to pull away again. When he didn't release her, she looked up at him. "I'd better say good-bye to my family, don't you think?"

He released her, and she walked to the sitting room door, opened it, and went inside.

Something was very wrong here. It appeared he'd miscalculated her reaction badly. He'd expected fire, and he'd gotten ice. He'd expected confrontation, and he'd gotten secrecy. Where *had* she been just now?

He'd better watch her very carefully from this point on. She was planning something. No doubt she was planning the exact same thing she'd once enlisted his own help for—escape. Reggie Montrose had offered her a way to South America. He could feel it in his bones.

Well, she couldn't get to South America without a ship, and all departures and arrivals were listed in the *Times*. He'd follow it for information about ships, and he'd follow his wife to find out what she was doing. Then, the minute the Derby was over, he'd pack them up and move them to the country, where he could start

Taming Angelica

making plans for his stables. And where he could keep her away from Montrose and ships and any other means of escape she might try.

Angelica Hamilton Claridge was his wife; and she wasn't going anywhere without him.

Angelica sat in her bedroom, waiting and listening. The clock had just chimed two. No sound of a carriage had come from the street for almost half an hour now. Surely Lord Montrose couldn't have come and gone without taking her. Surely he wouldn't give up early and leave her behind. Blast it, why hadn't they worked out some signal at that first meeting?

But then, how had she known that Will wouldn't leave her alone for a second after that afternoon? Every daylight hour he was either with her or had a servant trailing along after her. He almost acted as if he knew of her plans. Now she could only sit here and hope and pray that she'd know—somehow—that Lord Montrose had arrived. That she'd figure out—somehow—how to get to him without waking Will or Newsome. That—somehow—she'd make it through this night and end up where she wanted to be: on the *Peregrine*.

She checked her bags for at least the fifth time. She had so little to carry. Her complete lack of freedom for the past days had made any sort of shopping impossible. What little money she'd already had at the beginning of this enterprise still lay securely in her reticula. The rest of her luggage consisted of the satchel that held her jewelry and another bag with small clothes, a journal, and the miniature.

Oh, dear, the miniature. She opened the bag and took it out. Her husband looked back at her from inside the gilt frame. Even in the dim light of the single candle she'd lit she couldn't miss the charm of his smile, the blue of his eyes, the noble slope of his nose.

She'd married a handsome devil, no doubt about it. Memories of that devil and his smile and his skillful caresses would haunt her dreams all the way to Tierra del Fuego.

She rose, walked to her dressing table, and set the picture of Will down next to the candle. Then she walked to the window and glanced out. She looked up one side of the street and down the other, but there was no sign anywhere of a carriage.

Where could Lord Montrose be? Could Will have gotten to him somehow? Could Will have threatened him with violence if he tried to take her away? Could he have forged her signature and sent Lord Montrose a note saying she had changed her mind? Maybe the man had simply changed his own mind about taking her. If only she knew.

She turned, went back to the bed, and sat down again. Her traitorous eyes looked over toward the dressing table and the miniature. Will stared back at her, and in the flickering of the candle, his expression almost appeared hurt and full of reproach.

Don't leave me, Angelica, it seemed to say.

You're a painting, she answered in her mind. *You can't talk to me.*

Don't leave me. I love you.

Oh, yes. He'd said that, hadn't he? Twice. The first time after he'd made love to her on their wedding day—after he'd won her body through trickery. The second time in the library that day with Papa—after he'd won her money, again with trickery. If that was his idea of love, he could have it.

Don't leave me, Will's image whispered to her mind.

A painting, she repeated. *Oil on canvas. I don't have to listen to you.*

You don't want to go away with Montrose.

Taming Angelica

I wanted to go with you, her mind shouted back. Blast, now she was talking to the thing.

The last bit at least made sense. She didn't want to go away with Lord Montrose. She hardly wanted to cross the street with him. And here she was running away with him for two years.

Dear heavens, two years?

She looked around the room she'd occupied for so short a time, and her gaze fell back on the painting of Will. She'd miss him for those two years. She couldn't hope to delude herself on that score. His laughter, his kisses, his touch—they'd all become such an important part of her existence.

What would she do when she reached the Galápagos and he was here, so very far away? What would she do when she craved his loving then? Crave it she would; he'd made sure of that, curse him.

Don't leave me, Angelica.

"Oh, shut up," she whispered.

Just then the sound of horses' hooves and rolling wheels came to her from out on the street. She rushed to the window and looked out. A large, sleek carriage turned the corner and headed toward the house. Its finish shone in the light of the lanterns at the front, marking it clearly as the carriage of someone quite wealthy. It pulled up in front of the house and stopped, and Angelica could barely make out a family crest on the door—the same one as on Lord Montrose's handkerchief. He had come, after all.

She flew to the bed and grabbed her bags and then went to the dressing table. After glancing at the miniature one last time, she blew out the candle. Then she turned and went to her bedroom door. Once there, she hesitated for a moment, as if her feet didn't quite know how to proceed.

Oh, blast. She turned and looked toward the dressing table, where she could just make out the shape of the miniature standing there. Quickly she ran and snatched it up and then continued out into the hall and closed the door softly behind her.

She didn't dare run, even with the thick carpet runner under her feet. But she walked as briskly as possible, listening for the sounds of people stirring and hearing nothing but the tick of the grandfather clock. She reached the stairs finally, and descended as quickly and quietly as possible. At the bottom she tiptoed across the parquet floors to the huge front door.

Just to be safe, she looked around one more time, straining to hear if anyone was following. When no sound except for the clock answered, she opened the door and stepped outside, pulling it silently shut behind her.

A soft rain had just begun, and the light from the lanterns caught the mist and set up a glow in front of the carriage. The effect made the thing look huge—a dark, menacing shadow. The horses didn't nicker or stamp their feet but stood in silence, as if they recognized the need to keep such doings secret.

Dear heavens, what fancies. Angelica shook herself and walked down the stairs to the street. At her approach, a liveried footman jumped down from his post at the back of the carriage and opened the door for her. The shadow of his hat hid his face as he reached for her bags. She surrendered them, and he set them inside the carriage, then turned back to her, holding the door.

So this was it. This was how she left her husband and family for travel she'd always dreamed of. Sneaking away in the night like a thief. Any number of other ways to leave held more appeal—leaving with Will, or if not with him, with his blessing. Even announcing her intentions and simply carrying through on them over Will's objection seemed a great deal more honorable. But this was the only choice Will had given her, and this was the choice she'd take.

Still clutching the miniature of her husband in her hand, she lifted her chin and climbed into the carriage.

Chapter Eighteen

"Damn it," Will bellowed. "Newsome!"

Scuffling footsteps sounded from the floor below as Will stood and surveyed his wife's bedroom. Her empty bedroom. Where in hell was she?

"Newsome," he shouted again.

"Coming, my lord." Newsome charged into the room, breathing heavily. "I'm here, sir. What could be amiss to disturb you so?"

"Amiss?" Will repeated. "My wife. She's gone."

"Your wife, sir?" Newsome said, glancing blankly around the room.

Will grabbed his butler by the lapels. "My wife. Lady Claridge. She's bolted."

Newsome looked up at him, wide-eyed. "Are you quite sure, my lord?"

"Damn it." He dropped Newsome's lapels and gestured around the room. "Her bed hasn't been slept in, and her wardrobe door is open. And there's a candle here, where no candle belongs."

Taming Angelica

"My lady always takes a candle to bed with her when she retires," Newsome said.

"Bloody hell, I ought to know when my own wife has run off."

"Perhaps she only rose early to take a walk," Newsome offered.

"You and the staff are supposed to be following her," Will answered. "Did anyone see her go?"

"No, sir. Not that I know of."

"Well, then?"

"Oh, dear," Newsome said. "Oh, dear, dear."

Will went to Angelica's dressing table and pulled open one drawer and then another. "Where does Lady Claridge keep her jewels?"

"I don't know, my lord."

"Get Mary in here and have her search. I want to know what's missing."

"Yes, sir." Newsome walked to the door and called loudly for Angelica's lady's maid, while Will continued his search of the dressing table.

None of the drawers turned up anything that remotely resembled a jewel case, so Will walked to her dresser. Several of those drawers were empty—the sort that would normally hold small clothes. He searched the whole dresser and still didn't find any jewelry.

He went to the wardrobe and looked inside. Her clothes were there, at least as far as he could tell, but they'd been shoved to one side, as if she'd been searching for something on the floor. He pushed them even further and scanned the bottom of the wardrobe. She'd had a few small bags there, he was sure, and they were gone now.

Mary appeared then. Will could hear her huffing and puffing behind him. "My lady," she said. "Where is she?"

He pulled back out of the wardrobe and straightened. "When was the last time you saw Lady Claridge, Mary?"

"Last night, my lord. I combed out her hair and left her here, as I always do."

"And you haven't seen or heard anything of her since?"

"No, sir."

"Where does she keep her jewelry?" he asked.

"Here, my lord." She walked to the dressing table and looked into one of the drawers. "Why, they're gone. We've been robbed."

"Where else does she keep them?" Will demanded.

Mary pressed a hand to her breast. "Oh, sweet saints preserve us, we've been robbed."

"Think, Mary," he ordered. "Where else does she keep her jewels?"

"In the wardrobe, in a large cherry wood box."

"That's gone, too," Will said.

"Oh, my lady," Mary wailed. "My poor lady. Do you think the robbers got her, your lordship?"

"Not a chance," he said in a growl. "But I have a rather good idea where she's got herself to."

"My lord?" Newsome said.

Will didn't answer but pushed by them both on his way to the door. Newsome and Mary followed, although they had to run to keep up.

"Where's the *Times*?" he shouted as he headed down the hallway.

"The *Times*?" Newsome repeated.

"The *Times*, the *Times*. The London *Times*."

"In the morning room," Newsome answered. "But do you really want to read the newspaper just now?"

When Will reached the staircase he descended two steps at a time and headed toward the morning room. He burst inside and found the *Times* on a sideboard. He snatched it up just as Newsome and Mary entered the room. Hastily he turned the pages, searching for news of ship arrivals and departures.

"How did this happen?" he demanded, rifling through the paper. "You were to have someone watching her."

"We didn't think her ladyship would steal away in the middle of the night. We were all asleep, sir."

"I was, too," Will said. "Damn it, I should have stayed awake all night so that I could listen for her."

"On the night before the Derby?" Newsome replied. "You needed your sleep, sir."

"The Derby!" *Oh, bloody hell.* The minute he'd seen Angelica's empty room, every thought of the Derby had flown straight out of his head. Of all the nights, how could she choose this one to leave him? Never, as long as he lived, would he let her forget that she'd done this to him. But, damn, first he had to find her.

"Mary, go find a footman. James, if he's about," he ordered. "Tell him he's to go to the track and find Mr. Eustace Jones."

"Eustace Jones," she repeated.

"He's to tell Mr. Jones that I've been detained and he's to proceed with the race and Black Diamond without me. Now, repeat that."

"I'm to tell James to go to the track and find Mr. Eustace Jones and tell him to proceed without you," Mary said.

"Good enough. Off with you."

Mary picked up her skirts and ran from the room. Will turned his attention back to the *Times*. Angelica had left him. His own wife had left him. How could she, after all they'd shared? He could never in his wildest dreams leave her, no matter what she did. No matter how angry she made him. And he couldn't face the possibility of living without her. *Damn the woman, anyway.*

Finally he found what he was looking for. "Here it is," he said. " 'HMS *Peregrine* leaves today on a survey expedition to South America.' Oh, no." He set the paper down. "It's leaving from Portsmouth and isn't expected back for two years."

Dear God. Two years? He couldn't bear to be parted from Angelica for that long. And what if something happened to her and she never came back? No, he couldn't even let himself think about that possibility.

"Two years, sir," Newsome said. "Surely her ladyship wouldn't leave and not come back for two years."

"Not if I have anything to say about it, she won't." He looked at Newsome. "When did you fall asleep last night?"

"Shortly after midnight, sir."

"Yes, I did, too. She's had all night to get to Portsmouth." *Damn.* How could she do this? How could she? "Order a horse saddled for me."

"Yes, sir." Newsome started toward the door.

"And pray that I get there before that ship sails."

"Yes, sir!" Newsome ran off, leaving Will with a sick dread settling into his stomach. *Dear God, grant a poor sinner just one wish. Please let me get there in time.*

Angelica sat on a crate marked LIMES and shaded her eyes against the sun. The tang of salt spray filled the air, and crowds of gulls flew overhead, calling raucously. Laughing at her and her botched escape, most likely.

A fine lot of good it had done arriving here in early morning. She'd been sitting and watching the *Peregrine* being loaded for hours. The sun had climbed high in the sky and hung there like a beacon to show Will which way she'd come. She had no way of knowing when, or

Taming Angelica

if, he'd missed her yet. For all she knew, he might go all through his blasted horse race without even looking for her. On the other hand, if he'd figured out where she'd headed, he might be on his way right now.

"How much longer will it be?" she asked Lord Montrose.

"I'm sure I don't know that any better than the last time you asked," he answered, scowling at her with his very ordinary features. As he had for the last few hours.

"There's no need to be cross," she said. "We've been waiting a long time, after all."

"I got you passage," he answered. "I can't tell a captain of Her Majesty's navy what time he's to set sail, too."

"I'm very sorry to be such a burden to you, I'm sure," she said, knowing perfectly well that her tone would tell him the exact opposite. For heaven's sake, she'd been in his company for less than a day, and already she was finding the man insufferable. The moment they arrived in South America she'd get as far away from him as possible and let the glories of nature make up for the fact that she'd had to spend months at sea with such a boor.

"Things might move more quickly if you weren't sitting on the supplies," Lord Montrose said.

Angelica glanced around and noticed two seamen standing beside the crate. She rose and smiled at them, and they picked up the crate and carried it to where the rest of the supplies were being loaded.

"There are some things you need to know before we board," Lord Montrose said.

"Things?" she repeated.

"I told Captain Varney that we were married."

"You what?" She stared at him. "Why did you do that?"

"I couldn't tell him the truth—that I was helping you to run away from your husband."

"I'm not running away."

He raised one eyebrow and stared at her in silence.

"Well, he deserved it," she said.

"And Varney could hardly take an unmarried woman along on a trip like this; ergo, you became my wife," he added. "I hope you'll remember to answer to Lady Montrose."

Lady Montrose—how perfectly odious. Still, there were far more important matters to this hoax than her name. "And what sleeping arrangements did you make?"

"You'll have the cabin that was to be mine, and I'll be bunking with the cartographer."

"The captain didn't find that odd?"

"No, in fact he insisted on it." He cleared his throat. "He told me in no uncertain terms that we're not to give the appearance of engaging in any connubial bliss."

Connubial bliss? The mere idea of doing that with Reginald Montrose was enough to make Angelica's insides twist into knots.

"We'll be at sea for some time," he continued. "You'll be the only woman any of the men—officers and seamen—will see for very long periods. If they thought I was enjoying your pleasures, they'd go quite mad with jealousy."

"I see." Put that way, the captain's instruction made sense. But she hadn't considered what it might be like to be isolated with all that male lust all the way to South America.

"The crew will have strict instructions not to molest you, but you'd be kind not to become too great a temptation for any of them."

"I'll do my very best not to look too tempting," she replied.

Taming Angelica

"Good, he said. "I don't know whether Varney still has authority to flog his men or not, and I'd hate to find out."

Flogging? Dear heavens, what barbarity. Lord Montrose must be making it up to torment her. "Very well. I wouldn't want anyone flogged on my account."

"Don't seem too friendly with any of them. And certainly no sidelong glances, blushes, or lowered lashes."

"I may at least talk to the crew, I hope."

"I wouldn't do much of that, either," he answered. "And if you wouldn't mind, you might afford me the same thoughtfulness. At least until we've landed somewhere with a sizable female population."

Oh, for heaven's sake. She put her hands on her hips and glared at him. "Do you suppose I dare have an occasional conversation with Captain Varney?"

"He has his commission to think of, so he's safe, I imagine."

Of all the ridiculous conversations, this one topped the list. Lord Montrose either thought her hopelessly stupid, or he was convinced that all men had the same lack of control over their impulses that he had. Her Majesty's sailors had better things to do with their time than bother a woman traveling with her husband.

She scanned the ship again. It was rather small, and things would get cramped after a time. But surely the seamen had more honor than Lord Montrose thought, and if they didn't, she'd rebuff their advances kindly but firmly. She'd report one to the captain only if strictly necessary.

As to Lord Montrose—if he attempted any of his tricks, she'd toss him overboard. If the crew fished him out, he would have learned his lesson. If they didn't, well, certainly no one would mourn the likes of him.

And yet, she could have hoped for the ship to be

just a little bigger, if she was going spend two years on it . . . surrounded by all those men.

Another man appeared on the deck. His uniform sported more gold and braid than the others she'd seen, and he carried a definite air of authority. He looked down and spotted her and Lord Montrose. "Your lordship, if you please," he called. "We're ready for you and Lady Montrose now."

Lord Montrose took her elbow and made as if to lead her to the gangplank, but she held back. "What's wrong?" he demanded. "You've been pestering me about when we could leave for hours."

"I know, but the plank isn't wide enough for both of us. You go ahead."

"And look like a brute, leaving you to fend on your own? I don't think so."

"Really, I can walk on my own."

"Yes, yes, I know all about you and your damned independence," he snapped. "But I will not look like a churl in front a group of common sailors."

"Kindly take more care with your language, sir," she said.

"Kindly get on this ship," he said from between gritted teeth. "Walk ahead of me as I help you up."

"Oh, all right." She picked up her skirts, and her reticule bumped against her wrist. It was heavier than usual because it held the miniature of Will. Dear heavens she was getting on a ship full of strange men *and* Reginald Montrose for a journey of two years. She wouldn't see Will for two years, and she'd be staring at these men and Reginald Montrose for that entire time. The thought would daunt a lesser woman. It surely would.

"Well, are you coming?" Lord Montrose said.

"Yes, of course."

"Then you might try putting one foot ahead of the other."

Taming Angelica

"Of course." She tried again, and the miniature bumped her yet again. The blasted thing had taken on a life of its own ever since she'd gotten it out of her satchel the night before. Well, it wasn't going to order her around any more than the flesh-and-blood Will Claridge could.

"Is there a problem?" the captain called from the deck.

"No problem," Lord Montrose called back. He tightened his grip on her elbow until it hurt. "Lady Montrose, if you please."

She allowed him to guide her to the gangplank, although *push* might have been a better word than *guide*. She got to the base of it and turned, looking first at Lord Montrose's ordinary face and then over his shoulder. She found nothing of interest, of course. What could there be to interest her except the *Peregrine* and the travel she'd always dreamed of?

"Not mooning after Claridge, I hope," he said.

"Don't be ridiculous."

"If he cared about you he'd be here now, not at some bloody horse race."

"I must ask you not to swear like that," she said.

"Just get on the damned ship, or by God I'll leave without you."

"Now, how could I resist a lovely invitation like that?" she grumbled. But she did as she was told, turning and placing her foot onto the gangplank. The boards creaked and bent as she climbed them, but she managed with Lord Montrose's "help" to reach the top.

The captain greeted her there with a tip of his hat. "Captain George Varney, at your service, ma'am."

"Thank you."

He seemed young for such a momentous position as captaining a Royal Navy ship. As if to compensate for his youth, he'd grown thick whiskers along the sides of his face. They, and the light of intelligence in his brown eyes, suggested that she might at least have someone to talk to during the voyage.

"We've done what we could to make you comfortable, Lady Montrose, but this is no ocean liner."

"I'm sure it will suit wonderfully," she answered.

"Damn it, Angelica," came a shout from the dock. "Come down from there. This instant."

Oh, dear merciful heaven. Will. How had he found her?

She peered over the railing and spotted him. He looked perfectly wild, with no coat or hat and with his hair in windblown disarray. In one hand he held the reins of an exhausted and lathered horse. The other hand was raised in a fist in the air. In her entire life she'd never seen anything or anyone so beautiful as her own scheming, lying husband.

"Pay no attention to that man," Lord Montrose said to the captain. "He's little more than a troublemaker."

"Angelica!" Will shouted again. "Do you hear me? Come down from there. Believe me, you don't want me to have to come up and get you."

"Go away, Will," she called, but somehow her heart failed to put any conviction behind her words.

"Like hell I will." He dropped the reins and started climbing the gangplank. "I swear, I'll put you over my knee when I get there, and I'll turn Montrose's face into a bloody pulp."

"I say," Captain Varney said. "What's all this, then?"

"Don't come up, Will," she cried. "Don't hit anyone. For heaven's sake, I'm coming down."

She headed down the gangplank, her feet traveling far faster than they had on the trip up. Maybe that was because of some help from gravity, but maybe it was

Taming Angelica

because of the man waiting at the other end. How on earth had she ever thought she could leave Will Claridge for two years? Why hadn't she listened to her heart? Even her feet had tried to tell her she didn't want to go to South America without him. Thank heaven he'd arrived here before her head forced her to make a terrible mistake.

When she got to the bottom of the gangplank, she ran to his arms. They closed around her immediately, and she found herself surrounded with his warmth and his scent. How she'd missed it. She hadn't even been in his bed for days and days.

"Come back on board, *my dear*," Lord Montrose called from on deck.

"Not on your life, Montrose," Will shouted back.

"Never mind all this, Will," Angelica said. "Let's just go home."

He turned an icy glare on her. "I'll deal with you later."

"Would you explain what's happening here, please?" Captain Varney asked Lord Montrose. "This is most irregular."

"You're helping this bastard to steal my wife," Will called. "Would you like the Admiralty to know that, captain?"

"Your wife?" Captain Varney turned to Lord Montrose. "I thought she was *your* wife."

"She is," Lord Montrose answered.

"Stop lying, Montrose," Will shouted. "Or I'll be forced to come up there and teach you some honesty."

He headed toward the gangplank, but Angelica held on to him. "Please, Will, this isn't necessary."

Captain Varney stared at her over the ship's rail. "How many husbands do you have, madam?"

Oh dear, how absolutely mortifying. "One," she answered. "This one."

Alice Chambers

"Will someone please explain what's going on here?" Captain Varney ordered.

"Oh, damn it all to hell," Lord Montrose cursed. "She's yours Claridge, and you're welcome to her."

"You attempted to bring another man's wife onto my ship as your own?" Captain Varney demanded, now clearly upset.

"It's done all the time," Lord Montrose said.

"That's the most preposterous thing I've ever heard," Captain Varney shouted. "It's never been done on my ship."

"You're young yet," Lord Montrose replied.

Captain Varney straightened into a tower of rage. "Sir, any more disrespect and I must ask you to leave my ship."

"I wouldn't advise that, Captain," Will called. "If that man sets foot on this dock, I shall feel obliged to tear him into pieces with my bare hands."

Angelica held on to her husband as if her life depended on it. Perhaps Lord Montrose's did.

Lord Montrose looked over the railing at Will, and his face turned ashen. "No need, old fellow. We'll be leaving soon, won't we, Captain?"

Captain Varney huffed a few times. "That we will," he said finally. "The tide has turned."

"I couldn't have put it better myself, Captain," Will declared. "For the sake of your health, I'd recommend you stay away for a good long while, Montrose. Long enough for me to forget what you've tried here today."

Lord Montrose just glared at Will for a moment and then went belowdecks.

"And thank you for the use of your carriage to return to London," Will shouted.

He turned and grasped Angelica's elbow just as tightly as Lord Montrose had earlier, but he looked easily ten times as angry. She'd never seen Will truly furious before, and the fire in his eyes and the tension in his jaw made quite a sight. It was going to be a very long ride back to London.

Chapter Nineteen

Indeed, Will glowered all the way home—except for when he was too busy sulking to glower. Angelica couldn't blame him, at least not entirely. How would she feel if he'd run off and left her, not intending to come back for two years?

Still, she'd never given him reason to leave her, and he'd given her ample reason.

She sat and peeked at him occasionally during the long ride. He'd stare at her for a while with a world of hurt and anger in his eyes. Then he'd look out the window as though he couldn't bear the sight of her. *Blast him.* She'd left him with all that mattered to him—her money. That ought to have been enough. What else did he want of her?

After his sixth or seventh deep sigh, she'd had enough. "All right," she said. "Out with it."

He didn't answer, but only switched his features from anger to suffering.

"Very well," she continued, holding her head high

Taming Angelica

and meeting his gaze straight on. "Either we have this out or I'll go ride on that poor horse you hounded all the way to Portsmouth."

"You can't ride worth a damn," he answered.

"I don't care. I'll go get on him now and ride alongside the carriage. The atmosphere in here is stifling."

"In the name of God, give the poor beast some rest," Will said. "I had to drive him mercilessly since you took it into your head to abandon me in the middle of the night."

"Abandon you?" She clucked her tongue. "Aren't you being a bit melodramatic?"

"What would you call it?" he demanded as he leaned toward her, ice blue fury in his eyes. "When were you planning on coming back?"

Oh, dear. She rested back against the cushions and lowered her gaze.

"The *Times* said that ship wouldn't return for two years," he said. "Two years, Angelica."

He made it sound like an accusation, and maybe it was. In fact, it sounded perfectly heartless, and there wasn't a thing she could say to dispute it.

"Perhaps you had some plan for getting home earlier," he added. "Did you?"

"No," she answered.

"You'd leave me for all that time without so much as a word?" he said, and she could have sworn his voice broke. "You didn't even write me a note."

She looked up and found him staring, wide-eyed, at her. No one could have feigned the accusation and disappointment in his eyes. The look cut right into her. How could she have hurt him like that? What kind of unnatural female was she?

Oh, for heaven's sake, what was she thinking? He'd caused this situation, not her. He'd brought on his own unhappiness by treating her like a possession. If she'd tried to run away from him, he had no one but himself to blame. If he cared about her he'd have agreed to go away with her, rather than force her to seek out someone like Reginald Montrose. But all he wanted from this marriage was money.

Still, if he didn't care about her, why had he come after her? He'd not only followed her to Portsmouth, he'd ridden a horse to exhaustion to do it. And he'd looked ready to tear apart anyone who'd stood in his way. He'd acted positively possessive, as if he really did want her with him. As if he might truly love her.

Oh, blast him. How did he manage to confuse her like this?

He'd returned to staring out the window at the countryside going by. But he didn't see any of it, if she could read the bleakness of his gaze correctly, the tension in his jaw.

"If I hadn't found you in time, where do you suppose you'd be right now?" he asked.

"I don't know."

"Nearing Land's End, perhaps. With nothing but the Atlantic Ocean in front of you."

"Perhaps."

"What if something happened to you?" he said softly. "What if you never came back?"

"For heaven's sake, nothing would have happened to me."

He turned and glared at her. "You can't know that. Any number of things could have happened to you. Good God, you might have been killed."

She had no way of disputing that either. So she just kept silent.

"My own wife," he said. "Running away from me and getting herself killed. How do you think that would have made me feel?"

"I don't see why you'd care," she answered.

"You don't?" he said, his voice rising. "You don't see why I'd care?"

She raised her chin and looked him squarely in the eye. "No, I don't."

"Then you have an even lower opinion of me than I'd thought. Does our marriage mean nothing to you at all?"

"I didn't want to get married," she answered, her own voice growing louder. "I feared I'd lose any hope of freedom. It turns out I was right."

"I promised to do what you wanted. I only asked you to wait for a time."

"Three years," she shouted. "You're so angry at me for going away for two years. I'd have been back a full year before you'd even have had time to go with me."

"But we would have been together the whole time."

"As if you care where I am," she said. "You had my money. That's all you wanted."

His eyes widened in the perfect picture of rage. "If you believe that, you have an even lower opinion of yourself than you do of me."

"It's true. You would have had your stables and your tracks and your blasted horses. You wouldn't even have noticed I'd gone."

"I noticed very well, thank you. I noticed the moment you were gone. I felt your absence inside me."

"That's ridiculous," she replied.

"I know it is, but I felt it, nevertheless." He stopped, as though he'd surprised himself with that declaration. "I felt as if my heart had stopped somehow. Or my breath."

She sat and looked at him. Could he have really missed her so instantly and so intensely? Certainly she'd felt the presence of his miniature in her reticule, far out of proportion to its real weight. Had they really forged some sort of link between them in the short time they'd been married? If they had, she'd done him a great disservice by running away like that. Maybe even greater than any disservice she would have done to herself. After all, he hadn't run from her. Oh, why did things have to get so complicated?

"I was beside myself," he continued. "I couldn't sit still. I couldn't think about the Derby or anything else until I'd found you."

"The Derby," she said. From the moment she'd seen him on the dock at Portsmouth, she'd forgotten everything else, too. "I'm sorry you missed the Derby."

"Are you?"

"Of course. Do you think Black Diamond won without you there?"

"I don't know," he said. "We'll find out when we get home."

"I didn't mean for you to miss the Derby," she said. "I had no control over what day that ship left."

"But it did help you to make good your escape, didn't it?"

She could hardly deny that, so she didn't try.

He leaned back against his seat and studied her. "Just tell me one thing. Did you plan to sleep with Montrose?"

"No," she cried. "How could you think such a thing?"

He looked at her evenly, but the expression couldn't really hide his anger. "You were pretending to be his wife."

"Only to get on the ship. We were going to have separate cabins."

He laughed, but not pleasantly. "And how long do you think that would have lasted?"

"As long as I wanted it to."

His eyebrows rose.

"I mean for the entire trip. Oh, for heaven's sake. I have no interest in Reginald Montrose in that way or any other way."

"You would have been gone with him for a long time," he said. "You might have changed your mind."

"Never." *Curse Will.* How could he even entertain such an idea? "You must have an even lower opinion of me than you think I have of myself. Or you. Or us. Oh, never mind. You know what I mean."

"I might have thought I knew what you meant at one time," he said. "But I'm convinced now that I haven't the faintest idea of what goes on inside your head."

"I assure you, I feel exactly the same way about you."

"Fine then. We have nothing more to talk about."

She crossed her arms over her chest. "That's fine with me."

"Fine," he repeated and stared out the window.

She did the same. If she'd learned anything from the past few days it was that there was no point discussing anything with Will Claridge.

The sun's last rays stretched over London when they finally arrived back home. Will allowed the footman to help Angelica from the carriage and then followed her into the house. Jonesy was sitting in the foyer waiting for them, and he rose as Will and Angelica entered. "My lord."

"Hello, Jonesy."

Angelica crossed the foyer and started to ascend the staircase.

"How did Black Diamond do?" Will asked.

Angelica paused where she was, not looking at either of them, but waiting to hear the answer to Will's question.

"He ran second, my lord," Jonesy said. "Did us right proud."

"Quite so," Will said.

Well, that was that. The day had shattered more than

a few of his illusions. First, the wife he'd grown to cherish more than his own life had left him without a word. Now his best shot at winning the Derby had come up short, too.

Angelica didn't say anything but proceeded up the stairs until she was out of view.

"There wasn't anything you could have done, sir," Jonesy added. "Tim says Lad O'Day fouled him on the far turn, but we'll never prove it."

"So Black Diamond might have won a fair race."

"There's no point dwelling on these things, my lord. Racing's racing. What happens happens."

"You're right, of course." He clapped Jonesy on the shoulder. "Give Black Diamond some apples for a job well done."

"Already have, sir."

"And pay Tim a little extra for his trouble."

"He'll appreciate it," Jonesy answered.

"And give yourself a bit, too."

"Thank you, my lord."

Will dropped his hand. "I'll say good-bye for now, then. It's been a long and dreadful day."

Jonesy cleared his throat. "If you don't mind my saying so—I met her ladyship's aunt at the track today. She's worried about the two of you."

"No doubt," Will answered. "I'm worried about the two of us, too."

Jonesy blushed and nodded. "None of my business, that's sure. I'll just see myself out, my lord."

"Good day, and thank you for coming."

"Good day to you, sir."

Jonesy headed toward the front door, and Will turned and went into the sitting room. He walked to the cabinet and poured himself a stiff whiskey. What to do now?

He'd brought Angelica home but for how long? Would she try to run away again? Would he go after

Taming Angelica

her again if she did? What a stupid question. Of course he would. But would it hurt this much each time she tried to leave him, or would he get used to it after a while?

Oh, God. How could she care so little about him? Granted, she'd been angry with him about his plans for her inheritance, but how could she have done this? How could she cast aside the joy they'd shared? The laughter, the loving? Did he mean nothing at all to her?

To go off with Montrose, in the name of God. A man who'd tried to force himself on her. What could she have been thinking? Montrose would have tried again—force or persuasion, whatever it took. And again and again. It was a very small ship, after all. Would the bastard have succeeded finally?

No. No, he couldn't let himself believe she would have surrendered to Montrose, not if he wanted to keep his sanity. The mere idea of that man—any man— touching her would drive him quite mad.

He walked to the settee and sat down, not drinking, not moving, not allowing himself to think. He sat there like that for who knew how long when some noise from the foyer finally roused him. The front door opened and closed, and angry footsteps sounded across the parquet floor.

"Will, Angelica." Aunt Minnie's voice reverberated through the house. "Come out here this instant. Both of you."

He rose and walked to the doorway. Aunt Minnie stood at the base of the stairway looking like a goddess of vengeance. A plump goddess of vengeance in a ridiculous feathered hat, but still not someone a fellow would want to cross in this lifetime.

She put her hands on her hips when she saw him, and her eyes narrowed. "There you are, young man. Don't you dare move from that spot."

"No, ma'am," he answered.

"And put down that drink. There are times for drinking, but this isn't one of them."

"Yes, ma'am." He looked around for a place to set his whiskey and found nothing. As he could hardly put down his drink without moving from the spot, he just lowered his hand and held the glass at his side.

Aunt Minnie turned and looked up the staircase. "Angelica Roberta Hamilton Claridge," she bellowed loudly enough to set all the feathers on her hat to flouncing. "I know you're up there, and I want you to come down here. Now."

Angelica appeared on the landing above. Wearing a nightgown and slipping first one arm and then the other into a wrapper, she descended the stairs, wide-eyed and barefoot. When she got to bottom, Aunt Minnie shooed them both into the sitting room with fluttering but emphatic hand gestures.

"Both of you, sit down," she ordered, indicating the settee. Will set his whiskey onto a table and sat where Aunt Minnie had indicated. Angelica moved across the room toward a straight-backed chair. "Oh, no," Aunt Minnie said. "You sit beside your husband, young lady."

Angelica did as she was told, wordlessly crossing to the settee and dropping into it as far from Will as she could possibly get.

"Now, then," Aunt Minnie began, "Mr. Jones tells me the two of you have been off somewhere doing something you oughtn't to have been doing. I don't know what. You both missed the Derby, I know that much."

"Your niece—my wife—took it into her head to run away from me in the dead of last night," Will said.

"Angelica!" Aunt Minnie exclaimed. "Is this true?"

"I had my reasons," Angelica said. She pointed at Will. "Have him tell you what he planned to do with my inheritance."

Taming Angelica

"Only for a short while," he answered.

"Three years!" she shouted.

"You planned to be gone almost that long," he replied.

"Only two years," she said. "Two-thirds as long. Not nearly 'almost' as long."

"That would depend on who left and who got left behind, wouldn't you say?" he demanded.

"Stop it. Both of you," Aunt Minnie ordered. "Bickering will get us nowhere."

Angelica crossed her arms over her chest and let out an angry little huff. Her nightgown shook where one bare foot twitched under the hem.

"One at a time," Aunt Minnie said. "Will, what happened?"

"I woke up this morning to find her and her jewelry gone. No note, not so much as a good-bye. I discovered from the *Times* that a ship was leaving for South America today. So I rode like hell to Portsmouth, only to find your niece getting ready to sail off into the sunset—"

"It was afternoon," Angelica interjected. Aunt Minnie glowered at her, and she fell silent.

"As I was saying. She was getting ready to sail off into the sunset with a man who'd tried to force himself on her."

"Not that dreadful Montrose person," Aunt Minnie said.

"One and the same," Will answered.

Aunt Minnie turned toward Angelica. "Child, how could you?"

"You haven't heard my side of it yet."

"All right," Aunt Minnie said. "What do you have to say for yourself?"

"You remember our plan to get my inheritance," she said. "I was supposed to act like a docile little wife so that Papa would give us the money."

"I remember," Aunt Minnie replied.

"I did all that. I performed like a trained monkey to get that money, and what did he want to spend it on?" Angelica said, again leveling an accusatory finger at him.

"Well, what?" Aunt Minnie demanded.

"Horses," Angelica cried, as if the word were somehow obscene. "He wanted to buy horses and stables and practice tracks and all that nonsense and keep me here in England for three years while he did it."

"You're my wife," he shouted.

"Not your possession," she shouted back.

"And is this true, Will?" Aunt Minnie asked. "You convinced Angelica to act like someone she wasn't to get her inheritance and only afterward told her you didn't plan to go with her to South America?"

Put that way, it did sound underhanded, but he couldn't very well deny it. "Yes."

Aunt Minnie turned toward Angelica. "And so you decided to run away with another man."

Angelica's foot twitched furiously under her nightgown. "Yes."

Aunt Minnie huffed and glared at them both. "I must say that in my entire life I've never seen such a perfectly matched pair of idiots."

Will scrambled frantically for something to say that would prove Aunt Minnie wrong. Something like he'd had his own dreams that Angelica failed to recognize. Or like South America and the finches and the tortoises would still be there in three years. But it all sounded so hollow now.

He looked over at Angelica. She appeared to be suffering from the same internal struggle as she continued to hug her ribs and her foot kept up its staccato rhythm. But she didn't say anything either.

"The two of you are hopelessly in love with each

other but too stubborn to see it," Aunt Minnie continued. "Stubborn or stupid, I'm not sure which."

Angelica glanced at him out of the corner of her eye and then lowered her gaze. Her foot slowed its quivering but didn't stop entirely.

"I'll bet you haven't told each other how you feel, have you?" Aunt Minnie demanded.

"I told her twice that I love her," Will said. "She didn't believe me."

"Both times after you'd won something from me I didn't want to give," Angelica replied.

Aunt Minnie lifted her gaze toward the ceiling. "Give me strength." She looked back down at Angelica. "A wise woman doesn't discount a man's declaration of love. The poor fools don't know their own hearts most of the time."

"I beg your pardon," Will said.

"Most men will fight love from here to next Sunday," Aunt Minnie continued as if he hadn't spoken. "If you meet one who'll admit that he cares, you should believe him—no matter how much he'd lie about everything else."

"Thank you," Will said. "I think."

"Have you told Will that you love him?" Aunt Minnie said.

"Not in so many words," Angelica answered.

"So you haven't." Aunt Minnie huffed again. "Well, do it now."

"But dear heart," Angelica said.

"Don't 'dear heart' me," Aunt Minnie replied. "You always use that to get around me, and I won't be gotten around. Not this time. It's too important."

Angelica shifted in her seat for a moment and then turned to him. Her amber eyes got wide, and she nibbled on her lower lip for a moment. Finally she lifted her chin and looked at him full on. "I love you, Will."

"Oh, my darling." His heart melted on the spot. He pulled her into his arms and buried his nose in her hair. "My darling. My darling."

"And do you love Angelica, Will?" Aunt Minnie asked.

"With every breath. With every fiber of my being."

"None of your flowery speeches, young man," Aunt Minnie said. "Just tell her honestly that you love her."

"I love you, Angelica," he whispered.

She gave a tiny sob and ran her own arms around his ribs, pulling herself against him. He held her and stroked her back. Good God, how long had it been since he'd touched her like this? Not more than a fortnight, certainly, and hardly less than an eternity.

"Now, then," Aunt Minnie said. "As to your behavior. Angelica, you were very wrong to run away like that."

Angelica pulled her head from his shoulder but left her arms around him. "But Auntie," she said, "he tricked me."

"Yes, he did. And that was wrong, too. But you're his wife. That doesn't make you his slave, but it does make you the better part of his life. If you have problems, you don't run off with the first man who offers escape. You stay and solve your problems. Together."

Angelica looked at him. "I'm sorry I ran away."

What it must have cost her to say that. Her confession left him quite speechless. So he raised his hands to her face and stroked her skin.

"And you were doubly wrong to keep Angelica from her dreams," Aunt Minnie went on. "She needs to see the world before motherhood keeps her in England."

"Motherhood," Will repeated, all the air going out of him in a rush.

"Motherhood?" Angelica echoed, her eyes as wide as saucers.

Taming Angelica

"Motherhood," Aunt Minnie said again. "You've heard of it."

"Oh, my darling." Will stared into Angelica's dear, dear face as his heart nearly burst in his chest. "Oh, my darling. You'd have my child?"

"Of course she'll have your child. She can hardly avoid it, can she? Unless . . ." Aunt Minnie stopped, and her face registered shock. "You two haven't been practicing abstinence, I hope."

"Of course not," Will replied. "I'm not that big an idiot."

"Thank heaven," Aunt Minnie said. "One can never know for sure what perversity young people will think up next."

"But Aunt Minnie, what if Angelica were to become pregnant in some godforsaken place in South America? What would we do then?"

Angelica smiled at him indulgently, as if he were a silly child, and damn him if he didn't feel like a silly child. "There are cities and doctors in South America. Babies don't just pop in on you. They take months to develop."

"Yes. Very well, I suppose," he said. If she could feel so confident about this baby business, so could he. If he worked at it diligently, for some time. "But what will I do with my breeding program? Even running second in the Derby, Black Diamond's a promising stud."

"Mr. Jones seems like a capable man," Aunt Minnie said. "Leave things to him for a while."

"I imagine I don't have much choice," he said and took a deep breath. "Yes, I can do that."

"Oh, Will." Angelica threw her arms around his neck and brought her face to his for a kiss. He obliged. He crushed her against his chest and kissed her for all he was worth. Weeks of worrying and missing her and needing her built up in him until he thought he'd die if he ever had to let her go. Angelica, his Angelica. His wife. His life.

After breathless moments, he pulled away to thank Aunt Minnie, but she'd already gone. Just as well. He didn't want any witnesses for what would come next. Upstairs. In the bedroom.

Aunt Minnie's wedding was a very small affair, with only the vicar, both families, and a few of Mr. Foxworthy's business associates and their wives. Angelica had never seen a more beautiful bride than her aunt, nor a prouder bridegroom than Mr. Foxworthy. Even Mr. Foxworthy's sister and her grown son and daughter seemed beside themselves with joy at the union. And, miracle of miracles, Papa had behaved himself all day.

Now Angelica stood at the front of the room with her own husband, who had one arm draped casually around her waist. At his nod, several of the household staff circulated with trays of glasses, passing them out to all the guests. Angelica took hers and watched while Will helped himself.

"Ladies and gentlemen," he said, lifting his glass. "Family and friends," he added, nodding to Papa and Mr. Foxworthy's sister. "It gives me very great pleasure to offer a toast to Mr. and Mrs. Edward Foxworthy on the occasion of their marriage."

A cheer went up. Mr. Foxworthy put his arm around Aunt Minnie's shoulders and smiled so broadly his face positively glowed.

"May they live a long and happy life together," Will said. "May they find joy and peace in each other's companionship. And may the sun never set on their love."

"Hear! Hear!" Mr. Foxworthy's nephew shouted. The assembled group emptied their glasses, as did Angelica. The wine danced over her tongue and down her throat—sweet and happy, just like the occasion that had called for it.

Mr. Foxworthy cleared his throat. "We thank you for your generosity and hospitality, my lord," he said. "We'll do our best to live up to your well-wishes."

Aunt Minnie grinned and giggled and looked as pleased as humanly possible. "Let's go home, Edward."

The tiny throng laughed at that, and Aunt Minnie blushed. She gave her glass to a servant, walked to Angelica, and encircled her in a hug that smelled of rose water.

"Congratulations, dear heart," Angelica said.

"And to you, too, child. Be as happy as I am."

Angelica looked up at Will. "I already am."

Mr. Foxworthy joined them and took Aunt Minnie's elbow. "We'll be leaving then."

The two of them walked away, only to be replaced by Papa and Mama. "The rest of us will be leaving, too," Papa said. "England's given us two husbands now, and I guess that's enough for any Bostonian."

"We'll be right behind you, Lawrence," Will said. "I'm taking Angelica to South America—the Galápagos, Tierra del Fuego, wherever she wants to go."

"Now just a minute, young man," Papa said, bristling. "I'm not sure I approve of your taking my daughter somewhere so dangerous."

Will looked over at him. "I'm afraid I don't need your approval."

Mama reached out and touched Angelica's shoulder. "Do you think it wise, Angelica?" Mama said. "After all, there are snakes and Indians and volcanoes and things."

"I'll be fine, Mama."

"I'll take care of your daughter, Mrs. Hamilton," Will said. "I love her more than my life. I won't let anything harm her."

Papa grunted. "Harrumph. Come along, Katherine."

Papa strode off, but Mama hung back. "I don't know. It's one thing to leave you here in England. South America's quite something else."

Angelica took her mother's hand and squeezed it. "I'm not a child anymore, Mama. I'm a wife."

"We'll pay you a visit in Boston on the way back, Mrs. Hamilton," Will said.

"Oh, I'd like that," Mama said, and the unhappiness lifted from her face.

"Come along, Katherine," Papa yelled from across the room.

Mama stayed just long enough to give Angelica a quick hug and then rushed off after her husband. "I'm coming, my dear."

"Thank you for that." Angelica slid her arms around Will and looked up into his face. "Stopping in Boston will delay our return for some time."

He shrugged. "I'm a family man now. I have to consider other people's wishes."

The declaration was such a preposterous thing for the likes of Will Claridge to say, Angelica couldn't help but laugh. "I would never have expected the man I met in Lady Kimball's sitting room to say a thing like that."

"That scoundrel?" Will said. "I'm glad we're done with him."

"I don't want to lose him entirely," she said, grinning up at him. "He had his charm."

Her charming scoundrel smiled his most mischievous smile for her. "Did he?"

"I don't think I could have grown to care for anyone but him," she answered. "In fact, I think I was fated to love a scoundrel."

Epilogue

Head in his hands, Will sat in a chair in the hallway of the *estancia,* staring at the red tiles of the floor. If he had to listen to Angelica scream one more time, he'd barge into the bedroom. To hell with the doctor's orders. And the midwife's, too.

Would things have been easier in England? Would an English doctor have given her laudanum to ease the pains? Dear God, they had laudanum in this part of the world, didn't they? They must.

Why had he let her talk him into staying in South America to give birth? He should have packed her up the moment they'd discovered she was with child and taken her to Boston. Or even someplace half-civilized, like San Francisco. Bloody hell, he didn't even understand the language they spoke here. But one thing he understood—he'd run out of patience. Ten more minutes and he'd go in to be with his wife, no matter what any of them said in Spanish *or* English.

One last scream rent the air—louder and more prolonged than any previous. That did it. He shot from his chair and went to the door. That scream died away and, magically, none followed. He stood, frozen, his hand on the knob. It was good that she'd stopped screaming, wasn't it? *Oh, God, please, let it be good.*

Another moment of silence and another cry came to him. Not Angelica, but a baby. His baby. He turned the knob, but before he could go inside, the door swung open. The midwife emerged carrying some soiled linens in one arm. With the other hand, she pushed him firmly backward.

"My wife," he said. *"Mi esposa.* How is *mi esposa?"*

She said something he couldn't understand, pushed by him, and proceeded down the hallway. He turned back to the door, only to be interrupted again, this time by the doctor.

"My wife," he shouted this time. Bloody hell, wouldn't someone tell him something? "What about my wife?"

The little man stroked his goatee and smiled up at Will. *"Cálmese, Señor Claridge.* Your wife is a healthy young woman. She's fine."

"Oh, thank God." Will's knees went weak, and tears forced themselves up behind his eyes. Until this exact moment he hadn't dared admit to himself how terrified he'd been. "And the child?"

"A beautiful little girl," the doctor answered. *"Perfectamente linda."*

A little girl. Dear God in heaven, he had a little girl, and she was perfectly beautiful. Even Will knew enough Spanish to understand that. "May I see them now?"

"Por supuesto. Go inside."

Will opened the door and stepped into the bedroom. One maid remained, gathering up a few things before she slipped out of the room, leaving him with Angelica.

She looked tiny in the huge four-poster bed. And exhausted and as pale as the sheets. But she opened her eyes and gave him a smile so beautiful it took his breath away. He walked to the bed, sat down carefully, and planted a gentle kiss on Angelica's forehead. She kissed his cheek, and he straightened again so that he could look at her.

"I've been outside all night listening," he said. "I don't think I can endure anything like that again."

"Don't be silly. The doctor says I'll give you many more *niños*."

"Just don't ever leave me," he said, and he couldn't quite keep the sob out of his voice. "I love you, Angelica."

"And I love you, Will." She pulled back the cover of a small bundle next to her. "Would you like to see your daughter?"

"Oh, my, yes." She gently pushed aside some linen, showing him his little girl. The doctor hadn't exaggerated. She was perfectly beautiful. Red and wrinkled and just as exhausted as her mother. And perfectly beautiful.

"What shall we call her?" he asked.

"Miranda, I think. They tell me it means 'admirable one.' "

"Miranda," he repeated. "That'll make her quite exotic in London society."

"She will be anyway. She has my brown eyes and your blond hair."

"How can you tell? It's nothing but fuzz."

"I can tell," she answered.

"Very well. This came out all right," he said. "But I should never have let you have your way about continuing our travels. I should have made you go home as soon as we knew you were *enceinte*."

"But I would have missed so much," she said. "It was my only chance."

"Well, you're done with all that now. We'll leave for Boston when you're stronger, and then we'll go home. I won't hear any arguments."

"That sounds wonderful," she said.

"And you're to settle down in the country with me. And Miranda. And the horses."

"Yes, Will."

"For years," he added. "If not for the rest of our lives."

She smiled at him sweetly. "Of course."

"And we'll never—ever—take a chance like this with your health again. Do you understand?"

"Whatever you say."

He eyed her with some skepticism. "Is this my wife, or did they substitute some docile female in the night?"

"I'm only agreeing with you, dearest."

"Perhaps, but the woman I married was never this agreeable."

"But that was before I'd fulfilled my dreams. I have other adventures ahead of me now."

She held Miranda out to him, and he took her carefully into his arms.

"Besides," Angelica said, "from now on, deviling you is your Miranda's job."

Will looked down into his daughter's face, and he could swear she winked at him.

And Gold Was Ours

Rebecca Brandewyne

In Spain the young Aurora's future is foretold—a long arduous journey, a dark, wild jungle, and a fierce, protective man. Now in the New World, on a plantation haunted by a tale of lost love and hidden gold, the dark-haired beauty wonders if the swordsman and warrior who haunts her dreams truly lived and if he can rescue her from the enemies who seek to destroy her. Together, will they be able to overcome the past and conquer the present to find the greatest treasure on this earth, a treasure that is even more precious than gold. . . .

___52314-0 $5.99 US/$6.99 CAN

Dorchester Publishing Co., Inc.
P.O. Box 6640
Wayne, PA 19087-8640

Please add $1.75 for shipping and handling for the first book and $.50 for each book thereafter. NY, NYC, and PA residents, please add appropriate sales tax. No cash, stamps, or C.O.D.s. All orders shipped within 6 weeks via postal service book rate. Canadian orders require $2.00 extra postage and must be paid in U.S. dollars through a U.S. banking facility.

Name_____
Address_____
City_____State_____Zip_____
I have enclosed $_____ in payment for the checked book(s).
Payment <u>must</u> accompany all orders. ❏ Please send a free catalog.
CHECK OUT OUR WEBSITE! www.dorchesterpub.com

IMAGES IN SCARLET

SAMANTHA LEE

Allison Caine hardly imagined the road to Santa Fe to be picture perfect, but the headstrong photographer has to admit that she never expected a man sleeping in the middle of the road to bar her path. And for a man with no memories, the virile "Jake" sure seems built to make a few worth remembering. Snatches of his life are all Jake can summon of his fragmented past: swirling images of sheets of scarlet and a woman beneath. But now—a beauty that consorts with outlaws and whose lips promise passion untold—Allie makes him ache for the truth which is just beyond reach. Deep in his heart he knows that he is the man of her dreams and not the killer his flashbacks suggest. All he has to do is prove it.

___4578-8 $4.99 US/$5.99 CAN

Dorchester Publishing Co., Inc.
P.O. Box 6640
Wayne, PA 19087-8640

Please add $1.75 for shipping and handling for the first book and $.50 for each book thereafter. NY, NYC, and PA residents, please add appropriate sales tax. No cash, stamps, or C.O.D.s. All orders shipped within 6 weeks via postal service book rate. Canadian orders require $2.00 extra postage and must be paid in U.S. dollars through a U.S. banking facility.

Name_____
Address_____
City_____State_____Zip_____
I have enclosed $_____ in payment for the checked book(s).
Payment <u>must</u> accompany all orders. ❏ Please send a free catalog.
CHECK OUT OUR WEBSITE! www.dorchesterpub.com

ENCANTADORA

GAIL LINK

"Gail Link was born to write romance!"
—Jayne Ann Krentz

"Husband needed. Must be in good health, strong. No older than forty. Fee paid." Independent and proud, Victoria reads the outlandish advertisement with horror. When she refuses to choose a husband from among the cowboys and ranchers of San Antonio, she never dreams that her father will go out and buy her a man. And what a man he is! Tall, dark, and far too handsome for Tory's peace of mind, Rhys makes it clear he is going to be much more than a hired stud. With consummate skill he woos his reluctant bride until she is as eager as he to share the enchantment of love.

_4181-2 $5.99 US/$6.99 CAN

Dorchester Publishing Co., Inc.
P.O. Box 6640
Wayne, PA 19087-8640

Please add $1.75 for shipping and handling for the first book and $.50 for each book thereafter. NY, NYC, and PA residents, please add appropriate sales tax. No cash, stamps, or C.O.D.s. All orders shipped within 6 weeks via postal service book rate. Canadian orders require $2.00 extra postage and must be paid in U.S. dollars through a U.S. banking facility.

Name_____
Address_____
City_____ State_____ Zip_____
I have enclosed $_____ in payment for the checked book(s).
Payment <u>must</u> accompany all orders. ☐ Please send a free catalog.

ICE & *Rapture*

CONNIE MASON

Cool as a cucumber, and totally dedicated to her career as a newspaperwoman, Maggie Agton is just the kind of challenge Chase McGarrett enjoys—especially when he discovers that she hides skimpy silk underthings and a simmering sensuality beneath her businesslike exterior. Virile and all too sure of himself, Chase is just the kind of man Maggie detests—especially when she learns that he has no intention of taking her across the Yukon to report on the Klondike gold rush. Cold and hot, reserved and brash—Maggie and Chase are a study in opposites. But when they join forces in the frozen wilderness, the fiery sparks of their searing desire burn brighter than the northern lights.

___4570-2 $5.99 US/$6.99 CAN

Dorchester Publishing Co., Inc.
P.O. Box 6640
Wayne, PA 19087-8640

Please add $1.75 for shipping and handling for the first book and $.50 for each book thereafter. NY, NYC, and PA residents, please add appropriate sales tax. No cash, stamps, or C.O.D.s. All orders shipped within 6 weeks via postal service book rate. Canadian orders require $2.00 extra postage and must be paid in U.S. dollars through a U.S. banking facility.

Name_____
Address_____
City_____ State_____ Zip_____
I have enclosed $_____ in payment for the checked book(s).
Payment <u>must</u> accompany all orders. ❑ Please send a free catalog.
    CHECK OUT OUR WEBSITE! www.dorchesterpub.com

SUPERSTITIONS

ANNIE McKNIGHT

Beautiful young Billie Bahill is determined. Despite what her father says, she knows her fiancé won't just leave her. So come hell or high water, she is going to go find him. So what if she rides off into the deadly Superstition Mountains? Billie is as good on a horse as any of the men on her father's ranch, and she won't let anybody stop her—especially not the Arizona Ranger with eyes that make her heart skip a beat.

___4405-6 $5.50 US/$6.50 CAN

Dorchester Publishing Co., Inc.
P.O. Box 6640
Wayne, PA 19087-8640

Please add $1.75 for shipping and handling for the first book and $.50 for each book thereafter. NY, NYC, and PA residents, please add appropriate sales tax. No cash, stamps, or C.O.D.s. All orders shipped within 6 weeks via postal service book rate. Canadian orders require $2.00 extra postage and must be paid in U.S. dollars through a U.S. banking facility.

Name_____
Address_____
City_____State_____Zip_____
I have enclosed $_____ in payment for the checked book(s).
Payment <u>must</u> accompany all orders. ❑ Please send a free catalog.
CHECK OUT OUR WEBSITE! www.dorchesterpub.com

Marriage By Design

Jill Metcalf

Her sign proclaims it as one of a number of services procurable through Miss Coady Blake, but there is nothing illicit in what it offers. All a prospective husband has to do is obtain a bride—Coady will take care of the wedding details. But it is difficult to purchase luxuries in the Yukon Territory, 1898, and Coady charges accordingly. After hearing several suspicions about Coady's business ethics, Northwest Mounted Police officer Stone MacGregor takes it upon himself to search out the crafty huckster. Instead, the inspector finds a willful beauty who thinks she knows the worth of every item—and he finds himself thinking that the proprietress herself is far beyond price.

___4553-2 $4.99 US/$5.99 CAN

Dorchester Publishing Co., Inc.
P.O. Box 6640
Wayne, PA 19087-8640

Please add $1.75 for shipping and handling for the first book and $.50 for each book thereafter. NY, NYC, and PA residents, please add appropriate sales tax. No cash, stamps, or C.O.D.s. All orders shipped within 6 weeks via postal service book rate. Canadian orders require $2.00 extra postage and must be paid in U.S. dollars through a U.S. banking facility.

Name_____
Address_____
City_____State_____Zip_____
I have enclosed $_____ in payment for the checked book(s).
Payment <u>must</u> accompany all orders. ❑ Please send a free catalog.
CHECK OUT OUR WEBSITE! www.dorchesterpub.com

BEYOND BETRAYAL

CHRISTINE MICHELS

Disguised as the law, outlaw Samson Towers travels to Red Rock, Montana, where he finds the one woman that can knock down the pillars of his deception and win his heart—a temptress named Delilah Sterne. While the lovely widow finds herself drawn to the town's sheriff, the beautiful gambler suddenly fears she's played the wrong cards—and sentenced the man she loves to death. Her heart in danger, she knows that she must save the handsome Samson and prove that their love can exist beyond betrayal.

___52264-0 $5.50 US/$6.50 CAN

Dorchester Publishing Co., Inc.
P.O. Box 6640
Wayne, PA 19087-8640

Please add $1.75 for shipping and handling for the first book and $.50 for each book thereafter. NY, NYC, and PA residents, please add appropriate sales tax. No cash, stamps, or C.O.D.s. All orders shipped within 6 weeks via postal service book rate. Canadian orders require $2.00 extra postage and must be paid in U.S. dollars through a U.S. banking facility.

Name_____
Address_____
City_____State_____Zip_____
I have enclosed $_____ in payment for the checked book(s).
Payment <u>must</u> accompany all orders. ❑ Please send a free catalog.
    CHECK OUT OUR WEBSITE! www.dorchesterpub.com

Abiding Hope
Melody Morgan

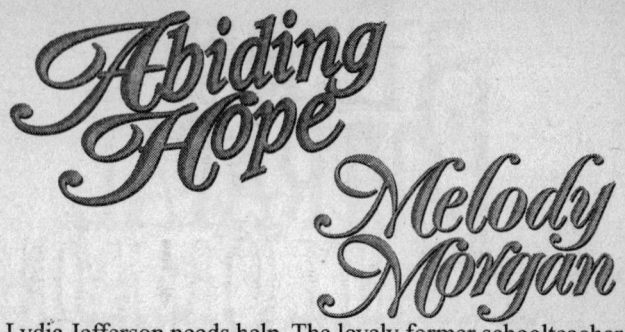

Lydia Jefferson needs help. The lovely former schoolteacher can't open her home for orphans without getting her house in order, and she can't afford the necessary repairs on the run-down estate. She needs Peaceful Valley's only woodworker: Nathan "Stoney" Stockwell. While beneath the handsome cabinetmaker's brusque facade lies a tender heart, the stubborn man with a mysterious past refuses to aid her, until she begins the repairs herself. And when Nathan pitches in and works alongside her, Lydia longs to feel his strong arms around her. Yet as the weeks pass, Lydia sees the hurt buried deep behind his warm eyes and knows that only her sweet kiss can provide him with an abiding hope.

___4493-5 $5.50 US/$6.50 CAN

Dorchester Publishing Co., Inc.
P.O. Box 6640
Wayne, PA 19087-8640

Please add $1.75 for shipping and handling for the first book and $.50 for each book thereafter. NY, NYC, and PA residents, please add appropriate sales tax. No cash, stamps, or C.O.D.s. All orders shipped within 6 weeks via postal service book rate. Canadian orders require $2.00 extra postage and must be paid in U.S. dollars through a U.S. banking facility.

Name_____
Address_____
City_____State_____Zip_____
I have enclosed $_____ in payment for the checked book(s).
Payment <u>must</u> accompany all orders. ❏ Please send a free catalog.
CHECK OUT OUR WEBSITE! www.dorchesterpub.com

TEXAS PROUD
CONSTANCE O'BANYON

Rachel Rutledge has her gun trained on Noble Vincente. With one shot, she will have her revenge on the man who killed her father. So what is stopping her from pulling the trigger? Perhaps it is the memory of Noble's teasing voice, his soft smile, or the way one glance from his dark Spanish eyes once stirred her foolish heart to longing. Yes, she loved him then... as much as she hates him now. One way or another, she will wound him to the heart—if not with bullets, then with her own feminine wiles. But as Rachel discovers, sometimes the line between love and hate is too thinly drawn.

___4492-7 $5.99 US/$6.99 CAN

Dorchester Publishing Co., Inc.
P.O. Box 6640
Wayne, PA 19087-8640

Please add $1.75 for shipping and handling for the first book and $.50 for each book thereafter. NY, NYC, and PA residents, please add appropriate sales tax. No cash, stamps, or C.O.D.s. All orders shipped within 6 weeks via postal service book rate. Canadian orders require $2.00 extra postage and must be paid in U.S. dollars through a U.S. banking facility.

Name_____
Address_____
City_____State_____Zip_____
I have enclosed $_____ in payment for the checked book(s).
Payment <u>must</u> accompany all orders. ❑ Please send a free catalog.
CHECK OUT OUR WEBSITE! www.dorchesterpub.com

ATTENTION ROMANCE CUSTOMERS!

SPECIAL TOLL-FREE NUMBER
1-800-481-9191

*Call Monday through Friday 10 a.m. to 9 p.m. Eastern Time
Get a free catalogue, join the Romance Book Club, and order books using your Visa, MasterCard, or Discover®*

Leisure Books

Love Spell

GO ONLINE WITH US AT DORCHESTERPUB.COM